"I THINK SHE'S TRYING TO TELL US SOMETHING..."

When Timmy was trapped in the mineshaft, Lassie had to resort to barking because human minds are deaf to canine eloquence.

In *The Voice of the Dog*, Farfel sets the record straight:

"Dogs can talk. We understand everything that people are saying, and—with a little practice—we're fully capable of answering back, carrying on a conversation, providing the sort of man's-best-friend feedback for which, I think, dogs were put on earth by our Creator. Every puppy, when he or she learns to speak, talks up a regular storm, innocently candid and eager to bond with master or mistress. Of course, we get nothing back but baby talk. By and by, we all give up, sometimes to the point where we lose the power of speech. The main problem with dog-to-man speech—or Dogspeak—is that dogs talk on a wavelength outside the range of human imagination. Scout, one of my buddies in the K-9 unit, had a theory that Dogspeak is not so much oral communication as a sort of telepathy that humans can't pick up on their mental radar."

LAST KID BOOKS
by David Benjamin

The Life and Times of the Last Kid Picked

Three's a Crowd

A Sunday Kind of Love

Almost Killed by a Train of Thought: Collected Essays

Skulduggery in the Latin Quarter

Summer of '68

Black Dragon

They Shot Kennedy

Jailbait

Bastard's Bluff

Woman Trouble

Fat Vinny's Forbidden Love

Witness to the Crucifixion

Choose Moose

Dead Shot

Bistro Nights

The Melting Grandmother and Other Short Works

Also by David Benjamin

SUMO: A Thinking Fan's Guide to Japan's National Sport

"I THINK SHE'S TRYING TO TELL US SOMETHING..."

When Timmy was trapped in the mineshaft, Lassie had to resort to barking because human minds are deaf to canine eloquence.

In *The Voice of the Dog*, Farfel sets the record straight:

"Dogs can talk. We understand everything that people are saying, and—with a little practice—we're fully capable of answering back, carrying on a conversation, providing the sort of man's-best-friend feedback for which, I think, dogs were put on earth by our Creator. Every puppy, when he or she learns to speak, talks up a regular storm, innocently candid and eager to bond with master or mistress. Of course, we get nothing back but baby talk. By and by, we all give up, sometimes to the point where we lose the power of speech. The main problem with dog-to-man speech—or Dogspeak—is that dogs talk on a wavelength outside the range of human imagination. Scout, one of my buddies in the K-9 unit, had a theory that Dogspeak is not so much oral communication as a sort of telepathy that humans can't pick up on their mental radar."

LAST KID BOOKS
by David Benjamin

The Life and Times of the Last Kid Picked

Three's a Crowd

A Sunday Kind of Love

Almost Killed by a Train of Thought: Collected Essays

Skulduggery in the Latin Quarter

Summer of '68

Black Dragon

They Shot Kennedy

Jailbait

Bastard's Bluff

Woman Trouble

Fat Vinny's Forbidden Love

Witness to the Crucifixion

Choose Moose

Dead Shot

Bistro Nights

The Melting Grandmother and Other Short Works

Also by David Benjamin

SUMO: A Thinking Fan's Guide to Japan's National Sport

THE VOICE OF THE DOG

BY DAVID BENJAMIN

LAST KID BOOKS

Copyright © 2024 David Benjamin

Last Kid Books
309 W. Washington Avenue
Madison, WI 53703

First Edition
March 2024

All rights reserved

No part of this book may be used or reproduced
in any manner whatsoever without written
permission from the author.

Printed in Wisconsin, United States of America

For more information or to order books:
visit www.lastkidbooks.com

Library of Congress Control Number: 2023952639

ISBN-13: 979-8-9876144-6-4

A NOTE ON THE TYPE

This book was set in Athelas, a serif typeface designed by Veronika Burian and Jose Scaglione and intended for use in body text.[1] Released by the company TypeTogether in 2008, Burian and Scaglione described Athelas as inspired by British fine book printing.

Printed and bound by Park Printing Solutions
Verona, Wisconsin

Designed by Kristin Mitchell, Little Creek Press and Book Design
Mineral Point, Wisconsin

Cover photo by Max Kleinen

This one is dedicated, lovingly, to the memory of my dogs,
Sashenka and Brandy

"When a wretch could no longer attract the notice of a man, woman or child, he must be respectable in the eyes of his dog."

—Jean-Jacques Rousseau

1

"Dogs do speak, but only to those who know how to listen."
—Orhan Pamuk

I used to be a cop.

I had to take early retirement because, according to my lieutenant, I lacked the requisite level of ferocity expected of an NYPD police officer. Of course, I disagreed. No one questioned my courage. Set me loose and I'll plunge without hesitation into the jaws of death—a burning building, a gang war crossfire of flying bullets, a trainwreck or a collapsed bridge. I'm there wide-eyed and pronto, without a thought for my own skin. I'm a little nuts that way, and I have the scars to prove it. But when cases came down to using force, I always leaned toward self-restraint. I guess my deep-seated predilection is that I like people and don't want to hurt them any more than necessary, no matter how volatile the crisis. I guess most cops, when they're on the job, see every suspect as already guilty, or else they wouldn't be hunting them down and arresting them. I never bought into that ethic. I just see people as people, all the same, even when they're resisting the cops, even when they're so whacked-out or juiced-up that they're a threat to themselves and everybody around them.

I mean, it's human nature—no, I think it's even more basic. It's animal instinct to fight capture and confinement, even if you're soaked in your victim's blood, holding the chainsaw, steeped in guilt and surrounded by police. The thing is, it's not up to cops to decide who deserves to be locked up or to start punishing suspects before they go to trial. Even as you're grabbing them, subduing them, forcing them handcuffed into a squad car, they're just people, the fallible children of God.

Not guilty, even if they look guilty, even if you've caught them red-handed. That's how I saw it when I was on the job. Not that I thought it out in so many words. Words, in those days, didn't always come to me fast and natural. But I felt that way, and because I did, I tended to back off and take it easy as soon as I saw that a suspect was under control. But the other cops noticed. They saw that I never tightened my grip one notch more to inflict a little extra pain. They shook their heads when my voice grew calm, or silent, while everyone else was still shouting and cursing. They were disappointed in me when I didn't draw blood, break a bone, or send a suspect into a state of terror so deep that he'd wet himself or vomit from fear. I could've done it. I know how to scare the wits out of a perp. I was trained to intimidate. We all are. But I never went that far unless I absolutely had to. And I never really had to ...

... Well, maybe not 'til Reggie.

It all started to become clear a month or so after I'd moved in with Reggie. This was when the big storm hit, and all of Lower Manhattan turned into a lake. Reggie and I were living in a basement apartment between Broadway and the FDR. I don't want to be any more specific because—since all the publicity about Reggie hit the fan—I'd rather not attract a lot of morbid tourists into a nice, quiet neighborhood.

That day, even though we were aware of the weather, we were unprepared and virtually helpless when suddenly a wall of water and mud exploded into our apartment. I'd been asleep in the back room and woke up half drenched. Reggie

THE VOICE OF THE DOG

BY DAVID BENJAMIN

LAST KID BOOKS

Copyright © 2024 David Benjamin

Last Kid Books
309 W. Washington Avenue
Madison, WI 53703

First Edition
March 2024

All rights reserved

No part of this book may be used or reproduced
in any manner whatsoever without written
permission from the author.

Printed in Wisconsin, United States of America

For more information or to order books:
visit www.lastkidbooks.com

Library of Congress Control Number: 2023952639

ISBN-13: 979-8-9876144-6-4

A NOTE ON THE TYPE

This book was set in Athelas, a serif typeface designed by Veronika Burian and Jose Scaglione and intended for use in body text.[1] Released by the company TypeTogether in 2008, Burian and Scaglione described Athelas as inspired by British fine book printing.

Printed and bound by Park Printing Solutions
Verona, Wisconsin

Designed by Kristin Mitchell, Little Creek Press and Book Design
Mineral Point, Wisconsin

Cover photo by Max Kleinen

burst in, followed by a flood that had been partly held back by the door.

He grabbed me and said, "Farfel! Come on! We gotta get out of here."

Before I could even get to my feet, Reggie had me in his arms, wading through the rising tide toward the door. He wasn't just fighting the water. Workmen had been digging up the street for several days, piling up dirt, rocks and broken pavement in a heap just opposite our doorway. Suddenly, a ton of sandy soil was flowing into our little three-room walkdown. I could see that if we didn't clear the door in maybe thirty seconds, we'd be trapped inside and drowned in our living room.

Reggie's a strong man. He got us almost to the doorway before a fresh surge, consisting almost exclusively of gummy mud from the construction site, hit us and sent Reggie stumbling back. For a moment, I struggled to get out of Reggie's arms, thinking I could swim and wallow my way out. But Reggie held on, wisely. He knew that there was no dog-paddling through this muck. Since I'm only about two feet, ten inches from my feet to the top of my head, I wouldn't have lasted long on my own.

Since I'm here to tell the tale, Reggie did get us through that last gush of brown slime. He waded through the doorway chest-deep in the flood, battled his way up the stairs and paused there on the street, knee-deep in filthy water, looking around, holding tight to me.

We were fleeing for dry ground a moment later. The water got shallower as we headed uptown. I was squirming again, insistent that Reggie should set me down. That's when we saw the woman.

She was as tall as Reggie but slender in the right places, round where she should be round. She wore a light raincoat that clung to her curves. I may be a dog, but I know a gorgeous human when I see one.

She was carrying a useless umbrella, destroyed by the

wind. Her mid-heel shoes were drenched and ruined, and her wet hair—probably a honey-like blonde when it was dry—lay on her shoulders in sodden gray ropes. But she was still a knockout. I could sense Reggie staring at her. She paused, looking into the distance uncertainly.

"Hey," Reggie called out to her. "Excuse me. Could you help—"

That's as far as he got. She turned at the sound of Reggie's voice. As soon as she saw us, she screamed. "Oh my God!" she cried. "Oh my God, no! Help! Help me!"

She flung her umbrella at us. And then she ran, jaloping through water that was still above her ankles, splashing and flailing, still calling for help, finally reaching a cross-street a hundred yards uptown and disappearing around the corner.

Later, I realized what she saw. Reggie—whose curly, unruly hair always needs a trim, whose physical bulk suggests a giant prehistoric sloth with a mild obesity problem—would have been a little bit scary even if he'd been standing there in a tuxedo with a top hat and cane. But he was covered to his knees in glutinous brown mud, his hair matted with a mixture of filth that probably included raw sewage and a variety of petroleum by-products, his glasses filmed over and cloudy with dirt, his shirt torn and hanging in strips, his pants halfway to his knees and his private parts all but exposed beneath his wet, clinging boxer shorts.

And then there was me, bunched up in his arms, also drenched and muck-frosted, my hair sticking out every which way, my eyes glassy with fear and confusion, tongue hanging out the side of my mouth, one of my canines visible and my tail hanging lower than half-mast, dripping glop.

Anyone seeing us would've probably screamed and fled. We looked like an apparition from a Wes Craven movie. But Reggie didn't see us that way. Reggie had never been an attractive guy—what with his pear shape, uncontrollable hair, bad eyes and recessive personality. Somehow, this moment of spontaneous revulsion inflicted by a beautiful stranger, I think, hit him worse than ever before. He staggered back a step and then just plopped down on his ass in the gushing street, letting me go and uttering a heartrending moan.

He remained like that for at least five minutes, just staring down, looking at his pants around his knees. People sloshed by. A few paused to peer at him briefly and, a little fearfully, at me. (I'm mostly German shepherd, with a black muzzle, dark fur and a sort of husky build. So I can be a little frightening even when I'm not trying.) Reggie cupped his hands over his privates out of modesty, I guess. But except for that, he didn't move or make a peep.

Until finally, this: "Bitches. Rotten, rotten bitches. They're all bitches."

I looked around, saw no one near, so I spoke. "Who? Who are you talking about, Reggie?"

• • •

I should explain.

Dogs can talk. We understand everything that people are saying, and—with a little practice—we're fully capable of answering back, carrying on a conversation, providing the sort of man's-best-friend feedback for which, I think, dogs were put on earth by our Creator. Every puppy, when he or she learns to speak, talks up a regular storm, innocently candid and eager to bond with master or mistress. Of course, we get nothing back but baby talk. By and by, we all give up, sometimes to the point where we lose the power of speech. The main problem with dog-to-man speech—or Dogspeak—is that dogs talk on a wavelength outside the range of human imagination. Scout, one of my buddies in the K-9 unit, had a theory that Dogspeak is not so much oral communication as a sort of telepathy that humans can't pick up on their mental radar.

So, by the time Reggie adopted me, at age five, through the NYPD canine retirement program, I had long since given up trying to converse with people. I was as mum as every other dog on the block. It was only by coincidence that I discovered Reggie had been feeding me canned dog food for my first two weeks with him, which I liked just fine. Then, one day, he went to this fancy pet emporium over by NYU and came home with a bag of specially formulated organic bio-kibble, composed, apparently, of wheat germ, fish oil, brewer's yeast, free-range chicken by-products and a lot of little green pellets that smelled almost exactly like Schnauzer piss.

Well, Reggie poured this stuff into a bowl, sprinkled a little olive oil over the top, and said to me, "There ya go, boy."

I sniffed this mess once, almost passed out, smelled it again from a safer distance, cocked my head toward Reggie and, resorting to profanity, blurted out, "What is this shit?"

I expected no reply, of course. But Reggie did this exaggerated double take, put his hands on his knees, crouched down so his face was almost even with mine and said, "Say *what?*"

This led to a brief dog/man staring contest, Reggie studying my mouth like it was some kind of alien orifice. I knew that even though people don't understand dogs or even hear us, they sometimes sense that we're communicating. I figured this was one of those occasions until Reggie said, "You don't like this food?"

Had he really understood what I'd said? Or was he just guessing, based on my refusal to eat this dreck? So, what the heck. I said, "It smells like piss."

Reggie sat on the floor, now gaping at me. Talking very slowly, as though I was a moron, he then said, "Did. You. Just. Say. This. Stuff. Smells. Like. Piss?"

"You don't believe me?" I said in a normal (dog) voice at normal speed. "Stick your nose in it."

Which he did and then said, "Holy shit. It does smell like piss. And you can talk. Jesus H. Christ, you're a talking dog!"

"We can all talk, Reggie," I said patiently. "It's just that people can't hear."

Anyway, that was the beginning. Reggie is one of those humans, maybe one in a million, who can understand everything his dog says. Not that he ever listens when he should, when a little listening to me could save him from a whole world of grief. But at least, for a while, before he went off the deep end, he knew what I was talking about, which is more than I can say about most other humans I've met.

. . .

Anyway, that was the beginning. Reggie is one of those humans, maybe one in a million, who can understand everything his dog says. Not that he ever listens when he should, when a little listening to me could save him from a whole world of grief. But at least, for a while, before he went off the deep end, he knew what I was talking about, which is more than I can say about most other humans I've met.

2

"I've seen a look in dogs' eyes, a quickly vanishing look of amazed contempt, and I am convinced that basically dogs think humans are nuts."

—John Steinbeck

I sometimes wonder. If the big storm hadn't landed us in Brooklyn, would Reggie have snapped the way he did? From our first meeting, I had sensed the fragility of his psyche, and I was drawn to him in sympathy. From the very first, I strove to be a calming influence in Reggie's life, soothing his anguish with my simple, unconditional affection. But the storm that took everything, punctuated by that screaming woman in the street, and then starting all over on the other side of the East River—all these traumas were beyond a mere housepet's ability to assuage.

He and I ended up in a new apartment, whose exact location I won't reveal because, again, the neighborhood would be crawling with voyeurs and morbid curiosity-seekers. I really wonder about humans sometimes.

I mean, a dog will go to the scene of a murder for one reason and one reason only—to sniff around the blood and guts left behind and lick up anything that smells the least bit tasty. And we don't do this out of curiosity. It's just instinct. We're compulsive carnivores. But humans, they'll show up months, or years later, long after the last whiff of residue has disappeared, where no sign of the crime, either visible or olfactory, can be remotely discerned. They'll hang around, talking about the horrible event that occurred there, pointing at things, imagining the carnage, gossiping about the killer or killers and the victims. They'll even start re-enacting the tragedy and laughing about it. Sick. A dog would never stoop so low.

This unnamed apartment of ours, on one of those obscure little streets off Bedford Avenue, was much nicer than Reggie's basement place over on the Lower East Side. We managed it because a) Brooklyn's cheaper than even the cruddiest parts of lower Manhattan, and b) Reggie had finally ended one of his feuds with his mother—whom Reggie referred to, when he was angry with her, as "that ball-busting bitch." When he wasn't inexplicably angry at Mom, he almost worshipped her, viewing her as a sort of empyreal ideal that no other woman could match.

I've never understood why Reggie seemed so schizophrenic about his mother. She's a nice normal human female with a kind voice, a steady temperament and a scent that reminds me of ripe apricots and butterfly wingdust. She had seemed almost preternaturally sweet the two times we visited her. And she pampered Reggie to the point where I was amazed that he could do anything for himself.

My guess is that Reggie made war with his mother because she's the only one who really cares how he feels about anything. She was, for most of his life, the only person he could hurt. He always made up with her, because she loved him thoughtlessly. After the flood, Reggie made peace with Mom—grudgingly, as usual—because he needed the security deposit on his new apartment and three months' rent. This became every month's rent after Reggie lost his job at one of the lower Manhattan branches of the New York Public Library.

On that matter, Reggie never made it real clear what happened to get him fired. It had something to do with him shouting at a woman, who'd been reading at one of the tables, "crossing her legs provocatively but never once looking at me."

That was the last job Reggie ever had. After we moved to Brooklyn and he pretty much gave up trying to make a living, his favorite place to take me for a walk was Fort Greene Park. This was copacetic with me because it was a nice long stroll both ways—past hundreds of nice, fragrant peed-on trees—and the park was overflowing with attractive bitches.

(Actually, knowing its human connotation, I've developed a habit of avoiding that word, preferring to call my female colleagues "lady dogs" or just "LDs.")

Trouble is, in our excursions to Fort Greene Park, Reggie's routine made me increasingly uneasy. He would sit at a bench, motionless, sometimes for hours. Now and then, he'd lean back, throw his arm on the back of the bench and sort of smirk at the world as it passed by. When nobody made eye contact with him, smirked back or paid him any mind, he'd slump forward, glaring out from beneath his eyebrows, and he'd mutter to himself profanely. I noticed that whenever a pretty girl or a crisp-looking businesswoman in heels passed by, he'd fix his gaze right on her and track her—like a human spotlight—'til she disappeared around the bend.

He'd be talking, under his breath, the whole time, saying stuff like, "Okay, go ahead, you snotty cunt. Don't turn your head, don't look, don't glance, don't you give a shit that there's a real man here, the lover you've been aching for, the romantic gentleman you'll never deserve. No, you go on, you strut your stuff, you high-heeled lesbian cocksucker. You'll get yours. There'll be a reckoning, slut. Just you wait ..."

I know. "Lesbian cocksucker?" But he'd go on and on like that, making no sense that I, in my canine ignorance, could fathom. Finally, once I said to him, in my softest, most

DAVID BENJAMIN

sympathetic growl, "Hey, Reg, man, why don'tcha, like, lighten up a little. Women aren't *all* that bad. Y'know?"

And Reggie just glowered at me with eyes that reminded me of this abused Airedale I used to know. And he said, "Don't you see what's happening, you dumb-fuck mutt?"

Of course, I ignored the insult because dogs are, by nature, the most forgiving of all quadrupeds. If we weren't, most humans would have been eaten by now. Instead of offering tit for tat, I said to Reggie: "Well, I guess I'm missing something, boss. But it just seems like a normal day in the park."

"Normal?" Reggie said. "Normal? When not one—not one!—woman, in two hours—two hours!—gives me even one lousy passing glance? Not one!"

"Oh, heck, Reggie," I said. "Don't be silly. It's all about location. Nobody makes eye contact in New York City."

To which Reggie grabbed me by the collar and yanked my nose right up to his face and said, "What the fuck do you know about New York City, you shit-sniffing fleabag?"

Again, I shrugged off the disparagement. "New York? Gosh, Reg, I've lived here all my—"

Reggie still had me in his grip. "All your life? Well, you're fucking lucky you've got a life. D'you know that the day after I took you away, they were planning to pump you full of phenobarbitol and put you out with the morning garbage?"

By that time, Reggie had mentioned my planned euthanasia so often that it was water off a retriever's back. Besides, I don't even think it was true. We retired police dogs are pretty popular among the adoptive public. But I let that remark go, too.

"Mangy mutt," said Reggie. "You've got no right giving me advice. You're barely superior to women."

Here was the paradox that made Reggie such an interesting master. On the one hand, he raged and fumed over the inferiority of all the women who had spurned, rejected and failed to appreciate him in all his masculine glory. On the other hand, he suffered, terribly and outspokenly, from a huge case of the constant hots for women—which I, of all people, being a dog, could understand.

Dogs—especially us males—are pretty much slaves to libido.

We live by smell, as you probably know. Among canines, my vision is pretty sharp, but if I were human, I'd be considered half-blind and couldn't get a driver's license. So my nose is my co-pilot. Every human has a unique olfactory signature—or noseprint—like fingertip whorls or DNA. Reggie, for example. I'd know him, sight-unseen, from at least a half-mile. His primary scent is a blend of slightly vinegary sweat and Kentucky Fried Chicken batter (extra crispy), with a *frisson* of 3-in-1 oil. Don't ask me to explain how a guy who almost never eats KFC smells like he rolled around in it. The chemistry of the human body is one of dogdom's deepest mysteries.

Of course, there's nothing that hits my nostrils, and goes straight to my gonads, like one whiff of quiff (excuse the expression), especially if we're talking about a bitch in heat, which is a term I prefer to avoid, by the way. The euphemism I've adopted to replace that crude construction is "ovulating lady dog," or just OLD. When we're walking and I catch the scent of an OLD—which is so powerful it can pierce walls—I get a little woozy and disoriented. Up close to an OLD, it's like I'm a giant, phallic B-52 winging my way blind, five hundred miles an hour, into a dense black thundercloud of raging lust. Can't see, can't hear. Can't smell anything but lady dog. Can't think. Can't function. I'm helpless. I love it but I hate it. And when it's over, whether I manage to bond with the OLD or—more likely—Reggie drags me away by my leash, I end up envying all my neutered colleagues, for whom the official term, among dogs, is "disabled American dog (DAD)." They can still smell OLD. There's nothing wrong with their noses, but DADs are not intoxicated and crippled by that miasma of raw, irresistible sex. A DAD experiences an OLD encounter as more of an aesthetic interlude, like a purple sunset or a fresh Shih Tzu turd on the sidewalk.

Of course, most OLDs, well, they can take us guys or leave us. The urge isn't nearly as overwhelming for them. So, you see, I had a sense of how Reggie felt as he watched all these busy, beautiful Brooklyn broads hurrying by, none of them wondering who he was or why he was smirking, not even noticing his existence. I got it. Reggie just didn't know I got it. He was wrapped up pretty thoroughly with himself.

Reggie let my collar go finally and patted me on the head—his way of apologizing. He was really a sweet guy. In a softer, more thoughtful voice, he said, "I wonder why I bother, Farfel. I mean, women don't deserve me. They're not people. They're more like beasts. I mean, not dogs like you, boy. They're worse. They're attracted to the most aggressive, tall, muscular, hairy men, the ones who'll seize them and drag them away into a dark place and shove themselves into them over and over until they've bred more great, hairy barbarians just like they are. Women hunger to be raped, ravaged and ruined. They lust to crawl on all fours and lick up the sperm of chest-thumping gorillas."

Carefully, I said to Reggie, "Gosh, Reg. Don't you think you might be generalizing a little too broadly?"

Reggie's eyes flashed dangerously. He said, "Oh yeah. Show me one who isn't a coldblooded slut!"

"Well ..."

"Look around, you dumb mutt! They treat me like I'm invisible. They can't see me because they're only interested in the surface. In big cars, fancy clothes, bulging muscles, six-pack abs and bulging pants. They don't want to be courted, romanced and pampered with roses and poetry. They just want to be fucked! Fucked brutally and suddenly. Fucked like animals. Animals!"

Again, I didn't take that "animals" reference personally. Reggie tends to get carried away.

Besides, I was curious about how Reggie had got this way—turned into a raving, one-note misogynist. So, rather than trying to argue with a master who was in no mood to listen to reason, I did a little trick every dog learns in early puppyhood. I cocked my head to one side, opened my eyes to full mast and hung out my tongue. All this creates an impression of receptivity that humans find just about impossible to resist.

Reggie started talking. "Okay, moron. Listen up. It all hit me at puberty," he went on. "Actually, before puberty, I had already sensed the cruelty of girls. As far back as third grade, when I was trying to impress the cool kids."

"There are cool kids in third grade?" I asked.

Reggie stared at me as though I'd just coughed up a hairball. So I pulled in my tongue and clammed up.

"As I was saying," said Reggie, "they laughed at me if my clothes were wrong or they thought my hair looked funny. I'm a large guy. I've always been large but not fat. But they called me fat. Girls pointed. They giggled. They drew big, fat pictures of me in their notebooks. They were vicious. But I didn't figure out the pattern then. I didn't realize the sheer evil of their behavior until puberty, when I was hit by this huge hunger, this overwhelming desire to have a girlfriend, to hold her hand, kiss her, court her and feel her love for me.

"That was when the inhuman cruelty of girls became clear—because they rejected me, all of them. Every one. Not because I'm large or fat or unattractive but because I'm good, caring, gentle, kind, respectful.

"I am the opposite of what women lust for. I am a gentleman in a ruthless world where girls are only attracted to barbarians."

"Whoa there, Reg," I broke in. "Isn't that sort of a sweeping generality?"

Reggie smiled at me indulgently. "You're forgetting what you yourself said to me, Farf."

"What I said? What was that?"

DAVID BENJAMIN

"Yeah, fuzzface. When we were still living in Manhattan, you said to me—I remember your exact words. I was talking about my loneliness and my lifelong rejection by women, and you said, 'Women are hard to understand. It's almost as though they're a different species.'"

I nodded sheepishly, hearing my own words thrown back at me. I remembered saying that. But Reggie had taken it out of its original context. I meant that a man, any man, has to look more closely at women, to listen and sympathize, because the experience of being a woman—or a lady dog—is so vastly different from growing up male in a society still heavily biased toward men.

Apparently, Reggie had forgotten all of that.

He went on. "Shit, man. I hate to admit that I could learn anything from a dog. But I gotta hand it to ya, Farf. That hit me like a claw hammer between the eyes—women, a whole different species! Abso-fuckin'-lutely!"

"But, Reg. That isn't really what I—"

"It all became clear, man. I understood—like a flash of revelation—why I had lived a life of misery and rejection. I am not just a higher species than women. I'm one of the *advanced* members of the superior species."

"You mean men?"

"Yeah!" said Reggie. "Don't you see? Women, being a lower order of beast, can't help but feel attracted to the lowest members of the male species—brutes, slobs, frat boys. Men hardly above the level of jungle savages, men who seize them, drag them away and beat them into submission while tearing open their vaginas and planting their degenerate seed."

"I see," I said (not really seeing, of course).

"After your amazing insight forced me to realize the terrible gap between me and my social enemies, I remembered a terrible experience I had," said Reggie, hunching down on the bench and talking between his knees in an undertone that seethed with shame and rage.

"It was one of those terrible hot days in August. A weekend. I was sixteen. I took the subway all the way out to Coney Island, desperate for companionship, hoping to meet some lovely girl who could appreciate me and love me for the quiet, modest, masterful lover that I know I am, because of my gentlemanly nature. But as I walked along the crowded beach, crawling with people, many of them young couples pawing at each other's bodies and filling me with disgust and hatred, I passed by one young girl who was like a Greek goddess descended from Olympus. She was walking alone, in her bright red bikini with her breasts tan and straining from her top, and her luscious blonde hair blowing in the wind. I tried to be subtle, but I stared. I stared at her beauty, and I was scared. I was terrified that she might view me as nothing but a creepy little bug that she was afraid might buzz too close and touch her perfect skin. Her beauty was terrifying and intoxicating! And then, just as we passed each other, she actually looked at me. She looked at me and smiled. Most girls never even notice me, or if they do, they sort of veer away from me. But she smiled. Smiled! I had never felt so euphoric in my life. One smile. One smile was all it took to change my mood and make the hot, crappy trip out to Coney worthwhile. The power that beautiful women have is enormous. It's awful, Farf. One blonde girl can turn a desperate boy's whole world around—if just for a minute—with one little glance and a polite smile.

"I stayed euphoric for the rest of that walk. But then, I was barely off the beach when it hit me. That girl was just a brief moment, and her smile was probably an accident or maybe gas in her stomach. If I had smiled back and approached closer, she probably would have screamed and run away. And I asked myself, *what's the use of living if I can never have a girl of such beauty?* There are millions of men, ugly and stupid, who get girls like that, get them and use them and then get another beautiful girl, and another one after that. But me? I knew I could never ever hope—hope!—to have even one girl like that, to love me, to hold my hand, to slip beside me in bed and have glorious, lingering intercourse. I knew that in my lonely heart. But until you made it clear to me, I didn't understand why my life was so desolate.

"As much as I want a girl like that, as much as I hunger and lust for her, I understand now that wanting her is a cruel trick that nature is playing on me, the cruelest trick of all. Because I could no more have sex with her—a blonde, beautiful beast without a soul or a sense of human morality—than an angel could have sex with a sow."

Unfortunately, I pictured this. The unsettling image distracted me long enough to lose track of Reggie's ramblings—which ended abruptly when a mother passed our park bench, pushing a stroller. Reggie went silent, careful not to be seen talking animatedly with a dog. When the mom was out of range, Reggie said, "They reject me and they hate me, and that's why I hate life, Farf. I hate it."

On that cheery note, we headed back to our place, where Reggie couldn't see any women. After a while, he seemed to calm down. He stopped raving about the injustices and rejections that women had inflicted on him. But I sensed that he was still upset. He reminded me, for the umpteenth time, that he was twenty-eight years old and still a virgin. "Never been kissed! Kissed, for Christ's sake! Never!"

That night, after watching his favorite Monday night shows on TV, he suddenly just up and bolted, leaving me alone in the apartment. At the time, I attached no importance to his abrupt departure. I was grateful for the peace and quiet. I have a rag rug where I like to curl up and chase golden retriever and Irish setter OLDs in my sleep.

When Reggie returned, there was something new and disturbing in the air. In the dim light of a single small lamp in our living room, I couldn't really make out the stains all down his jacket and pants and splashed on his shoes. But the

scent was unmistakable. It was blood, and it wasn't any sort of dog's blood I could recognize, nor another type of animal blood. Even your dumbest, slowest dog—and there are lots of them (don't get me started on Dalmatians)—is a regular encyclopedia of animal blood. We can distinguish a bleeding chipmunk from a roadkill raccoon at a mile's distance from either one.

This stuff smeared all over Reggie was no animal. When Reggie, who was making some not-very-human noises deep in his throat, staggered toward the bathroom and dropped this huge, jagged-back Bowie knife, he confirmed my worst fears. One sniff of the gore-smeared blade told me not only that this was human blood. The unique chemistry that filtered into my brain and left me slightly dizzy was—unmistakably—the essence of female. This knife had been inside a woman.

"Darn," I said to myself.

3

"Snarling people have snarling dogs, dangerous people have dangerous ones."
—Arthur Conan Doyle

If you're a human, you can't truly imagine the ethical crisis faced by a dog who discovers that his master might be a murderer. This is because we all live by "the Code of the Dog."

My fidelity to the Code was sorely tested only a few days later.

After the night Reggie came in with the bloody knife—and then cleaned up after himself frantically 'til not a visible vestige of his "adventure" existed in our apartment, although I could still smell it—he hunkered down in a corner of the bedroom that he called his "office." I knew he was very upset with himself because he sank into a binge of playing the latest version of his favorite video game, "Zombie Slaughterhouse." His only breaks were to feed me and take me for brief walks—to a vacant lot just across the street from our building.

I kept hoping that Reggie would turn on the TV so I might be able to catch a newscast, hoping—and dreading—to hear something that might explain the blood all over his clothes. (My best-case scenario? He had interrupted a bloody assault on the street, inadvertently pocketed the knife used in the attack, then messed up his clothes while giving mouth-to-mouth resuscitation to the bleeding victim.) But Reggie had no interest in anything but annihilating digital zombies, and—bright and resourceful though I am, being a German shepherd—I lack the dexterity to manage a television remote. Of course, I could have knocked it onto the floor and stepped on it, probably landing on an episode of "SpongeBob Squarepants." However, if I'd done this, the sudden burst of noise would have merely angered Reggie, who would have scolded me, clicked off the TV and put the remote on a shelf beyond my reach.

When they say it's a dog's life, they're not just whistling Dixie.

Those were a pretty tense three days. I kept my distance, sticking close to my rag-rug bed and making no fuss when my water dish was empty. As long as there's a toilet, I'll never die of thirst.

Then, suddenly, after Reggie had forgotten to eat any dinner—again—he stood up and said, "There's going to be a reckoning. There must be. Someone has to pay."

I raised my head and spoke carefully. "A reckoning? What do you mean, Reg?"

"Vengeance," he said. "A hard reckoning is due for every one of them who have humiliated, belittled and tortured me."

"Tortured?" I said. "Who—?"

"Come on! You'll see!" said Reggie, snatching my leash off its hook. "They're everywhere."

"Who's everywhere?"

"Oh, you'll see! You've never noticed 'cause you're a fucking ignorant animal. But I'll show you."

With that, he rummaged in his closet for a heavy khaki rain slicker and put it on, even though it wasn't raining outside. He grabbed something from the top drawer of his bureau and shoved it into the pocket of his slicker. Then he snapped the leash, rather violently, onto my choke chain and nearly dragged me out the door as I tried to gather my feet and match Reggie's violent purposefulness.

Going out the door, I didn't have a good feeling.

Reggie, pulling me away from every appealing smell I came across, prowled Brooklyn's streets like a jungle cat, pausing only to glare at couples as they hurried by. Half the time, I could hear him utter the word *whore* as he turned to watch a woman pass. Then, in a quiet block on what I think was Willoughby Avenue (being lower to the ground, with bad eyesight, I can't read street signs too well), he just halted in his tracks and glared.

The objects of his regard were a man and woman walking close together. They were both perhaps twenty-five years old. The male had an arm around the woman's waist, his hand sliding down several times to caress her bottom—a trespass that seemed to afford them both a little shiver of pleasure. Being a sentimentalist, I thought the scene rather sweet and charming. But its effect on Reggie was, apparently, the opposite.

Reggie began to talk under his breath in a high-pitched whine that people could only hear if they got very close to him. But I heard him easily, even though what I heard was very disturbing.

"Look at him," Reggie whispered. "He's a barbarian, a knuckle-dragging cretin."

"Who?" I replied. I admit I was a little befuddled.

"That fucker rubbing that whore's ass," Reggie snapped back.

I looked back at the couple. All I could discern were two typical twenty-first-century Brooklynites. The man was dressed in scruffy-seeming but expensive and fashionable clothes. He'd bathed (I could tell with one sniff) within the last three hours. He had angular, attractive features and well-groomed hair redolent of coconut-oil mousse. He conveyed an overall physical softness that suggested a white-collar career. He was probably a graduate student, an office worker, maybe even a first-year associate at a law firm. A similar profile fit the girl, who was a pretty thing with long, clean-smelling hair cascading down her back and a mild, pleasant aroma of freesia, "unscented" moisturizer and pungent sexual arousal. "Barbarian" didn't seem to apply.

But Reggie was rambling on about how "women are savages, incapable of intelligent thought. They're completely controlled by the constant hunger they feel in their cunts. They're hungry for attack and devastation. They want to be ripped open …"

"Oh no, Reggie. I don't think … I mean, look at them. They're probably in love. They look nice."

"Nice? Nice? They're degenerate, Neanderthal, slobbering animals, pawing each other."

I have to admit that all this editorializing against "animals"—me being regarded generally as an animal myself—irked me just a little. I would have mentioned this to Reggie, but he was yanking my leash. The choke chain cut off my breath for a moment, rendering my speaking voice inoperative. By the time I could talk again, Reggie had dragged me around a corner, the offending couple was out of sight and Reggie was quietly fuming. I decided that discretion was the better part of shutting the heck up.

I'd have ample opportunity to critique Reggie's anti-animal biases later, at home.

Meanwhile, Reggie was zigzagging in a northerly direction, almost as though he were seeking something—or someone. It seemed as though we were on some sort of hunt. I started feeling queasy.

"I'm gentle, I'm thoughtful," Reggie was muttering as we walked along. "I have the best manners of anyone I know. My face is kind. My eyes are large, chestnut brown and intelligent. You've seen that, Farf."

Surprised to hear my name, I hesitated to respond. Reggie was quick to pounce.

"Haven't you, you fuckin' mutt?"

I said, "Reggie, I agree. Your eyes are ..."

"The mirrors of a pure soul. Too fucking pure! I'm the most desirable man I know, and I'm a virgin! A virgin because women are too depraved and foul to appreciate my refinements, my gentle manners, my superior nature. All they want is to crawl in the gutter and lick the gonorrhea germs off the balls of hairy sadists."

Reggie went on like this for about twelve blocks, but I stopped listening after a while. Having worked up a lather, he couldn't calm down. He kept getting angrier and louder as we walked along. He wasn't talking in that dog-whisper that was only audible to me. He growled and shouted, calling women whores and sluts and guttersnipes.

It was right after "guttersnipes" that he stopped in his tracks, giving my choke chain an entirely gratuitous snap. I tracked his gaze and saw what he was looking at. We had gotten well over toward the Navy Yard, in an area not heavily traveled and now, 'round midnight, pretty much deserted. On the far side of a broad street—which was probably Flushing Avenue— and around a corner, a car was parked but not motionless. It was easy to guess what was going on behind the fogged-up glass. I caught the distinct odors of Jack Daniel's and human sex seeping from a slim opening in the rear window.

Human sex, in case you weren't aware, has a fragrance unlike any other creatures in coitus. The difference between dogs humping, for example, and humans copulating is like the difference between pots of *cioppino* and *ratatouille* simmering on the same stove. If your nose is experienced, there's no mistaking one for the other.

And cats humping? More like bratwurst boiling in urine.

Anyway, a subtle erotic hint of *ratatouille* was wafting from the back seat of the parked car.

DAVID BENJAMIN

"There!" hissed Reggie. "There they are! Barenaked and fucking and degrading the gene pool."

"Gene pool?" I said.

"Shut the fuck up, mutt!"

There it was—my problem in five words. If I'd been, say, a familiar buddy of Reggie's, a human, and he had spoken to me that way, I'd be in his face like a flash, and I'd be poking his chest with my finger and saying something like, "Where the fuck do you get off, motherfucker? Talking to me like that? I'm your fuckin' best friend, fucko!"

And he'd have to apologize, out of friendship.

But it's different if you're "man's best friend," by which I mean a dog, any dog. We have to take all the abuse our masters hand out—verbal, physical, even fatal—because we live by the Code, which dictates absolute loyalty to one's master. I mean, absolute. You cannot betray—or even question—your master in any way, shape or form. You can't even doubt him, although I admit I had to struggle pretty hard to suppress a few misgivings about Reggie, especially after what happened next.

Reggie dropped my leash and started toward that rocking Ford Taurus like a flaming angel after an ovulating cow. As he did, he yanked from the depths of his canvas slicker this great big Bowie knife—the same bloody weapon he had dropped on the rug a few nights before.

At first, I barely kept up with him as he charged the car. But I speeded up, knowing I'd better be quick to the spot.

In a few seconds, Reggie had both hands on the car. He pressed his nose to the glass, trying to see through the condensation inside. He peeked through the slim crack at the top of the window. "Shit," he said under his breath, frustrated.

Then it came out of him like the cry of a raging bear with its foot in a trap, a scream like I'd never heard before. All my hair stood up, my ears flapped down flat and my tail slapped up between my legs so hard that I bruised a testicle.

With the polished steel butt of that hideous knife, Reggie bashed at the window, punching a whole the size of a cantaloupe.

Suddenly, a girl was screaming inside, and a male voice grunted and said, "Hey! Jesus! What the fuck?"

But Reggie drowned them out as he continued to whale away at the window and scream. "Kill you, fucking whore! Kill you and your rutting pigslobmoron savage! Cut you to fucking shreds, you fucking slime!"

He kept going on like that. No need to provide a complete transcript, particularly because I believed Reggie. He was definitely out to kill these people. I didn't really understand why, but I knew—as a former police dog and a firm believer in the preservation of all life, but especially the lives of humans, without whom dogs would still be out in the woods, chased by vicious wolverines and gnawing on carrion—that I didn't want him to kill these innocent sweethearts whose only evident offense was their failure to get a room.

On the other hand, there was the Code of the Dog, which prevented me from doing anything to intentionally interfere with my master.

Wham, wham, wham! The hole in the passenger window was getting bigger. The window was going to collapse at any second. The mostly naked girl was shrieking and floundering in the back seat. From my vantage point, I could only glimpse parts of her as they popped up in the car's rear window—an arm, a shoulder, her head, her bottom. I saw bits of the man, too, but the girl seemed to have worked her way on top of the male and was struggling to escape Reggie. The main sounds from the man were more grunts and the occasional outcry of groin pain (which, as all dogs know, sounds more urgent than pain incurred in other parts of the anatomy).

The man was shouting, "Ouch, Jesus! Goddammit! Who the fuck?" when it hit me. Although I could not interfere with Reggie, there was a way I could interfere with these two hapless shmucks in the Ford. So, with the grace natural to my breed, I stood up on my hind legs, shouldered Reggie aside and stuck my magnificent but intimidating head right through the hole in the window. The prevailing odors inside hit me like a pot of boiling Provençale veggies poured over my head.

But I ignored that.

I started barking and snarling like White Fang. When I really work up a good growling fit, my saliva kicks in, and pretty soon I have slobber flying in great loops around my head—which is what happened. Of course, Reggie, with his giant elephant-gutting knife, wanted to get at the two lovers and was trying to push me aside. But now I had both feet planted now on the window ledge, raving and raging away like I'd gone completely around the bend.

As I expected, my interruption gave the man and woman time to recover their senses and find the opposite door handle. They might have moved faster if they weren't so scared of me. They were clambering over each other to escape the car before I could breach the window and start to shred them like cornered gerbils.

In twenty more seconds, they had shoved open the door and scrambled onto the sidewalk. In two more seconds, they were sprinting down the street, both without their pants. I noticed that the woman was a little heavy in the hips, but the man had beautifully formed, tightly muscled buttocks built for speed. By the time he turned the corner at the end of the long block, he had a ten-yard lead on his erstwhile lover. She might have been able to keep up if she hadn't persisted in screaming the whole way.

The important thing is that they got away.

"Jesus Christ, Farfel. What the hell's wrong with you?"

I dropped back to the ground, breathing hard. I did a quick end-to-end body shake and lapped the saliva from around my mouth, looking as content as I could manage under these dire circumstances.

"They got away, ya mutt!"

Although he was miffed, Reggie had recovered. I could tell. There was a note of pride in his voice, as though—with all that barking and drooling—I had joined his crusade against women.

"We'll do better next time, Farf. Thanks for tryin' to help."

"Aw," I said, "what are friends for?"

As Reggie reached down to pat my head, he said, "Yeah, but I've learned my lesson, Farf. Thanks to you."

"Lesson?" I asked.

"Yeah," said my master. "I gotta get a gun."

Oh my God.

4

"Slowly, deliberately, the dog turned from the black wolf and walked toward the man. He was a dog, and dogs chose men."
—Jim Kjelgaard

Your serious dog (by which I mean the sort of dog who can resist the urge to lick every human face he sees) lives by the Code of the Dog, even if he doesn't remember the exact wording. Different breeds have different formulations, but the one I learned at the police academy from my canine mentor Scout is more or less the King James Version:

I pledge absolute, lifelong allegiance to the master who has rescued me from the jungle, the back alley and the call of the wild, who has saved me from the needle, who has vaccinated and wormed me, who brushes my coat, pulls out my ticks and kills my fleas, who fills my bowl, picks up my shit, rubs my belly and glorifies me above all other creatures—cats especially—as Man's Best Friend, and to the species for which he stands, one humankind over all dogs, pedigreed and mongrel, champions and mutts, with twice-daily walks and rawhide chew-toys for all.

Serious dogs don't just give lip service to the Code. We believe it fervently because we know, without it, without devotion to the blind loyalty enshrined in the Code, we'd be no higher on the pet scale than barn cats or hamsters. With our speed, size and cunning, with our powerful jaws and sharp teeth, with our exceptional communication skills and ability to operate in packs, I mean, think about it! Without an expressed commitment to mindless loyalty, we'd be too treacherous to keep around the house. We'd have to live in crawlspaces, in woodsheds or, God forbid, one of those drafty, cramped, lonely doghouses. If you've ever sat down and had a conversation with a doghouse dog or—even worse—a chain-in-the-backyard dog, you have no idea how miserable life can be.

So, we live by the Code. We survive by it, and we thrive by it.

Which became my dilemma ever since I saw Reggie go ape and attack the two lovers in the Taurus.

Mind you, after that incident, I remained unequivocally true to Reggie. He was my master. However, I was beginning to suspect, from the accumulation of fairly strange evidence, that Reggie might be just a little bit *loco en la cabeza*.

Not that this bothered me terribly. Lots of crazy people own dogs. In fact, some psychologists regard an intensely close bond with one's dog, or any pet, as a form of mental illness. But, you see, dogs are pretty tolerant of lunacy in people because we deal with it so often in our fellow dogs. I can't even count the number of my good friends who suffered from canine distemper, and I've never met a Yorkie who wasn't crazier than an outhouse rat. Besides, as a rule, crazy people tend to feed us better.

So crazy, in humans? No big deal.

But crazy enough to kill? Well, loyal though I am, Reggie's apparent homicidal tendencies got me thinking.

Certainly, I could understand Reggie's slippage into the Twilight Zone. I mean, the guy hadn't had sex in his entire life—twenty-eight years. Being a dog, I could hardly imagine.

Dogs, like humans, believe in love. All that shmaltz, candlelight and violin music in *Lady and the Tramp*, for example, was perfectly accurate. Dogs regard Walt Disney as one of cinema history's great realists. However, dogs don't normally associate sex with love. For us, sex is pure instinct. When I spot an unspayed LD with her tail in the air, I don't worry about introductions, small talk or boxes of chocolate. I just wag right up to her and start drinking in the pungency of her relevant parts. If she's normal, she starts sniffing away just as eagerly around my nether regions. Then, before we can be yanked apart on our respective leashes, I get the world's fastest erection, mount the bitch—er, LD, and bango, she welcomes me in, and we take a quick trip to the moon on eiderdown wings. Twenty seconds, max. No emotion, no dilly-dallying, no second thoughts or weepy recriminations. Just wham-bam, thank you, poochie, followed by a nice full-body shimmy to clear our sinuses and shake off any clinging body fluids.

Reggie, alas, being human, lacked the instinct and the *chutzpah* to just grab a woman, rip off her undies and plunge. Not that I wanted him to do that. But what's worse: he was totally bereft of the simple gumption to walk up to a girl and say, for Pete's sake, "Hi." Consider, for example, his usual routine when we stroll over to Fort Greene Park. He finds a bench on the footpath with a view of the benches across the lawn. He sits there in the open—exposed, vulnerable and looking totally pathetic, like an emotional panhandler. He watches the girls go by, follows their passage like a tracking shot in a Hitchcock movie, and all the while, he's yearning, pining, hungering away at this oblivious female who's got someplace to go and wouldn't look at Brad Pitt if he was sitting on a bench in Fort Greene Park—because this is New York. In New York, you keep your eyes to yourself and never, ever, invite any sort of human response. Ever.

Which Reggie just does not grasp.

He sees New York women behaving like normal New York women—I mean, surviving—and he thinks each one of them is personally shunning him.

And he does nothing to break down that barrier. Doesn't talk, doesn't move. He peers at them surreptitiously and doesn't show any more interest in these women than they show in him. But Reggie expects them to be drawn over to him on some sort of psychic tracking beam of gentlemanly allure. And when they fail to be sucked mystically into his orbit, Reggie crashes. He starts to rave about the bestiality of women, their attraction to the most aggressive, least refined males of the species.

You know, the kind of lothario who, while walking out of church, turns to the woman next to him and says, "Hi."

Well, I've given you an idea of the way Reggie talks about women. For a long time, I thought he was just rationalizing his bashfulness, creating a philosophy that soothed his feelings after being rejected by women who had no idea that their mere existence was tantamount to Regicide (pun intended).

That *status quo ante* changed the night Reggie came home covered with blood. Which was followed by the attack on the Taurus.

If women had a decent sense of smell, maybe they'd notice. Reggie, after all, gives off a huge cloud of want. Dog friends of mine have noticed this from blocks away, and they've mentioned it to me. After the two lovers fled the Taurus, it began to dawn on me that Reggie was neither putting himself on women's radar nor coping well with his romantic deficiencies. He had slipped the bonds, I realized, of normalcy. I worried what he might do next.

All right. Truth is, I was worried about what he had already done. The bloody knife. That remark about getting a gun.

It was the night after the Taurus incident that I got up from my rag rug and laid my head on Reggie's leg as he was watching a re-run of "Friends" on Nick at Nite (the episode where Ross takes the bald girl to the beach). I said to Reggie, sort of offhand, "I have to admit, Reg. You have some fairly unconventional views on women."

"Fucking bitches." He said this softly, like the beginning of prayer, like "Hail Mary" or "Our Father." It gave me a chill. I could feel the hair rise up across my shoulders.

Then he stabbed the remote, shutting off the television.

"I'm not going to let them do this to me."

Inadvertently, I realized that I had set him off.

"Do what?" I asked. I sat back then, looking up at Reggie, my eyes round with loyalty and respect. Dogs do this really well. It's one of the many ways we regulate human behavior.

"Kill me," said Reggie.

"Kill you? Who's trying to kill you?"

"All of them. Every one of those sluts and whores who think they can crush me and destroy me."

"Gosh, Reg," I said as soothingly as I could, "I haven't really noticed any women trying—"

"Jesus, Farfel, what the fuck do you know? You're a fucking dog."

Well, there it was again. Bigoted inter-species disparagement. And please don't imagine that it didn't hurt—especially coming from my master. But he was my master. That's just the point. And I was living by the Code. So, nobly—with a power of forgiveness unique to dogdom—I shrugged it off.

I said, "Well, you have a point, Reg. I am only a dog, and my perceptions are limited by my inferior intelligence ..."

Yes, I know. I was sucking up shamelessly. But this was an emergency. I had accidentally triggered his anger. Now, it was my responsibility to calm Reggie down and keep him out of trouble.

I went on, "But maybe the solution is more like your responsibility, Reg, than these women you don't even know, women you've never met or spoken to."

Reggie nodded almost violently. "Well, you're right about

that, mutt. I gotta take the situation at hand by myself. I can either let those rotten whores drag me down and force me to kill myself in despair. Or I can take the war to them. I can take my vengeance while I still have the strength and purity of a twenty-eight-year-old virgin!"

This didn't make a lot of sense to me, so I asked Reggie to elaborate.

"The hour of reckoning, Farfel!" said Reggie. "No, no! These are hours of reckoning. There are thousands of women, millions of them, throwing themselves at men no more worthy of their beautiful bodies and flowing blonde hair than an orangutan or a dog like you."

Again, the dig. Again, I took it like a dog.

"I will wreak my vengeance, but I will wreak it quietly, artfully and graphically. I will do it again and again. I will write my message on the bestial forms of the women who say to me—in their every movement, in their words and gestures and the spreading of their thighs for inferior men—'No, Reggie! Not you! Anybody but you! Would I screw an AIDS carrier? yes! A syphilitic madman? yes! A sadistic sodomist with a broken beer bottle? sure! Why not? But Reggie? No, not Reggie! *Never* Reggie!'"

By this time, Reggie was standing up, screaming at the ceiling and crushing the TV remote in his fist. As he did so, the television came back to life, and I glanced at it, then turned with horror. The show that Reggie had turned on, in the dying throes of his remote control, was "Dating Naked." Here were happy men and women, buck naked (but strategically pixillated), flirting, laughing and getting to know each other (preliminary to off-camera canoodling) in ways that Reggie could never imagine for himself.

As soon as Reggie saw what had popped up on the screen, he shrieked painfully (to me) and flung the mangled remote at the TV, where it bounced off harmlessly. A naked couple on the screen was toasting with champagne flutes and sneaking peeks at each other's goodies.

Failing in his first salvo, Reggie pushed me aside, strode to the TV—a state-of-the-art fifty-four-inch Samsung his mother had bought for his birthday—and lifted it over his head. In another instant, the TV lay smashed at Reggie's feet, sparking and smoldering. A string of drool escaped Reggie's lower lip and hissed when it made contact with an exposed wire.

"Fucking bitches," said Reggie in that scary "Hail Mary" tone.

I decided it was not a good time to continue humoring Reggie. He had not only failed to get my drift but had shifted it in a totally different direction. So, in one of my more cowardly moments, I slunk back to my rag rug, lay my head between my paws and tried to be as inconspicuous as an eighty-pound police dog can manage.

Reggie stalked around our living room for a while, muttering and cursing, mentioning the "reckoning." Finally, he lunged toward the door, burst through, slammed it so hard that it didn't latch and thundered down the stairs. I had watched to see if he grabbed that awful knife on his way out. But he'd left it behind, and I breathed a premature and ultimately foolish sigh of relief.

In Reggie's absence, I remembered the troubles of my former police partner, Marilyn. She had trained me from a pup, and I loved her more than I will ever love anyone, dog or human. I think she felt almost as strongly toward me.

In many ways, I offered Marilyn a refuge from her life at home, with a husband, Alec, who abused and belittled her verbally and—when he was drunk—attacked her physically. I often wished Marilyn would just once take me home with her, where I could lie in wait in a quiet corner of her living room. Then, as soon as Alec said one vile word to Marilyn, or raised a hand to strike her, I'd be all over the son of a bitch (excuse my language) like a killer whale on a baby seal.

But Marilyn had always left me behind at the police

kennel. When she came to work with bruises on her body and tears in her eyes, I couldn't do a thing to heal or console her. Sometimes, I think the distraction of loving Marilyn affected my performance on the force. My anxiety about Marilyn's domestic problems might be the reason I had to retire early.

The one blessing from Marilyn's abuse by that prick (excuse my language) Alec was that Marilyn often took me along to her sessions with the police department's psychologist, Dr. Adrian Menzies.

Dr. Menzies coaxed Marilyn toward breaking from Alec without ever once telling her directly to get away before too late. Every time Marilyn expressed her fear or even the slightest desire to escape, Dr. Menzies encouraged her to explore that feeling, to look deeper into her own needs and unleash her suppressed emotions. When Marilyn finally admitted to Dr. Menzies that she was afraid the bastard (excuse my language) might kill her and that she needed help to leave him, it was all I could do to resist jumping up off the floor and licking Dr. Menzies' face 'til his mustache wore off.

My greatest regret is that I was mustered out of the force and placed with Reggie (after a powerfully emotional parting from Marilyn, the eternal love of my life) before Marilyn actually took the plunge and left Alec once and for all. I hoped, with all my heart, that she would go through with it and then find a guy who's really deserving of her.

But I had no way of ever knowing.

Still, having learned the basics of therapy from Dr. Menzies, I thought I could at least try to steer Reggie away from the worst consequences of his twisted celibacy. If I could talk to Reggie the way Dr. Menzies counseled Marilyn, I might yet save my basically kind and well-meaning master from the demons who haunted him.

Hey, I had a right to hope—and more important, I had a responsibility to Reggie.

5

"The conclusion I have reached is that, above all, dogs are witnesses. They are allowed access to our most private moments. They are there when we think we are alone. Think of what they could tell us. They sit on the laps of presidents. They see acts of love and violence, quarrels and feuds, and the secret play of children. If they could tell us everything they have seen, all of the gaps of our lives would stitch themselves together."
—Carolyn Parkhurst

Reggie had come home that night—the night he smashed the TV—with a spanking-new gun, a vicious-looking 9-millimeter with a fifteen-round clip. It reeked of fresh oil, a cloying scent but also redolent of a faint citrus tang that lingers on freshly milled high-carbon steel. If I got too close, it irritated my nasal passages. Cop though I was, I've always deplored guns.

For a while, he just sat stewing in his chair, staring at the wreck of his television. Then he picked up the phone and called his mother.

"Hello, Mommy? ... Oh, is it that late? I'm sorry, Mom ... No, no, it's good to hear your voice, too ..."

I'm never sure Reggie loves me or ever loved anybody—except his mother. Her he's crazy about, even when he's calling her names. I suppose he wants all women to be like Mom, but I'm not sure he has even seen her as she really is. For one thing, he has a brother and sister I've never met nor ever heard Reggie talk about, but he seems to think his mother is still a virgin.

He told her his television had gone haywire and could she give him the money for a new one, to which she answered—as usual—that, no, he shouldn't bother going to some tacky big-box store and shopping for a TV set. She would order one for him and have it delivered the next day.

Which she did, another fifty-four-inch Samsung HD monster that was up and glowing by noon. The deliverymen even cleaned up the wreckage of his old TV and carried it away.

The rest of Reggie's conversation with Mom that night was the usual pack of lies.

Mommy asked Reggie if he had a new job.

"Oh, I don't have time for that now, Mom. I'm programming and scripting a new video game called 'Intergalactic Hitman' ... Oh, well, yes, it is time-consuming—not to mention a real mental challenge—but it's fun, and when it's finished, well, Mommy, we'll both be living on Easy Street. A real good video game is worth millions ... Oh, thank you, Mommy. It's all in the genes, Mom. Your genes, not Dad's ..."

Reggie's mother thought he was a creative genius. She believed he was on the cusp of immortality in whatever endeavor he finally set his brilliant mind to. I agreed that Reggie is a pretty bright guy, but I also suspected that he lacked the sort of occupational focus to succeed as easily as his mother expected.

"Besides, Mom, I have to study ... Yes, I'm in school again. Taking courses at Pratt ... Yes, Pratt Institute. It's not far away ... Architecture. My professors are thrilled with my aptitude ...

Yes, even though now I'm just a part-time student. They want me to enroll full time. I might even qualify for an academic scholarship based on my grades and recommendations from my professors ... Well, thanks, Mommy. If it wasn't for you ... Girls? Oh, well, I do have a girlfriend ..."

At this, I almost choked. As it was, I made a rude noise that caused Reggie to send a dirty look my way.

Then he went on lying.

"Antoinette ... Yes, it's a beautiful name. And she's a beautiful girl. She always wears white or light blue dresses, trimmed in satin—she never wears slacks or shorts. She's blonde and very pale, with perfect skin with huge blue eyes, and she paints impressionist aquarelles ... Yes, watercolors. She's really gifted. Beautiful little paintings of flowers and landscapes and kittens ..."

Why not puppies? I thought. Why are kittens always the apotheosis of cuteness? Puppies are cute—plus, they're honest. There's nothing on earth more devious than a six-week-old cat. Oh, well ...

"Well, she's very shy and innocent. She was home-schooled by Christian Scientists ..."

Oh, for God's sake, I thought. After that whopper, I stopped listening to the conversation. It ended about ten minutes later, with Mommy promising to transfer money into Reggie's bank account for tuition, art materials, rent and groceries. Honestly, if he'd asked for a car, there'd be a brand-new BMW parked on the street in front of our building the next morning. But like all good spongers—dogs, as the leaders in the field, know how it's done—Reggie never got extravagant. He asked only as much as he needed from his mother, plus a little bit more. And the tap never went dry.

• • •

That was April. Reggie had used his mother's money to buy his gun. He didn't buy it legally, of course. He was too smart to buy a traceable weapon. He kept the gun in a drawer next to his bed. I could smell it, oozing an oily fragrance and a faint suggestion of burnt flesh.

After the big purchase, every day, I feared that Reggie would rush out in a rage, looking to use his new gun as quickly as he could. But the gun seemed to quiet his anger just by its presence. Maybe it scared him (it sure scared me). But, over the days that followed, I was able to talk with him and explain that many people were lonely, some because other people rejected them, but also because of their own insecurities. Many people were lonely simply because they had fallen, unconsciously, into a solitary lifestyle.

I spoke with him about these things, saying nothing critical or disparaging, just as Dr. Menzies had conversed gently with Marilyn, my sweet, patient trainer. Reggie seemed to be getting better. I sensed that he was confronting his demons, recognizing that his problem with girls was not a vast conspiracy in a world that had turned against him.

Reggie, I think, really was making progress until the iced-latte incident in Fort Greene Park. It all started out as a normal walk. I had discreetly pooped on the grass, underneath my favorite linden tree. Reggie had deftly swept up the evidence in an Associated Supermarket plastic bag and dropped it into a trash receptacle. Then, as usual, we strolled to the heart of the park, where Reggie took up his surveillance post on a bench, waiting for some lovelorn beauty queen to discover him there, the man of her fevered nightly dreams, fling herself into his lap and cover his face with burning kisses.

As long as that imaginary woman didn't make her fantastical appearance, Reggie would conduct his usual stakeout, tracking every attractive woman who came in sight, following each 'til she disappeared around the bend. After what happened that day, I realized I should have been more vigilant. But I was so used to Reggie's sad, passive routine that I'd grown complacent. I actually dozed off and didn't notice the couple who settled onto a bench right across from us.

When I awoke from my nap, I could sense the tension coursing through Reggie's body, and I looked around for the source.

There they were. It was a warm spring day. The girl, a blonde in a filmy sun dress, had her arms around the man's neck and she was nuzzling his cheek, turning his face frequently to kiss him. The man was tall, slim and dressed head-to-toe in the sort of casual slacks, jacket, polo shirt and loafers (without socks) that had cost him four figures at Ralph Lauren or Armani.

Actually, being a working-class type of dog (not your indolent housebound Scotty or penthouse dachshund), I admit that once in a while, I've intentionally slobbered on guys in outfits like that.

But I digress.

The man, who was evidently as much in love as the girl, had one hand on her waist while the other would creep up her thigh until she would squirm and giggle and slap the probing hand playfully. Besides the pheromones pouring off both of them, the young man was redolent of Brut and Right Guard. The girl was all Aveeno, with a hint of cucumber. To an objective observer like me, they posed a tender portrait of young love among humans at the peak of their reproductive powers. As a dog, my only regret in seeing these two young people obviously primed for sex was that human social norms prevented the male from dropping his $400 slacks and mounting the woman right there on the bench.

(I know. People are not dogs. But really, wouldn't everything be simpler if they were?)

Knowing Reggie, I sensed that he wasn't responding well to this tableau. His eyes were wide, his face was livid with boiling blood, and his fists were clenched between his knees. Having discussed his feelings with him, I knew that he regarded the woman, irrationally, as his own God-given mate, stolen unjustly from him only because this other guy was shapelier, more muscular, more handsome, more glib and charming, smarter, richer and more romantically aggressive than he.

I was about to speak softly to Reggie, to calm him if I could, or simply to divert the seething fury I could smell emanating from him like a steaming vat of ammonia. I mean, really, anger stinks so bad it burns your eyes. If humans could smell themselves, they'd think twice about picking fights and waging wars.

Already, I was too late.

Someone who'd been on our bench before us had left behind an extra-large plastic cup from Starbucks, still half-full of what used to be—judging by my nose—an iced two-percent latte with too much sugar, a dash of cinnamon and a lot of superfluous foam (What is this human infatuation with foam?). In a single movement, Reggie swept up the cup and stood, glowering ferociously at the lovers on the opposite bench.

"Um, Reggie, wait."

I know. Pretty lame. But I had no idea he would move so fast. Suddenly, I was skidding along on the end of my leash while Reggie strode over to the couple, who didn't notice his presence until his shadow covered them.

The girl said, "Oh!" Also pretty lame. That's the only word she managed before Reggie covered her with lukewarm latte, splashing some on the guy's $800 sportcoat and $250 polo shirt.

The guy was more expressive. He said, "What the fuck?"

This I only heard at a distance because, as soon as Reggie had delivered his *coup de grace*, he began cheezing it out of the park as fast as his ponderous legs could carry him. To suggest that this was an embarrassing experience for me—as a former officer in the New York Police Department—would be to understate my shame immeasurably. I mean, as long as I was on the job, it was my duty, my oath, to run toward any public disturbance, to quell it before anyone's life or safety could be further imperiled. But here I was, accessory to an incident that I could have prevented. Technically, this was an assault. Here I was, turning tail and galloping, like a greyhound out of Hell, away from the scene of the outrage. Within a few seconds, I had actually passed Reggie. Straining at my leash, gagging on my choke chain, I was dragging him, stumbling and floundering, toward Dekalb Avenue as fast as I could go. With every leap and every jerk on my leash, I was terrified of hearing the once-comforting wail of NYPD sirens.

Once I'd gotten Reggie safely out of the park and made several turns, ending up on Cumberland Street heading toward Lafayette, I slowed us both down and tried to look like your average innocent pooch doing his walkies and snuffling at hydrants.

Then I said, "Reggie, what were you thinking?"

But Reggie didn't answer—or couldn't. All the way home, his conversation consisted of little outbursts that made no sense. Occasionally, he would growl juicily, like a pug with a sinus problem (actually, all pugs have sinus problems). His most comprehensible utterances were the usual stuff about "animal lust," "bitches," "rotten bitches," "ball-busting cunts," "vengeance," "the hours of reckoning," etcetera. Most disturbing, even after all that exertion and time to reflect on his impulsive attack on this blameless pair of young lovers, I couldn't even begin to calm Reggie down.

When we got back to our apartment, Reggie retreated to his favorite chair, staring into the distance and kneading his hands. This went on so long that, despite my anxiety about what he might do next, I wearied of the vigil. Exhausted by the day's exertions, I slipped over to my rag rug for a (pardon the expression) catnap. I intended to just doze a little, for maybe ten minutes.

Two hours later, awakening from a sound sleep, I was alone. Reggie had locked me in. I did a complete tour of the apartment but found no sign of where he had gone or what he might be doing. I knew where he kept his new gun. I loped into the bedroom. The bedside drawer was closed tight. I could smell the gun, but this meant nothing. Even if it were not present, its oils and residues remained there to confuse the most reliable of my six senses.

Hours later, as I was licking my balls pensively for about the fiftieth time (a nervous habit), Reggie burst through the door. Seeing him across the room, I breathed a momentary sigh of relief because—in the faint light of the only lamp Reggie had left burning—I could see that there was no blood on his clothes. To confirm my admittedly myopic impression, I inhaled deeply—and almost gagged. I was overwhelmed by a veritable stormcloud in which, at first sniff, I could discern the distinct odors of nitrocellulose, diphenylamine, bismuth and potassium—all of which I had studied at the police academy, as elements in human police simply call "gunshot residue" (or GSR).

Reggie, his eyes bloodshot, his whole body trembling, slammed the door and threw himself into a chair. As he did so, he slammed his 9mm onto the end table, almost knocking over a lamp.

I approached him gingerly.

"Did it," he muttered as I sat, facing him. I adjusted my face, assuming a look of absolute loyalty and dumb-dog affection. To sell the impression, I hung my tongue out the side of my mouth.

"Did what?" I said ingenuously.

"The reckoning." He didn't seem to be talking to me. He was lost deep inside himself.

"I gather," I said, "that you've done some shooting."

This wasn't the right approach.

"Fuck you," said Reggie.

Of course, this rolled right off me. I said, "Listen, Reggie. I don't know what happened out there, man. But I'm your friend. Y'know?"

Reggie grunted.

"I mean," I said, in my smoothest impression of Dr. Menzies, "if there's something you want to talk about, something to get off your chest, man, I'm here for you."

Finally, he looked into my eyes. Progress?

"Wha'd you say, boy? *You* are here for *me*?"

"Yes, Reggie."

"So, you've got my back?"

"Absolutely, Reg."

"Shit. You're just a fuckin' dog!"

Okay, maybe not progress.

I backed away from Reggie. He sat ruminating.

A moment later, Reggie lifted his chin, caught my eye, and said. "No. You're not just any fuckin' dog."

Here was a ray of hope. I said, "That's right, Reggie. I'm not just any—"

"You're a fuckin' delusion, is what you are!" said Reggie. "You're a talking dog. Dogs don't talk. If you're talking and I can understand you, you know what that means?"

"Wait," I began.

"It means I'm fuckin' nuts!" Reggie shouted. "Jesus Christ! Maybe if I shoot you, I'll be cured. Whaddya think, Farf?"

At this, he grabbed the reeking gun and pointed it right between my eyes.

Fortunately, I have police training. From day one at the academy, police recruits learn to show no reaction, no fear, no anger, especially no sudden movements, in life-threatening situations. So, far more calmly than I felt, I gazed into Reggie's eyes, over the gun barrel, cocking my head ever so slightly to one side.

We held that pose for a while until I said quietly, "On the contrary, Reggie."

Wrinkling his brow, Reggie peered more closely at me as though trying to see inside my head. "You just say, 'On the contrary'?"

"Yes."

"Oh yeah? Whaddya mean by that, fleabag?"

"I mean, it's just possible that your ability to understand me is the sanest thing about you, Reggie."

"Oh yeah?"

"Yes," I said, noting that Reggie's finger was still tensed on the trigger, "because you see in me your most sympathetic listener. While you have difficulty speaking to anyone else—"

"I don't have difficulty, you dumb fuckin' dog. I won't talk to those assholes because I can't trust 'em. They're all out—"

"But you *can* trust me," I said quickly. "Can't you?"

"Well, you're a dog. Dogs are stupid. They can't fool anybody."

This remark was so idiotic that I almost barked. But this was no time to calibrate the cunning of the canine mind.

So, I just said, "Even if I could, I couldn't even think about fooling you, Reg. You're my master."

"Yeah." Reggie's hand relaxed. "I'm your master. I may not be anybody else's fuckin' master. But I'm yours."

"That's right," I said. Reggie lowered the gun. I quickly closed in so Reggie could scratch behind my ears, which he did. I had myself back in his good graces.

That was close.

Unfortunately, in saving my own pelt, I'd missed an opportunity. Reggie was clearly tuckered out by his evening's experience. I made a few gentle efforts to nudge information from him, but he was back to mumbling about "reckonings" and "justice for gentlemen."

In less than ten minutes, he was asleep in the chair. He didn't budge all night long.

In the morning, without saying a word, he replaced his gun in the bedside drawer and took me out for a refreshingly uneventful walk through our neighborhood. Unsurprisingly, I was constipated.

DAVID BENJAMIN

6

"Oh, why can't dogs read?"
—Nancy Mitford

That morning in the park, in an effort to loosen my bowels, I was gnawing on a selection of greens common to New York City and referred to generally by the vast majority of humans as "grass." If people knew the unique medicinal qualities of the variety of grasses right under their feet, they could rid their species of a thousand illnesses, cancer foremost among them. But whenever a dog tries to explain this, it falls on anthropoid ears.

I was beneath a sycamore tree, blending one of its leaves with an astringently-flavored subspecies of burdock into a sort of laxative salad, when my nose encountered a newspaper. The headline covered half the front page. Even with my faulty eyesight, I could read it clearly. It said:

HAMBURGER HILL!

Underneath was a grisly photo of two people, sprawled on the street in a lake of blood. The bodies were beside a car. The photo caption read, "Are the shootings of a young couple in

Clinton Hill related to the slasher who has set Brooklyn on edge, or is a new killer on the rampage?"

Yes, I know. You had no idea that dogs can read. But think about it. It's only natural that we would, since most of us spend our first six months of life standing around on newspapers. We'd be bored to tears if we didn't try to figure out what all those chicken scratches mean. I've known a few dogs who prolonged their paper-training period for months and refused to pee outdoors simply because they were literally addicted to *Calvin and Hobbes*, *Spiderman*, even *Garfield*. I once met a Belgian sheepdog who wouldn't talk about anything but David Brooks' latest column in *The Times*.

Anyway, I nosed open the paper and found out more. The victims had been parked on Adelphi. They'd been forced out of the car and executed in "Bonnie and Clyde fashion," meaning, I guess, a lot of bullets. I wanted to read more, but Reggie yanked my chain and dragged me away.

As we strolled the park, my mind was in turmoil. The murder had occurred last night, during the period that Reggie had left me alone in the apartment. He had come home drenched in GSR and seething with adrenalin. A hundred clues made me suspect, with all due reluctance, that Reggie was the killer cited in the *Daily News*.

Could it be? Was my master a murderer?

I groped for an alternative to this supposition as we completed our second lap around Fort Greene Park. Although I hadn't actually witnessed Reggie killing anyone, the evidence seemed overwhelming. My nose told me that Reggie had done these horrible deeds, and my nose, darn it, has never failed me.

"But what did it matter?" I said to myself as we started Lap No. 3. Reggie's my master. He's the center of my world and the object of my unquestioning loyalty. Even my allegiance to the NYPD, where Marilyn raised and trained and taught me to serve and protect even at the cost of my own life, does not supersede the Code of the Dog. I was with Reggie, body and soul, for better or worse, 'til death do us part.

Not that all this sophistry made me feel any better.

In fact, it made me—literally—sick. Suddenly, I felt as though my tummy was going to explode.

"Oh, my goodness, Reggie, here it comes."

"About fuckin' time," said Reggie.

"Quick, quick," I said. "Over by the fence."

I dragged Reggie to the fence, where the sycamore/burdock combo did its work in a veritable brown explosion.

"Jesus," said Reggie. "I'm not pickin' that up."

Relieved, I did a few desultory back-kicks and led Reggie quickly away from the scene of the crime. And then, as though the sudden end of my intestinal blockage had unfettered my brain, it came to me.

Actually, she came to me.

She was a medium poodle, perhaps one-quarter my size, off-white in color, with lovely black eyes and an overbite that gave her canines a subtle, lovely prominence. I had barely noticed her before she touched my nose with hers, after which she exhaled rather indelicately, as though clearing something unpleasant from her lungs.

"What have you been doing, snorting gunpowder?" she said.

I realized that a little of Reggie's GSR shower had rubbed off on me. To a poodle's refined sensibilities, this must have been a shock.

"Oh, I'm sorry," I said.

What a way to start off with a girl! Stinking of cordite. The first thing I should have done when I got to the park was a thorough, cleansing roll in the grass.

DAVID BENJAMIN

I said, "My master, he was …" What could I say? Out murdering lovers on Adelphi Avenue? "He was practicing at the gun range."

"Oh, really?" She backed away. "He doesn't look like a policeman."

"Oh, he isn't. He's just, well …"

"A gun nut?" she said.

This wasn't starting off well. And now Reggie was tugging on my choke chain, cutting off my voice. Suddenly, I was silent.

The poodle and I had been speaking in standard dog English, which Reggie couldn't understand. Every dog is at least bilingual. We learn both our master's tongue and the canine dialect common to most of the dogs around us. When we meet a dog from a foreign country, we resort to the instinctive language of our ancestors, which involves a lot of body movement, inarticulate vocalization and a certain amount of what we call "dog music." Humans hear dog music as a sort of multivariant high-pitched whining, punctuated with a vocabulary of urfs, woofs, snorts and plosives. While I was with the NYPD, I was able to expand my linguistic range to dog-Chinese, dog-French, dog-Spanish and—strangely enough—dog-Afrikaans and dog-Swahili. These last two languages I learned from a Rhodesian ridgeback named Tiny, who was in my academy class through an exchange program from the Pretoria PD.

As Reggie was struggling to disengage me from the poodle, I looked up and noticed the poodle's mistress, blonde and slender, dressed in jeans, t-shirt and tennis shoes. I caught a quick breath between Reggie's tugs and determined that the female human was young—in her twenties if my nose is any judge—and, unless my nose was failing me, a daily dabbler in "Light Blue," a slightly fruity *eau de toilette* from Dolce & Gabbana. She wasn't notably pretty, but she had a pleasant Kerry blue terrier face despite a look of mild distress. (And she had good taste in fragrances.)

She said something.

"Doesn't that hurt him?"

Reggie stopped pulling on me. He froze in place, staring at the woman.

"I mean," she pointed at my neck. "Isn't he choking?"

"Er, well ..." said Reggie.

To help Reggie out, I backed up, slacked the leash, sat, and hung my tongue out. To complete the performance, I cocked my head and looked the woman suavely in the eye.

"Oh, well," she said, "I guess he's okay."

"Well, well, big boy," said the poodle. "You're a real lady-killer, aren't you?"

"Um, yeah, he's ..." said Reggie to the woman.

The poodle was smirking at me, sarcasm virtually dripping from her pointy little snout. She had a natural coat, meaning she hadn't been trimmed into what people call a "poodle cut." Absent the ridiculous haircut, most humans wouldn't even recognize her by breed.

Ignoring the poodle's dig, I said, "Well, I don't know about that. But I get along okay with women. I used to have a mistress."

"Oh, really?"

"Yes. In the NYPD."

"Your mistress was a cop?"

"Well, yes. I was, too."

Her tune had changed.

"What's his name?" the woman asked Reggie.

"Huh?"

"Your dog."

"My dog? Him?"

Reggie was hopeless with women.

"Yes. What's his name?"

"My dog?"

"Yes."

"What is this guy?" the poodle asked me. "Retarded?"

"Farfel," Reggie finally said.

"No, Reggie's just scared," I said.

"Of what?"

"Oh, what an interesting name."

"Women," I said to the poodle.

"My little sweetie here is called Cupcake," said the woman.

"Oh," said Reggie.

"Your name is Cupcake?" I said to the poodle.

"Don't rub it in," said Cupcake.

"Hey, Farfel's nothing to exactly put up in neon lights in Times Square, y'know?" I said.

The poodle wagged, indicating that we'd broken the ice.

"Well, bye," said Reggie.

And suddenly, I was being dragged away just as I was formulating a brilliant remedy to Reggie's urge to kill. The poodle watched us depart, head cocked curiously. I caught a glimpse of the woman, whose brow was wrinkled with amusement.

• • •

It was more than a week before I spotted Cupcake again in the park. During the week, Reggie had gone out on another of his post-midnight hunting expeditions—from which, thank God, he'd come home unbloodied and irritable. I had tried to humor the poor guy, get him to loosen up and unburden. But he withdrew deep into himself and gave me no opening.

So I was thrilled at the sight of Cupcake, who possibly represented Reggie's salvation. You see, I had a theory.

Reggie hated and despised women whom he saw as hostile to him for his pathological bashfulness while being drawn to macho men. I thought that if I could find him a woman he doesn't hate, he might stop taking out his frustrations on strange girls and their collateral-damage boyfriends. Cupcake's mistress seemed as likely as any woman to help cure Reggie. She wasn't exactly a knockout, but I saw the silver lining. Her plainness suggested low self-esteem and a stagnant love life. This placed her, hypothetically, within Reggie's limited range. Moreover, as I'd already determined, she was polite and kind and smelled of Dolce.

However, I didn't know if she was available—which was why I dragged Reggie laboriously in her direction.

The woman was on a bench. Cupcake had been lying down, but she caught my scent and sat up. Luckily, Reggie was busy scanning the territory for women to hate. So, he didn't pay the woman much notice 'til I'd gotten him to the bench. I halted there and touched noses with Cupcake.

We went through the obligatory business of sniffing under each other's tails, although I had figured out at our first meeting that Cupcake hadn't yet been fixed. But I sublimated my carnal inclinations, so as not to distract from my higher purpose of saving Reggie from himself (and a whole lot of women from Reggie).

"Oh, hello!" said the woman.

Reggie changed colors, a weird human behavioral trait that has always mystified me. Are people somehow related to geckos and squids?

"Well," said the woman, holding up the conversation entirely on her own, "Cupcake and Farfel seem to like each other."

"Do we?" I said to Cupcake.

"You're all right."

"Thanks."

"Um," said Reggie.

Jesus. This was going nowhere.

"Still retarded?" Cupcake asked.

"No, but he acts like it, doesn't he?"

I had to intervene. Reggie was squandering a golden opportunity for cross-gender contact.

"Listen," I said to Cupcake, "I'm going to do something that might seem a little crazy. But I have my reasons."

"You're not going to go bite Gloria, are you?"

"Is that her name?"

"Yes. Are you?"

"No, of course not," I said.

"Okay, go crazy, ya big lug."

I did. Whipping my tail into a frenzy, I barked once in a happy tone and bounded into Gloria's lap, licking her face and nuzzling her about the neck and ears. She struggled to fend me off but laughed as she did so, showing no fear.

"Oh! Jesus Christ!" Reggie exclaimed. He yanked me back violently, although I was able to execute one excellent countersurge and regain the woman's lap, getting one more big lick in on her kisser.

This was, of course, fun. Face-licking is one of dogdom's greatest thrills. For some deep primordial reason, going back to when we were all wolves, dogs have found the human face one of the most lickable things in our universe of tactile sensations. As soon as we see a new face—especially when we're puppies—we just want to lick it 'til we wear it down to the bone. As we get older, we learn to control this temptation, and we only lick the faces who know us best, and then just as a form of affectionate greeting. But the pleasure never dies, and a good, prolonged face-licking will leave any dog glowing with satisfaction for hours.

So, even though there was an ulterior motive to my licking, it felt terrific. Gloria tasted like butter brickle ice cream. I could tell that Cupcake was envious.

"Was that good for you?" Cupcake sneered.

I just urfed, evocatively.

Meanwhile, Reggie was performing as I'd expected, sitting me down and yelling at me for being a "bad, bad boy." He apologized repeatedly and abjectly to Gloria. Gloria waved off Reggie's apologies, smiling and wiping her face as demurely as possible, considering the amount of saliva I'd left there.

(I am, as I might have mentioned, a world-class salivator.)

My ace-in-the-hole in this little scene was that Reggie happens to be one of the last guys on earth who carries a handkerchief—in his left hip pocket. He pulled it out. I breathed a sigh of relief when I saw that it was relatively clean. He handed it to the woman.

"Oh, thank you."

She rummaged in her bag and pulled out a plastic water bottle. She poured a little water on the hankie and looked up at Reggie, who was standing over her, bent into a sort of paralytic crouch.

"Do you mind if I wet your hankie?"

"Oh no. No no no no no no," replied Reggie obsequiously.

"Oh, please," she said. "Sit down for a second."

This hit Reggie like a Muhammad Ali uppercut.

"Huh?" he said, trembling with terror and indecision.

"Please," said the woman. "Sit by me. I won't bite, I promise. Let the dogs get to know each other."

Reggie didn't move.

"Let's get to know each other," said Cupcake, starting to nuzzle my face coquettishly.

Cupcake was biting me, rather ungently, on the neck.

"Not now," I said. "I've got to keep a close eye on—Ouch!"

Reggie, apparently inspired by the intimacy blossoming between Cupcake and me, shifted toward the bench and—with agonizing slowness, like a two-toed sloth closing in on a ripe fig—lowered himself to the edge of the bench, three inches west of the woman.

The woman was swabbing her cheeks with the wet handkerchief rather—I thought—fetchingly. "I'm Gloria, by the way," she said.

Reggie, of course, didn't answer.

"Gloria Greenbaum," she prompted.

Nothing from Reggie.

"My dog's Cupcake," the woman continued with admirable pluck. "Your dog—who's a sweetheart—is Farfel. I'm Gloria.

And you ..."

Reggie's forehead puckered. She had teed up the ball for him. It was his swing.

"Um," he said.

Gloria waited. In the meantime, she finished with the handkerchief, folded it, handed it to Reggie and searched her bag again.

"Uh," said Reggie.

Gloria removed a compact and began doing all those fascinating, fragrant things that women do with their faces. Reggie watched all this wordlessly.

I barked at him.

"Oh!" said Reggie, as though waking from a twenty-year nap. "Reggie."

"Oh, pardon," said the woman, who was obviously surprised to hear anything intelligible from Reggie.

"I said," said Reggie barely above a whisper, "my name's Reggie."

"Oh. Nice name!"

"Ya think?"

"Oh, yes. Short for Reginald?"

"Oh, no. Just Reggie. My mom, um ..."

"Liked it?"

"Yeah," said Reggie with a slight infusion of warmth. "Yeah, she did."

"Well, I do, too."

This began a halting conversation that went on for five more minutes, which I can't record because Cupcake started up with me.

"You're cute," said the poodle. "But I'm wondering."

"Wondering what?"

"Why should I trust you?"

I said, "What do you mean?"

"Listen, Gloria's nice. It's my job to look after her. Now, you bring this guy over to her. This Reggie. And well, no offense, but he seems a little strange. And he smells funny."

"Smells funny?"

"You live with him. You're probably used to it."

"Used to what?"

"Well, he's a little musty. A sort of sickly sweetness, like old mushrooms," said Cupcake. "There's a hint of decay. And is that chicken I smell?"

I could only sigh. She had an accurate nose.

"So, I'm thinking, what if Gloria takes up with your guy? Should I worry?"

What could I say? *Yes, worry your ass off! Drag her out of the park, never look back and never come here again! My master's a homicidal psycho!*

Instead, I said, "You're right, Cupcake. He is a little strange."

"Call me C.C. It's easier."

"Okay," I said. "But he's mainly just really shy. If he can make just one friend, someone who might be able to pull him out of his shell, I think he'll be fine."

"And you picked me and Gloria to unshell him?"

"Well, we happen to visit the same park."

"Along with a few thousand other dogs," said Cupcake.

But I was distracted. "Hey, listen to this," I said.

A little chemistry seemed to be percolating between Gloria and Reggie.

"Gee, I have to drop off Cupcake and get back to work, but ..."

Reggie, somehow sensing that Gloria's "but" was leading somewhere, said, "Yeah?"

I was proud of him. A regular Casanova.

"Well," said Gloria, staring down at her lap, "every day after work, I stop in for coffee at Connecticut Muffin, over on Myrtle. You know it?"

"No, but I know the, um ..."

"Neighborhood?"

"Right."

DAVID BENJAMIN

"So, I thought you might like to join me for coffee some day."

"Oh."

"Like, tomorrow?"

"Tomorrow?"

"About 5:30?"

"5:30?"

"Is that a date?"

"Uh."

"Will you be there?" asked Gloria.

I barked at the idiot.

"Oh. Okay," said Reggie.

"Oh, good. Thanks."

"Uh huh."

"I'll be looking forward to it."

"Um."

"Now don't stand me up."

"Stand you up?" said Reggie. "No, I wouldn't do that. Ever."

"No, of course not. Just kidding."

"Oh."

This disjointed bumbling seemed like it might go on for quite a while, so I started pulling on Reggie.

"Oh, I better go," he said.

"See you tomorrow," said Gloria, smiling and doing a finger waggle.

"Um, yeah."

"Well, C.C.," I said, "I'll be seeing you."

"Not if I see you first," she said, turning away and flipping her tail. She had a really cute little bottom, and she knew it.

• • •

A moment later, I said, "Well, Don Juan!"

"Whaddya mean by that?"

"Hey, an actual date, man," I said. "Way to go."

"Yeah, I guess."

"She's nice," I said.

"I guess," said Reggie.

"You guess? What was wrong with her?"

"That's the whole issue, isn't it?" said Reggie. "They're devious. They're killer angels. They lure you into their web, and you let down your defenses. They feel you out and find your weaknesses. Like spiders with their proboscis, looking for a soft spot between your armor plates. And then they plunge it in, like a hollow needle, sucking out all your juices."

Ignoring Reggie's tendency to mix metaphors brutally, I replied, "My God, Reggie. All she did was invite you for a lousy cup of coffee," I said. "She's nice."

"Yeah, well, she seemed okay."

"That's better," I said.

"But I'll be on my guard."

"Well, yeah. Anybody would. With a shameless floozy like that one."

Reggie ignored this.

"I bet there's a guy," he said.

"A what?"

"Another guy. She doesn't want me. She's trying to make him jealous. Some tall, Teutonic muscle-builder type. Some alpha prick!"

"Oh, for God's sake, Reggie!"

He went on like that all the way home.

But the next day, he kept the date.

7

"The dog has seldom been successful in pulling man up to its level of sagacity, but man has frequently dragged the dog down to his."
—James Thurber

Not only did Reggie keep the date. He met Gloria a few days later, for coffee again and then agreed to have dinner with her.

"Who asked?" I said.

"Huh?" said Reggie (his favorite word).

"Who proposed the dinner date, Reggie? You or Gloria?"

"Oh, it was her idea," said Reggie. "I wouldn't've. I mean, she's all right. But she's not that tremendously attractive, y'know? I mean, I could do better."

By "better," of course, Reggie meant the mythical Antoinette.

If you've never seen a dog roll his eyes, you've never seen me listening to Reggie. I rolled 'em over once and said soothingly, "Reggie, hey. You've got to walk before you can run. Think of Gloria as your training wheels before you move up in class to Kate Upton and Penelope Cruz."

"Who?" said Reggie.

Hopeless.

"Never mind."

"Yeah, well," said Reggie. "It's just dinner. It's not like I'm committed to anything."

"God forbid."

. . .

The date took place on a Friday night in mid-July at a very nice little bistro called Paulina's (chosen, of course, by Gloria) on Dekalb. I'd never been there, of course, but we had passed by, and the tendrils of scent that wafted from the kitchen—tarragon, fresh *chèvre* and roasted *Gruyère, béarnaise, moules, bouillabaisse* and just a faint suggestion of *truffe*—were sublime. I envied both of them their little feast.

Imagine my surprise when, both a little tipsy from wine (one sniff told me it was a thrifty but ingratiating *sauvignon blanc* from the Touraine domain), they came upstairs and walked right into our apartment just after 11 p.m.

"This is my place. It ain't much," said Reggie.

"Oh, it's very nice," said Gloria. She was being polite, but she shouldn't have said this. Reggie knew the place wasn't nice. It was stark, dark and haphazardly furnished, with no charm, no art on the walls except for a torn and flood-stained Keyshawn Johnson poster that harked back to Reggie's youthful enthusiasm for the New York Jets. I'd grown accustomed to the fishy pong that seemed to emanate from the paint and plaster—added to which was the dog smell that I couldn't help but contribute—but I could tell, as soon as she set foot inside, that it hit Gloria like a wet slap with a dead flounder. Her politeness in praising Reggie's fetid grotto would have been, normally, praiseworthy. But I feared Reggie might see it as a calculated deception meant to throw him off his guard and entice him into Gloria's deadly feminine web.

"Oh, yeah?" he said suspiciously. His eyes searched her face for the hidden proboscis.

I got up, wagged my tail and got Gloria to massage my

forehead and dig around sensuously behind my ears. Ah!

"Well," said Gloria smoothly, "it could certainly use a woman's touch."

"Yeah, well, I'm not a woman," said Reggie, with a note of belligerence. I turned to look at him, a little worried.

Gloria laughed rather musically. I looked up and gave her the once-over. She verged on lovely in a summer dress with a store-bought hairdo and a little makeup. Besides a stronger dose of Light Blue mixed with *sauvignon blanc*, residue of *boeuf bourguignon*, feminine perspiration and pheromones, I caught a hint of macadamia, probably from a high-end volumizing shampoo in a beauty salon. To my trusty nose, it was evident that Gloria had splurged for this date.

Unfortunately, Reggie was just about the last guy in New York who would appreciate this sort of effort.

I broke from Gloria's caress and padded over to Reggie. In whispered tones, I said, "Hey, Reggie. Come on. Cut the gal a little slack. She went all out for this date."

Reggie, who figured he'd caught Gloria subtly mocking him, just grunted.

An awkward pause followed. Reggie stood in front of his kitchen door. Gloria was more or less a statue in the middle of the living room, clutching a little beaded bag in front of her skirt, half-smiling at Reggie, waiting for him to do something, say something, extract his foot from his mouth and his thumb from his bunghole.

"Listen, Reg," I whispered. "Why don't you offer her a drink?"

"A drink?" said Reggie.

"Oh, yes," said Gloria. "That would be lovely."

"Oh." Gloria's answer to my question caught Reggie unawares.

"Anything would be fine," said Gloria, moving toward the hassock next to Reggie's only decent chair, a La-Z-Boy with a duct-tape strip across the seat.

"Oh, well, all I got is beer," said Reggie. "Well, there's some orange juice, but I'm not sure about the expiration date."

Gloria fielded this one like a pro. "Oh, a nice cold beer would be a nice change of pace after the wine," she said.

She hovered a moment before settling onto the hassock. I thought of a hen finding a bed of straw and priming herself to lay an egg.

"Okay, just a minute." Reggie turned abruptly and bustled into the kitchen. I went along.

"Listen," I said. "Relax. She's being very sweet."

"She fuckin' lied to me," growled Reggie. "This place is a dump."

"She's not lying. She's being polite."

"Yeah, well, that's how they start, how they set you up, how they suck you in."

"The beer," I said. "Get the darn beer."

Reggie pulled two bottles from the fridge. Bud Light. He twisted off the tops and headed back toward the living room. I got in his way.

"Glasses," I said. "Pour it in glasses."

"What the hell for?"

Eye roll. "Because she's a lady. And you're a gentleman."

That got him.

"Yes, goddammit, I am. You're right for a change. Good idea, Farf."

From then on, for almost an hour, the whole experiment unfolded smoothly. Reggie went into gentleman mode—which he had probably also done at the restaurant—and carried on an almost intelligent dialog, which included the weather, the tourists (who are everywhere in the summertime and seem to make New York even hotter than it is), the food at Paulina's, the waiter at Paulina's, the popularity of Paulina's, and a fair amount of dog stuff—mostly comparing poodles to shepherds. I'm always amazed at how people use us—their dogs—as conversational crutches.

They were into their third beer when Gloria made her fateful blunder.

She set down her glass, carefully and gently, on a napkin (which she had earlier requested) on Reggie's beat-up end table, next to Reggie's dilapidated lamp. She put her hand on Reggie's arm and said, "Reggie, I don't know when I've had a lovelier evening."

Her voice was slightly slurred.

With no warning, she leaned straight into Reggie's face and laid her lips on his, gently and lingeringly—while Reggie pressed his head into the back of the La-Z-Boy, staring bulge-eyed at Gloria.

When she was finished but still hanging very close to Reggie's mouth, I had a bad feeling.

Uh-oh, I thought.

Reggie said, "What the fuck was that?"

The question startled Gloria. But she held her ground and smiled very pleasantly. Did I mention that her smile is her best feature? Well, it is.

"I just had the urge to kiss you, Reggie."

"Why, because you knew I was no good at it?"

"No good at it?"

"Because you wanted to shame and humiliate me?"

Gloria, now bewildered by the anger in Reggie's voice, backed away. "Oh no, Reggie. It was just a kiss. Just—"

"Bullshit! I know what you're up to!"

"Up to?"

I was on my feet now, watching with alarm, trying to guess what Reggie might do next.

But Gloria stayed cool, looking sympathetically at Reggie. By this time, she had figured out how naïve and vulnerable he was.

But Reggie saw nothing in Gloria's expression but cruelty and guile.

"You were gonna tease me, weren't you?"

"Tease you? No, Reggie. I—"

"Don't you fuckin' lie to me.? You wanted to give me a hard-on, get me all worked up and then laugh at me."

"No!"

"Well you got your hard-on, bitch. You wanna see it?"

He did, actually, have an erection. I could tell, even though Gloria was courteously unaware.

"Reggie, please."

For a moment, he clawed at his pants, trying to get hold of his zipper against the pressure exerted from within. Gloria backed away, finally appreciating Reggie's demented state. Suddenly, he launched himself from the La-Z-Boy, hands outstretched. He clawed at Gloria's bodice, trying to rip the fabric. But it defied his efforts. Her dress held, although a little crookedly.

I know I should have been doing something to help Gloria. But this all happened a lot faster than I'm describing it. And, besides, as you know, Reggie—not Gloria—was my master. Technically, if he was going to rape and ravish Gloria, it was my duty to consent to the whole travesty, even help out where I could, perhaps by clamping my canines around her trachea.

While indecision wracked my psyche, Reggie tackled Gloria, landing on top of her and reaching under her skirt.

"Laugh at me?" he shouted in her face. "Go back to your friends? Make jokes about me? Tell them you got me hard? Tell them I came in my pants before I could unbuckle my belt? Oh, Jesus!"

For a moment, Reggie froze atop Gloria, biting his lower lip, grinding his molars and clenching his eyelids. I recognized the symptoms. He was coming in his pants.

Now I was embarrassed.

This brief respite allowed Gloria to slide to her right, almost escaping from beneath Reggie. But he broke from his ejaculatory trance and clamped her shoulders. "You lying bitch."

"Reggie, please."

Then he hit her, fist closed, across her face.

Oh my God, I thought. Instinctively, I barked.

Gloria was bleeding, tears pouring now from her eyes. She whimpered with terror. I couldn't blame her.

Suddenly, Reggie was on his feet, standing over Gloria. She held her hands out in front of her face. She was trembling. "Don't," she said. "Reggie, don't."

Of course, he couldn't. He had already shot his wad. A dark wetness spread on the front of his best pair of Dockers.

"Don't let her move," he said to me. "Keep her there. If she moves, rip her throat out."

Reggie thought I'd been trained by the NYPD to rip out people's throats. Actually, what we learn—as a sort of last resort—is to hold people by the throat, not even breaking the skin, merely immobilizing them with fear. Reggie's command, therefore, to rip out Gloria's throat was—in my interpretation as a veteran law enforcement officer—invalid.

Lucky for Gloria because, a few seconds later, Reggie was in the kitchen, noisily rummaging through a drawer.

I said to Gloria, "Look, you have to get up. Get moving. He's looking for a weapon. He's going to kill you, Gloria."

She just lay there, dazed, blood drooling from her nose, gazing at me dumbly. All she had heard me say, of course, was, "Urf, urf, urfety urf urf urf," etcetera.

A bellow of rage from the kitchen, followed by thumping footsteps, and Reggie barreling past us, toward his bedroom. Toward—I guessed—the bureau drawer where he kept that huge, jagged-back, razor-sharp Crocodile Dundee hunting knife.

"Shit," I said, resorting to vulgarity. I had remembered that there was another—even scarier—drawer containing Reggie's new gun. Reggie was armed to the teeth, and Gloria had nothing—except me. And I was statutorily neutral.

DAVID BENJAMIN

I gave up talking to Gloria. Instead, I just went right up to her face and started barking my brains out. I kept it up, loud and slobbery. Her eyes bugged out, she flailed at me.

"Good," I said between barks. "Keep moving. Snap out of it! Get on your feet!"

Then, "Bark bark woof, woof bark bark, grrr."

Gloria, still shaking with fear, her fingers feeling where the blood still bubbled from her nose, finally got onto her feet, leaning on the hassock. She stood, still unsteady but erect.

"Good. Great," I said. "Now, the door! Get the heck out!"

Oops. Reggie was back, filling the bedroom doorway, clutching that ghastly knife. I swear the dumb cluck was foaming at the mouth.

"You fucking, scheming, evil—"

"Okay, now, Gloria! Go. Fast!"

But she was talking to him. Honest to God, trying to calm him down.

"Reggie, I'm sorry," she said. "It's my fault. I had too much to drink. I moved too fast because I liked you. Really."

"Please, Gloria," I said. "You've got to get out of here. He's nuts. He'll kill you."

Yes, I know. All she heard was "Urf urf urf." Humans, they'll drive you bananas!

"I led you on," she said.

"No, you didn't," I said.

"Aaar-aar-aar-yaagh!" said Reggie, after which he choked on an excess of phlegm, coughing violently.

"Okay, this is your chance, Gloria! Run!"

Still, she didn't run. Coughing and gasping, Reggie was advancing on her.

I had a brainstorm. It was my job to protect Reggie, right? Gloria could represent a threat to him. What if, for instance, he stabbed her in an artery, causing an explosive spurt of blood that hit him in the eyes, blinding him, causing him to stagger and fall right on top of his knife, killing him?

I know. Not a likely scenario. But I needed a pretext for "saving" Reggie—from Gloria.

I started barking even more fanatically, snarling and raving at Gloria, baring my fangs and bouncing on my front paws, threatening her with the sort of mangled flesh and sundered veins that only the glistening white teeth of a healthy adult German shepherd could inflict.

Finally, Gloria screamed.

Sweet music!

She backed up to the door, groped for the knob and clumsily turned it. It took her a while. My throat was starting to hurt from all the noise I was making. She pulled open the door.

By this time, Reggie had closed the gap. He would have grabbed her and plunged the gigantic blade into her bosom, covering us all with gore, but he couldn't get past me. I was jumping up and down, ranging back and forth, growling and snarling like Old Yeller after the wolf bit him, protecting helpless Reggie from this dangerous woman with every ounce of my energy 'til finally she managed to squeeze through the door and stagger down the hall, while the neighbors—this was New York, after all (Remember Kitty Genovese?)—didn't even bother to open a door to see what all the ruckus was.

"She got away. She got awa-a-ay!" Reggie wailed.

"Reggie, my God," I said. "You can't invite people up to your apartment for a beer and then stab them to death."

"You're a fuckin' dog. You can't see evil when it stares you in the eye. She was evil! Oh, shit shit shit! She got awa-a-ay!"

As usual, my efforts to calm Reggie and make him see reason were futile, at least while he was in the throes of his frenzy. As an example to him, instead, I trotted over to my rag rug, did a few desultory circles to disperse the bad karma, and laid down.

Reggie, still overwrought, paced for ten minutes. I stayed still. Finally, I think he got the message. He threw down the knife, point first. It stuck in the floor, swaying with inanimate menace. Reggie collapsed into his La-Z-Boy, scowling and muttering, but was asleep in five minutes.

Exhausted, I followed his example.

Next morning, he called Mommy. He told her he was thinking about proposing to Antoinette, but not 'til he got his BA in architecture. He knew Antoinette would wait for him.

"She sounds like a wonderful girl," said his mother to Reggie.

"Oy," I said to myself.

8

"My mind reels with sarcastic replies."
—Snoopy

At times, Reggie can be pretty dim. He seemed to have no idea that assaulting and trying to rape a woman in his apartment might cause him a little trouble with the NYPD. On the other paw, I did. For the next few days, I was on tenterhooks, expecting detectives to bang on the door any minute.

However, as the uneventful hours passed, I found myself remembering what Marilyn had explained to her male colleagues over and over again. The vast majority of sexual assaults by men against women—at least eighty percent—go unreported. She explained many reasons for this but emphasized every woman's abiding fear—that male police officers would scoff and say that she was "asking for it" ... she let herself get sloppy drunk ... she was wearing provocative clothes ... she flirted and teased, kissed and caressed, led the man on, encouraged his arousal and toyed with his manly needs.

I guess this was going through Gloria's mind, and it's why she didn't report Reggie to my former brothers in blue at the

NYPD. And why Reggie was free to continue—and escalate—his wayward crusade.

Most amazing to me was that Reggie, within two days, was walking me again in the same park where we had met Gloria and Cupcake. He seemed to think that he'd done nothing wrong and had no reason to fear an encounter with the woman he undertook to eviscerate in his living room.

It was June then, hazy, hot and sticky in Brooklyn. After about fifteen minutes of meandering and sniffing, I sensed that Reggie was ready to take me back to the apartment. I preferred to stick around for a while. I was hoping to encounter Gloria and Cupcake—although I had no idea what would happen then. So, to prolong our time in the park, I made a sudden lunge toward one of the local squirrels—in whom I had a philosophical disinterest. My real purpose was to yank the leash from Reggie's grip and run free.

It worked.

"Hey!" Reggie shouted as I bounded across the lawn and up the hill toward the Prison Ship Martyrs Monument. This was great. This was the way it's supposed to be. Once upon a time, we all were wolves, woolly, ravenous and unfettered, ranging across the wilderness, devouring everything alive or dead that came across our path. We feared nothing and no one. We ruled snow-covered hills and grass-deep valleys. Elk and buffalo scattered at the mere sight of us as we crested a ridge, paused and howled fearsomely at the sky. Even bears and cougars ceded us their turf as we passed through.

"Goddammit, Farfel!" Reggie, slow afoot and prone to chafing, was in pursuit but way behind me. Even if he caught up, I could run circles around him, frustrating him to exhaustion.

I skidded to a halt. Right in front of me, also in flight, was a little boy, perhaps eight years old. He stared at me, frozen, frightened, but also curious.

Without thinking, I said, "Oh, sorry."

A second later, shocking me more than I had shocked him, the tyke said, "You can talk?"

I cocked my head wonderingly.

He peered at me. I saw his mother hurrying toward us. Reggie, from another direction, was also closing ground.

"Quick," I said. "Pat me on the head."

"Wow," said the kid, reaching out for my ears. "A talking dog."

"We all talk, kid. But most people can't understand us."

The boy went on rubbing my head a little awkwardly.

"What's your name?" I asked.

"Jesse."

"I'm Farfel," I said just before the mother and Reggie converged on us.

The little boy, going at my head now with both hands while I sat down and lolled my tongue around, said, "Hey, Mom, this is a nice dog. He talks!"

"Oh, Jesse, you scared me to death. You shouldn't pet strange dogs."

"Oh, he's not strange, Mom. His name is Farfel."

"Farfel?"

Just then, Reggie arrived. He heard the mother and looked at her with a piercing gaze. "That's his name. How'd you know that?"

Jesse spoke up. "Oh, he told me!"

Reggie turned his piercing gaze toward Jesse, who just smiled upward, glowing with pride.

Reggie snatched up my leash, glared at both Jesse and his mother, and dragged me away. As I looked back, Jesse waved and said, "See ya, Farfel!"

I tried to nod meaningfully at Jesse, but I'm not sure he caught the drift. He was just a little kid.

But, as we headed back home, I thought about how surprising humans can be. I had come to suspect that Reggie could only understand me because he was mentally disturbed.

DAVID BENJAMIN

A screw loose, somewhere in his cranium, had opened a fissure—long since sealed up in sane human beings—where Dogspeak slipped through into Reggie's consciousness.

Now, there was Jesse. Either the little kid was as crazy as Reggie, or it was possible that children—or perhaps just some of them, whose imaginations had expanded to the point where it opened all sorts of cracks—were somehow receptive to dog-human dialog.

I wondered if I would ever see Jesse again, and if I did, what would I say? Could this kid help me with my Reggie dilemma?

• • •

As we entered the apartment (ah, the faint fragrance of decomposing fish!), Reggie said, "Okay, fur-brain, what the hell was that? With that little brat in the park?"

"Tell you the truth, Reg," I said, "I'm still trying to figure it out myself. But that little boy, Jesse—"

"Jesse? How do you know his name?"

"He told me."

"Told you? Why?"

"Because I told him mine."

"Jesus Christ. You talked to the kid?"

"Well, it was sort of an accident."

"But he understood what you said?"

"Yes, he did. Amazing."

"Well, I don't want you talking to him anymore."

"Why not?"

"I just don't want you talking to anyone but me. You got that, fleabag?"

I shrugged, figuring what's the difference? I'd probably never see Jesse again.

But I couldn't help wondering. If Jesse could handle Dogspeak, were there other (sane) humans out there I could talk to?

Maybe, but not many. And how would I find them?

. . .

That night, Reggie was restless. He squirmed in his La-Z-Boy, muttering unintelligibly, kneading his crotch and drinking beer. Suddenly, he crushed a still half-full can of beer, splashing Brooklyn Lager all over himself and adding to the generally sour odor of our quarters.

"Gotta. Fuckin'. Get. Outa here!"

I knew this wasn't good.

I uncurled from my rag rug and trotted over to Reggie.

"Wait, Reggie," I said. "It's late. You're tired. Why not just—"

"Gotta! Get! Out!"

I thought of a possible diversion. "Okay, but before you go," I said, "why not call your mother?"

"My mother? That bitch!"

"Well, well. Aren't *you* in a good mood?" I said, sinking to sarcasm. Nobody likes an ironic pet.

"Fuck you!"

See?

I shifted into Dr. Menzies mode. "Hey, I know Mom can be difficult sometimes and insensitive to your feelings. But if it weren't for her, you might just be on the street."

Reggie was poised on the edge of his La-Z-Boy, and I was sitting up. So we were basically face-to-face. He glared at me. Then he crunched an eyebrow. And sighed.

"Yeah, well," he said.

He shambled over to the table by the door, where he always kept his mobile phone. He punched in Mom's number and slouched back to the La-Z-Boy. His mother picked up on the first ring. She was always close to the phone. I listened from my rag rug.

"Hello, Mommy ... You are? Oh, well, that's too bad. Do you want me to come over? ... Oh, okay, but maybe tomorrow ... Oh, okay then. Next week sometime ..."

The odd thing about Reggie's mother was that, even though she spoiled him ferociously, she didn't seem to want him around her house. Reggie regularly offered to visit her—she lives in Manhattan, on the upper West side—but she always found excuses to put him off.

"Oh, yeah, school's going great. I talked to the dean about my scholarship, and he said it was in the works. They don't want to lose a student like me ... Oh, yeah, we meet every morning in the quad and have coffee in the Student Union. She's just a wonderful conversationalist ..."

This, of course, was the phantom Antoinette. She represented the impossible standard that Reggie had set up for Gloria—which almost got her killed.

"Well, I had a part-time job lined up, servicing computers and consulting on IT. But I had to turn it down because I realized it would interfere with my studies, y'know. Architecture is a really challenging discipline ... Yes, it's a tough balance to manage, Mom. But my studies have to come first. I really need to concentrate ... No, no, it's okay, Mommy. I have enough money now, at least 'til the new semester ..."

The conversation went on like this—dull, meandering and largely mendacious. I dozed off. When I awoke, Reggie was embedded in the big chair, holding the now-silent phone, scowling grumpily. But he was pacified. His mother usually had a sedative effect on him. In every conversation, she plied him with unconditional affection, assuring Reggie that there was no one on earth quite like him. He was so special that few people, other than his mother, could appreciate him. So, he never had to feel bad about being different or fat and not being able to hold a job, pay attention in school or finish anything he started, or—excuse the expression—get laid.

Reggie sensed my misgivings about him, to the point where suddenly he seemed to be reading my thoughts.

I raised my head from my paws, listening warily.

"Jesus Christ, why should anybody get laid?" he said.

Of course, to a dog, this is an illogical figure of speech. We couldn't possibly copulate lying down. And if we tried, the position would be so ludicrous that we'd be unable to finish, instead just tumbling apart, wracked with amusement.

But I replied as earnestly as I could manage.

"Well, it's necessary to the species, isn't it?"

"No! Shit, no. We can make babies in test tubes now."

"Well, theoretically."

"Think about it, you goddamn moron mongrel. The whole process is crude, it's ugly, it's degrading. Nine times out of ten—no, 999 times out of a thousand—sex doesn't have anything to do with love, or babies, or romance or any of that happy horseshit. It's just animal instinct. The strong prey on the weak. The beast eats the beauty alive. It's like taking a dandelion in your fist and grinding it 'til it's just a wet yellow stain on your hand. That's what you do with a woman, rip her out of the ground, tear off her blossom and squeeze and squeeze 'til she drips all over the ground and makes a stinking mess."

There was a certain grim lyricism to what Reggie was saying, but I found it troubling nonetheless. I tried to enlighten him with the logical consequence of this dark vision.

"You mean people shouldn't have sex at all?"

"Yeah. Hey! Yeah, that's right!" Reggie exclaimed. "Jesus Christ, Farf. You put your finger right on it!"

I was thinking about how nice it would be to actually *have* a finger as Reggie bounded from the chair and spread his arms, almost shouting as he said, "Wouldn't it be better? Wouldn't everyone be kinder—more civilized? Sex is an evil and barbaric act. If we could wipe it from the earth, erase it from our lives, society would be more just to people like me, who've been denied sex because of our gentle nature. Life would be more fair."

"Fair?" I said. "Life?"

"Yeah, if I can't have sex—I mean, women won't let me. I mean, I could rape them. Put a knife at their throat or shove a gun in their nasty little lying mouths, and make 'em fuck me.

DAVID BENJAMIN

But I'm a gentleman, Farf. I can't bring myself to do that. And I can't get them to like me, or love me, or even look at me."

"But," I interrupted. "Gloria—"

"You fuckin' dumbass dog. You don't understand a fuckin' thing, do ya? She was a pig. A pig and a whore. She felt sorry for me and teased me, and then—just as we were ready to make beautiful love—she ran away. She was homely and not worthy of a gentleman like me. But I was willing to give her my virginity. I was ready to make the sacrifice for her sake. But what did she do? Huh? What? She played with my feelings, embarrassed me and ran away. I wish I'd killed her."

As I saw it, Reggie wasn't making much sense. But, cockeyed optimist that I am, I thought I could steer him out of his emotional maelstrom and into a safe harbor.

"Reggie, you're right. You are a gentleman. You're sweet and you're shy. But that's not a handicap. You shouldn't be so despairing. A lot of women are attracted to just your sort of guy," I said. "You'll find one. Or she'll find you."

"You are so full of shit," Reggie hissed at me.

Of course, this was water off a shepherd's slightly oily coat. "You've been patient all this time," I assured him. "Your time will come."

"And what if it doesn't, dog-breath? What if I spend my whole life waiting for this woman who isn't attracted to all these ass-grabbing alpha gorillas who grab up all the women while they're still teenagers, ruin them and whorify them?"

Whorify?

He kept talking. "Shit. Okay, let's say there's a woman out there looking for shy little old Reggie. And she sees me. And she's walking toward me—until this tall, handsome football captain intercepts her, sticks his tongue in her mouth, leads her to his Porsche and drives her to his beach house in the Hamptons, fills her with champagne, pulls down his pants and shoves his cock in her mouth, and she likes it! And she likes it when he throws her on the floor and fucks her and sodomizes her and invites his board of directors over to fuck her, too, and she likes that, likes being crushed and ruined and turned into a whore? And then, the weekend is over, and he drives her back, drops her in the park, brings her right over to me, all bruised and sticky and smelling like the twenty gorillas who've just destroyed her, and he says, 'Okay, Reg, here she is. It's your turn.' Do I want her now? She was the one—the one woman you're talking about. Right. Farf? But here's what you don't see because you're a dumb fuckin' dog. It doesn't matter if there's one woman meant for me or a million of 'em. Those assholes always get to her before I do. And after them, after the alpha creeps and fratboy rapists have crawled all over her and ripped her open like a grapefruit, she doesn't have any use for a gentle, civilized man. She just wants to be seized and stripped, subjugated and mounted again by cavemen, by thugs and bulls, by herds of horny horses. She's like a mirage on the highway, Farf. Beautiful in the distance and gone before I get there. Just a fuckin' stretch of asphalt laid down and run over."

I shook my head to clear it of all the bleak images Reggie had just put there. For a moment, I couldn't think of what to say.

Finally, I tried. "Reggie, it's not always like that."

"It's always like that," Reggie replied flatly.

"It doesn't have to be."

"That's how it is. Sex is exploitation and destruction. People are vicious animals, more vicious than the meanest dog in the world."

Reggie had a point. People commit unspeakable deeds against people—and against dogs—that no dog could even think up.

While I was pondering this, Reggie said, "They have to be stopped."

"Stopped?"

"From having sex?"

"Yeah."

DAVID BENJAMIN

"Reggie. You want to ban sex?"

"That's what I'm talkin' about, fuzzface. If I can't have it, why should anybody?" Reggie said. "And besides, it's fuckin' obsolete."

"Reggie, come on. You can't outlaw sex. That would be—"

"Impossible. You're right, Farfel. Smart dog."

"Thanks," I said. Then, foolishly, I continued. "I mean, what would you do, Reg? Catch a couple in the act and put them in prison? Or execute—"

"That's it!" said Reggie. "Catch them and kill them on the spot. To set an example!"

I bowed my head in frustration. Somehow, I'd led Reggie back around, unintentionally, to his worst behavior. It was almost as though I was encouraging the violent impulses to which, I feared, he had already succumbed more than once.

"You gotta do it over and over 'til they get the message!"

"No, Reggie, I didn't mean—"

"You're right, Farfel. You're not dumb. You're a smart dog. A brilliant dog!"

"Reggie, please. I didn't say what you think I meant."

"I gotta admit, Farf," said Reggie in a confidential tone that set my nerves on edge. "I've wondered about myself sometimes. Was it me? Am I crazy—going out there, wanting to hurt people? I was thinking, *Jesus Christ, what the hell am I doing*? I was like a chicken with his head cut off. But you've made it all clear, Farf. I was finding my way and clarifying my values. I realize now that I'm doing what I have to do."

"No, Reggie. Killing people isn't something anybody has to—"

"Thanks, man," said Reggie. He scratched behind my ears.

"But, Reggie—"

"I wasn't a chicken. I have my head. Farfel, you found my head!" He laughed more genuinely than I had heard in months. He held his head in both hands and rocked it from side to side.

"Well, no ..." I tried to say.

"It's like the Bible says," Reggie rejoiced, sitting back down and holding my face. "And a little dog shall lead them."

"Reg, I think you're misquoting Isaiah."

He wasn't listening to me.

"Jeez, y'know, I was right all along. I had a vision, but I didn't see it. I didn't have faith in myself. I didn't see the importance of my work. I didn't see the power I have to change things, to make people see how degenerate and filthy they are, to save us all from our worst selves."

"Reggie, wait. I think we need to discuss this some more. You're going off half—"

"I can't talk now. I gotta write this down."

"Oh my God," I said.

(You've probably noticed my occasional references to God. Dogs don't just believe in God. We hear him up there once in a while—usually on a really quiet, clear morning before dawn. For us creatures on Earth and all the things we do, he's like a studio audience, watching benignly, occasionally applauding, chuckling at the funny parts. He's compassionately silent when things turn sad and completely irrelevant to the whole circus. Sometimes I wish he'd step in and help us out a little. But that wouldn't be fair.)

Reggie bolted from the chair, dashed to his little desk and started clattering away at his computer.

I was pretty bummed. I had done my darnedest to channel Dr. Menzies, but the whole effort had backfired. There are few breeds worse than an amateur shrink.

9

*"We are alone, absolutely alone on this chance planet;
and amid all the forms of life that surround us, not one,
excepting the dog, has made an alliance with us."*
—Max De Pree

Reggie spotted the couple on Nassau Street, near Commodore Barry Park. He stayed about a half-block behind them, tugging at me if I did anything to slow him down. It was close to one in the morning, and the quiet streets were utterly abandoned.

• • •

Sensing a buildup of tension, I had tried to keep Reggie home that night. He had even dozed off in his La-Z-Boy. But just after midnight, he sat up, wide awake and tight as a drumskin. "Gotta go," he said.

"It's late, Reg," I said.

"That's why I gotta go. They're out there."

"Who's out there?"

"Whores. Sluts. Fratboys. Alpha males. Sensualists and savages!"

"Aw, c'mon, Reg. It's Tuesday. It's quiet. Tomorrow's a

workday," I said. "I mean, if you want to stop people from, you know, foolin' around, wouldn't it be better to wait 'til the weekend?"

He didn't hear me.

"Wait here. I'll be back."

He was shoving his battered gumshoes onto his feet. He stood up, patting a pocket for his keys. There was no stopping him. And God knows what he'd do once he got outside. He lumbered to the bedroom bureau, opened the top drawer and peered inside. I knew what was there.

Reggie grabbed the big, evil Bowie knife in its leather scabbard. He pushed it into the waist of his trousers. He turned to rush out the door.

Reggie was my master, and I had no power or pretext to challenge him in any way. But I dreaded what might happen out there if he was alone. As long as I lived by the Code of the Dog, he could do whatever he wanted without my interference. But my canine intuition told me that if I were just present, alongside Reggie, I might be able to alter the course of events.

"Hey, listen," I said.

"What?" Reggie turned on me, a falcon glint in his eyes.

"Well, I was just thinking," I said. "It's pretty hot in here. It'd be nice to go along. Do ya mind?"

"What?" Reggie looked confused.

"Besides," I said, rambling on as amiably as I could manage, "it's dark, it's late, it's New York City. It could be dangerous."

"Dangerous?"

"Sure," I said. "You don't know what kind of nuts are wandering the streets at this hour. But if we're together, nobody'll mess with us."

"Oh," said Reggie. He scowled thoughtfully.

"You can't be too careful," I said. "After all, there's some guy out there stabbing and shooting people."

I waited for him to say, "That's me, dumbass!"

But he didn't—which, of course, troubled me. Because then

he said, "I guess you're right."

He took down my leash, hooked me up and out we went. I took a deep breath.

• • •

If the male half of the couple in front of us didn't have his hand pretty much glued to the girl's bottom, I think Reggie might have ignored them. But her posterior was a wonderful thing, in sprayed-on blue jeans with pastel flowers on the pockets. You could be hypnotized just watching those little blossoms swaying back and forth.

Through vibrations in my leash, I could read the effect of that guy's hand fondling the girl's derriere. Reggie's rage was like voltage in a frayed wire.

"Fucking filthy pigs," he muttered as we followed them. The woman had clean, nut-brown hair that hung halfway down her back. Besides her jeans, she wore a lacy white top with three-quarter-length sleeves. The evening breeze carried her scent—which suggested dying roses and the sharp musk of bumblebees. He was also in jeans, slung low, revealing two inches of BVD, and a faded maroon t-shirt. His hair was cropped short. He smelled of talc, elastic, hemp and foot odor. She wore two earrings, he just one. Among the neo-hipsters of DUMBO, they were as normal as gluten-free, vegetarian buckwheat-crust pizza pie. While nobody else had reason to even notice them, Reggie was fixated—and mountingly furious.

"Fucking son of a bitch isn't gonna even wait 'til they get home," grumbled Reggie. "He's just gonna bend her over a fuckin' bench. Or push her up against a wall. Or stick his ..."

"Honestly, Reggie. They just seem like regular—"

"Yank down her tight little fuck-me jeans."

"Reggie, why don't we turn here?"

"Rip off her panties."

"Reggie, man. Hey, mind if I stop to take a leak?"

"Clamp his grubby hand over her mouth, spread her legs ..."

"Hey, perfect. There's a fire hydrant."

Suddenly, Reggie stopped and turned on me. "Will you shut the fuck up? Dogs aren't supposed to talk at all, goddammit. You talk too fucking much!"

"Well, I just needed to pee."

But Reggie yanked my choke chain, propelling me again toward the couple. Truthfully, I didn't really need to pee.

Reggie kept up with his running rape monolog all the way to the East River, where the couple, for a moment, disappeared into the shadows. I entertained a brief hope that we might have lost them.

But they emerged again into a shaft of moonlight, where the guy halted and turned the girl. Massaging her bottom with a lot of vigor, he kissed her. She lifted up onto her toes and reciprocated. As the kiss continued, with no sign of ending, Reggie's pace speeded up.

"Hey, Reggie, where's the fire?" I said as I skidded and stumbled along behind Reggie on the end of my leash.

Reggie was whispering as we neared the man and woman, still locked together in oblivious osculation. "Shut the fuck up, dog-breath."

This didn't bother me, of course. Sticks and stones. What concerned me was that Reggie had unsnapped the knife's sheath. Within ten feet of the unaware couple, just as the man was lifting the woman's top and feeling for her breasts, Reggie drew the knife.

The blade flashed melodramatically in the glow of a streetlight. I caught, faintly, the delicate burnt fragrance of freshly sharpened steel. The edge, if Reggie were to use it, would be keener than a new razor.

"Oh, hell," I said.

And I started barking like a Lhasa Apso on speed.

"Jesus!" Reggie said, lurching to a stop and staring at me.

I ignored him, instead lunging against my leash, getting my front feet up off the ground and menacing the kissing twosome as best I could. As I'd expected, the man and woman leapt apart. I got a good look at them then and saw that the girl was seriously gorgeous, and the guy wasn't too bad either, although he could have used a shave and a competent hairdresser.

"Hey, whaddya doin'?" said the man to Reggie. Not very articulate, but I had lots of experience in this situation, and I wasn't surprised. People tend to get rattled by the sudden appearance of a large dog, barking and snarling like a hyena defending a half-eaten zebra.

I paused only a second to put in a word to Reggie. "I got 'em scared, Reg," I said. "Go get 'em."

"What the fuck?"

"C'mon, Reg. Attack!"

Then I went back to barking even more violently than before.

As I'd hoped, Reggie was nonplussed by all the commotion and paused his attack. The complication that I didn't expect was the valiant and completely idiotic reaction by the male. Instead of grabbing the girl and high-tailing out of Reggie's range, he placed himself between me and the girl and straightened to his full height.

"Don't worry, Sandy," he said. "He's just barking at us."

Just my luck. The guy thought he knew dogs. But he didn't know Reggie.

The guy caught Reggie's eye. He said, with remarkable sangfroid: "Beautiful shepherd. Is he pedigreed?"

Reggie pulled at me, and I backed off a little. I kept growling and straining, keeping up the act as best I could. But it was hard. The guy just said I was beautiful. Marilyn used to tell me that, too. I loved that woman.

The guy spoke again. "Can I pet him?"

Oh, for Pete's sake.

"Pet him?" said Reggie. "Pet him?"

The guy couldn't have made a worse suggestion.

"Um, yeah," said the guy, a little puzzled by Reggie's sudden belligerence. That's when the guy, no longer looking at me, noticed the knife in Reggie's hand. His eyes widened.

Reggie, "Pet my dog? Pet my dog? Why don't you just pet your whore there, you fuckin' sicko?"

"Hey, just a second—"

Famous last words, because faster than I had ever seen Reggie move, he did a *grand jeté* across thirty feet of pavement and raked across the guy's throat with the tip of that gruesome knife.

A terrible second later, the guy was reaching for his neck, blood gushing down and instantly soaking his t-shirt. Sandy began to scream. As Reggie poised to shred the poor girl, I came to my senses and charged at her, raving and bellowing, baring my teeth and clawing the air. She staggered back just far enough to elude a roundhouse swing of Reggie's blade.

With one mighty desperate surge, I tore the leash from Reggie's grip, coiled myself, barking murderously, and gave the horrified girl the full view of my glistening canines. This did the trick. Staggering several steps backward, Sandy turned and fled. After stumbling over a curb, she picked herself up and ran away from the river and up the street.

I followed, barking away, keeping pace 'til I knew she wasn't going to do anything foolish, like rush back to nurse her boyfriend, who was sprawled in a lake of his own blood, dead after less than twenty seconds.

I felt terrible for the guy, but I couldn't dwell on that. I concentrated on hounding Sandy to safety. It occurred to me that she would probably hate dogs for the rest of her life.

"God DAMN it, Farfel!"

As Sandy put distance between herself and Reggie, who wasn't as fast as she was, I slowed to a trot, breathing a sigh of relief.

The girl had seen us both clearly. Reggie was unmistakable, a sort of ambulatory manatee. When the NYPD put her description of him together with me—a German shepherd—my whole awful experience would soon be over.

As I heard Reggie thudding up behind me, I took a final look at Sandy—who slowed for a moment and turned to look back. As she did, her foot slipped on the edge of the curb. I watched as her ankle—she was wearing heels—bent at a right angle. She cried out and tumbled to the pavement.

"Oh, for Lassie's sake," I muttered.

When she got up hurriedly, her face was white with pain. After one step on the wrenched ankle, she fell again, landing on her hands and knees, whimpering.

Oh, come on, sweetheart, I thought. *Suck it up.*

Reggie, shouting jubilantly, galloped past me, waving his knife at the suddenly helpless woman.

"Darn," I said weakly.

I won't describe the rest. Sandy had been beautiful, buxom, healthy and bursting with vitality. Afterward, she was little more than a torn, bloody slab of warm matter.

Of course, being a dog—attracted to rare meat—I found her unfortunately more alluring in this condition than when she'd been alive. But this was not an impulse that made me glow with pride.

I suppressed my instincts and turned away, angry at myself for my failure to save either the young man or his girlfriend, annoyed at Sandy for that fatal hesitation. Why did she stop?

"What the fuck d'ya think you were doing?" said Reggie, returning from the scene of the crime. "She almost got away."

"Just trying to help, Reggie."

"Help? How the fuck—"

"Listen, Reg, you shouldn't stick around here," I said. "You could get in trouble."

"Huh?"

"Well, Reggie, you've got blood all over you. Your knife

is big enough to skin a whale, and it's dripping blood. Two people are lying dead, and this is a public place."

Actually, I hated explaining all this to Reggie. As a former officer of the court, I understood my duty was to keep Reggie right here in hopes that the girl's screams might have triggered a 911 call from one of the dark apartments all around us. If I let Reggie hang around the crime scene in a blood-drunk haze, I still might end his spree of violence right then and there, serving and protecting according to the oath I had sworn when I joined the NYPD as little more than a pup.

But now, unfortunately, I lived by the Code of the Dog. Reggie was my first priority.

"Oh. Right," said Reggie. "Yeah. Jesus Christ. I'm a fuckin' mess. Let's go."

I looked back once at the boyfriend, face up on the sidewalk on the dark, empty waterfront. One hand still clutched his neck, his fingers stained dark pink from the gallons of blood that had gushed through them. I couldn't look at Sandy at all.

Under a street light, Reggie stopped to stare at me.

"What is it?" I asked.

Reggie dropped to his knees and dug into the fur just behind my collar. I felt a grating pain.

"You're bleeding, Farf!"

I did a quick body shake and felt the cut. While swinging the knife, Reggie had nicked me. It wasn't a deep wound, but Reggie was suddenly all guilty and weepy.

"Oh my God, boy, I'm sorry. I'm sorry. You're such a good dog, and look what I did. Oh my God."

He went on like this for another minute or so, eventually folding me into a bear hug and smearing my coat with the girl's blood. "I love you, boy. I'm so sorry," he said. "Jesus, what the hell is wrong with me?"

"Hey, don't worry about it, Reg. It's just a little cut."

"I could've killed you, man! Jesus Christ, what's wrong with me?"

I finally got him moving again by asking him to clean the wound and paint it with iodine when we got home. But he went on apologizing and sniffling for two more blocks.

Meanwhile, true to Reggie's luck, the only person we encountered on the way back was a homeless drunk who bumped into a tree and fell over as we passed him.

10

"Everything I know, I learned from dogs."
—Nora Roberts

I don't envy much about humans, but I wish I could sweat like they do. On a July day in New York, when everything seems to be melting, and the air smells like a stew made largely of boiled fat, garbage and asphalt fondue, I look around longingly at all the sweat-soaked suits, shirts and dresses on passing people, wishing I had more than my tongue to cool me off.

I also wish, like humans, I could just pull off my coat and hang it over the back of the park bench, the way Reggie did with his shirt the day after the bloodbath in DUMBO. He plucked his undershirt away from his damp tummy, leaned back, spread his arms and closed his eyes. He sighed. I plumped down on the sidewalk in a shady spot beneath the bench. I waited for him to talk. He hadn't said a word to me since we got back to our apartment the night before.

He had hurried into the bathroom, where he got the iodine to treat my cut. After playing nurse with me, he stripped down and spent half an hour in the shower, scrubbing away the evidence. Then, as I observed from a safe distance, he bagged up all his bloody clothes (which is getting to be a disturbing routine) and set the bag by the door for a later trip to some distant trashcan. Before going to bed, he cleaned up and bleached all traces of blood from the floors. When he was done, the apartment was immaculate, which was totally out of character from its normal condition. Murder was doing wonders for Reggie's household hygiene.

The next morning, we detoured about nine blocks before Reggie dropped the bag into a dumpster behind a Chinese restaurant. Then he guided us back to Fort Greene Park, where we'd met Gloria and Cupcake and the little boy, Jesse.

Seeing no one familiar, Reggie and I settled onto a shady bench, where the heat and humidity were slightly less oppressive. After a while, I couldn't contain my curiosity. I had to know what was going through Reggie's head.

So, I said, "Well …"

Without moving, Reggie snapped back at me. "What?"

"Well," I said, "I mean, that wasn't what you'd call a smooth operation last night."

"What the fuck you talkin' about, dog?"

It's not a good sign when Reggie calls me "dog." He had recovered from all that loving remorse he'd lavished upon me over that tiny cut. In the spirit of Dr. Menzies, I decided to examine his misbehavior from an entirely tactical point of view, leaving the thornier moral concerns for a future conversation.

"For one thing, the girl almost got away."

"That's not my fault, you fuckin' mutt."

Clearly, Reggie calling me "fuckin' mutt" is scarcely an improvement from "dog." But I persevered. Bound as I am by the Code, my best option for steering Reggie away from continued mayhem was diplomacy.

"I'm only suggesting that things didn't turn out the way you planned," I said. "It was almost as though you didn't plan it at all."

Reggie sat up straight, opened his eyes but didn't look at me. This was customary when we were in public. A human carrying on a detailed dialog with a dog, face-to-face, tends to draw unwelcome scrutiny. Prejudice plagues the dog/human interface—which is, I think, one reason why so few humans actually understand what we're saying to them.

"Oh yeah? Well, I planned."

"Oh, I know that, Reg. You honed your knife. You knew where you wanted to go. You picked the right time of night and waited patiently 'til you were completely alone with your victims ..."

"Victims?"

"I mean, urf ... " I paused. "Well, what would you call them?"

"Well, they're not victims, man," said Reggie. "They were guilty. They were fornicators facing their reckoning. I was, like, the exorcist of their evil, man."

"So," I said, "they were more of an objective."

"Yeah, but not victims, man. Victims? No way. They had it comin'."

"Right, well, semantics aside, Reggie, you were definitely ready to achieve your objective. But you didn't manage real well afterwards. I mean, what was your exit strategy?"

"Exit strategy? Well, shit, Farf. I got the hell out of there."

"True, but the girl, whom you didn't kill right away, ran off screaming, alerting perhaps hundreds of people, including the police, of your actions—while you were still on the scene. Right?"

This brought on a few seconds of reflective silence.

"Well, I guess," said Reggie grumpily.

"And if the police had been able to respond more quickly, and they'd caught you there, well, you were soaked in the blood of your, um ... objective."

"Fornicators."

"Yes, fornicators," I said. "And then you carried the murder weapon. All the way home. What if someone had seen you?

Maybe someone did see you."

Reggie seemed to consider this possibility. "Ya think?"

"Well," I said, "I didn't smell anyone—except that homeless guy who paid us no attention. Did you see anybody along the way? Maybe on the opposite side of the street?"

"No. It was really late."

"Okay, but the point remains, Reg, that you've been careless after your ..." Again, groping for a word. Finally, I said, "... excursions."

"Careless?" Reggie seemed to be having second thoughts. Was I getting through?

"I understand why you feel you have to do these things. But you need to consider the practical aspects of being a serial murderer, Reg."

"Whoa," said Reggie. He sat back on the bench, his mouth forming a pink "O" flecked with saliva. "Is that what I am? A serial murderer."

"Well, technically ... yes."

I actually did not believe this. I regarded Reggie as a randomly violent person who overreacts to delusional stimuli. He was suffering from poor impulse control, which was exacerbated by a deeply warped outlook on human sexuality. But a serial murderer? I had my doubts. But I thought it wise to simplify the issue for Reggie.

"You do meet all the criteria," I added.

"Hm," said Reggie. "Like on TV, huh?"

"Yes," I said. "Jack the Ripper, Jeffrey Dahmer, Hannibal Lecter."

"Cool," said Reggie.

I hadn't expected this. I thought maybe describing his criminal status bluntly might awaken him to the gravity of his situation. "Well, I don't know if that's how most people—"

"Hannibal Lecter? He's, like, an icon, isn't he?"

"Well," I said, "the word *icon* has been grossly devalued

by its overuse. Using it to characterize Hannibal Lecter is a typical—"

Reggie cut me off just as I was beginning to unbreast one of my linguistic pet peeves. "Y'know, Farf. I've never been *anything* before. I mean, I don't exactly have a career. Or even a job."

"Uh huh."

"I mean, I've had ambitions. And I've told Mom about my aspirations and all ..."

"Right," I said.

"But until now, I wasn't really anything you could put your finger on. I had no, like, vocation. No career. No title. Just kind of a blank slate. Right, Farf?"

"Oh, not really ... blank."

"But now! I'm something. I'm a serial murderer. I'm a fuckin' unsub, man. I'm an *icon!*"

"Well, Reg, that's—"

"And you're right, Farf," Reggie continued, sitting up and leaning toward me. "I haven't been going about this whole business professionally, y'know? It's like I'm goin' off half-cocked half the time. All the time. And if I get caught, well, then my work would go unfinished forever. My career would be over before I hardly even started it, right?"

"Reggie, doesn't it seem obvious that the longer you go on with this ... career, the more likely you'll get caught."

"Yeah, I know. Unless I get really good at it. Like the Pink Panther! He never got caught."

"The Pink Panther?"

"Yeah. But not the cartoon. The guy in the movie. Except he just stole jewels," said Reggie. "If he got caught, what the heck? No big deal. It's just jewels. But I can't get caught. I've got to plan these things better, Farf, because my mission is way more important than jewels."

This conversation was trending in the wrong direction. My

effort to appeal to Reggie on practical grounds was blowing up in my muzzle. I wondered if Dr. Menzies had this sort of problem. I decided to shift direction.

"Mission?" I said. "What mission?"

"Come on, Farf. You know what we've gotta do. We talked about this."

"I do? We did?"

"Look at me, man. What am I?"

I looked at Reggie as curiously as I could. I cocked my head, licked my nose, perked up an ear. As far as I could tell, I was looking at the same old giant doughy Reggie.

Reggie sighed. "I'm a fuckin' virgin, man," he said oxymoronically. "But that's just the fact, man. The question is, *why* am I a virgin—after all these years? I mean, how many guys my age have never, ever, once, got laid, Farf?"

"No idea."

"Well, shit. It's not many, is it?"

"I guess not."

"So, there's gotta be a reason, man. A plan. From above. I've been chosen!"

"Wait a minute!" Reggie kept surprising me with logic-defying U-turns. "Chosen?" I said.

"Yes! Chosen. Selected, Anointed!"

"Anointed. By whom?"

"By God. By fate. Whatever," said Reggie. "But I can see it now. I am pure, untouched, virginal, not because I'm unattractive, or unmanly, or unsexy, or antisocial. Right, Farf?"

"Well, you are painfully shy," I suggested.

Reggie considered this. "Okay, maybe. But that's not the reason I'm as pure and unsullied as the day I was born into this shitty world."

"Well, then," I began.

"It's because," Reggie rolled on, "I've been given a mission. The most important mission of the twenty-first century, the century when humanity will finally rise above the animals and abolish the bestiality of sexual intercourse."

Here we went again.

I took a deep breath and said, "Well, Reg, that would be a pretty big mission for anybody. But I'm just wondering. Are you the one? I mean, you don't seem like someone who's especially well situated to carry out the most important mission of the century."

"Was Noah well situated?"

Another U-turn. "I beg your pardon?"

"I mean, what was Noah? A fuckin' farmer or somethin', right? God said to build a giant boat, right? Noah wasn't a sailor. And God said, 'Collect two of every animal.' Was Noah, like, a zoologist or somethin'? No way, man!"

"So, you're going to build an ark?"

"No, you dumb fuckin' mutt. Abolishing sex—that's my ark. That's what I'm supposed to do."

I succumbed momentarily to sarcasm. "Really, Reg. Abolish sex?"

"No more fornication. No more intercourse of any kind. Just test tubes and Petri dishes. No more rape or lust or prostitution. No more pedophilia. No more sodomy. None of that."

"That's a tall order, Reggie."

"What? Noah's ark wasn't a tall order?"

Another harrowing U-turn, and we were back into the book of Genesis.

"Look," said Reggie, "God told Noah to build the ark, right? Why?"

I thought about answering this but decided against it.

"Because God," Reggie explained, "realized that he had screwed up. He'd created people wrong. They were basically rotten, and he needed to get rid of everyone except for a few guys, like Noah, who hadn't gone rotten. Okay?"

"I see your point," I replied, not really meaning it.

"Ya see, that's the great thing about God," said Reggie. "He makes mistakes, huge ones, right? Because he's God, right? He doesn't do anything small. But when he sees how he fucked up, he isn't afraid to come up with a huge solution—like making it rain for forty days and drowning every living thing on the face of the earth. So we could start all over again with one family and a boatload of giraffes and elephants."

"Wait," I said. "So you're saying that God has decided that sex was one of his mistakes? He doesn't want people to—"

"That's right, dog-breath. Now you got it."

"And God picked you, Reggie, to fix this huge mistake?"

"Yeah."

"You're sure?"

"Yeah."

"But how can you be so sure?" I said. "Did God speak to you?"

"No no no no no no!" said Reggie. "Don't be a moron, dog. God doesn't speak to people directly. He never did—'cause we'd never be able to understand him, anyway. There's nothing in the Bible where God talked to Jesus, right? His own son."

"Reggie, you're not comparing yourself to Jesus, are you?"

"No, I'm more like Moses. Jesus never killed anybody. God didn't want his son to do that kind of stuff. But Moses, he was a regular mass murderer. I mean, think of all the Egyptians he killed when he lowered his staff and drowned 'em all in the Red Sea. And then there were all those Canaanites he had to slaughter—men, women, little kids—to clear out space in the Promised Land."

I shook my head. Reggie had run me through a series of hairpin turns that led through Hannibal Lecter, the Pink Panther and Noah to Jesus and Moses. And now I was arguing with someone who thought God wanted him to purify the Promised Land.

"Listen, Reg," I said. "My trainer took me to church a few times. From what the priest said, I seem to recall that Moses didn't make it. God wouldn't let him into the Promised Land."

"Yeah, I know that, dog. You don't think I don't know that? Moses' mission was to get everyone else there. And that's what I'm gonna do."

"How?" I said. "And what is it, exactly? What do you mean by the Promised Land?"

"Okay, look. I've never had sex. Pussy was my Promised Land. Shit, it's every guy's fuckin' Promised Land. But I never got laid. Ever. Not gonna, either. God won't let me into the Promised Land, just like Moses couldn't get in. But that's what qualified Moses to lead the Israelites into the Promised Land—because there was nothin' in it for him. He was excluded by God. He was pure. Ya get it? Like me. I can lead everyone, even those soiled by carnal knowledge, from pussy to purity. To the Pure Land."

My brain was exhausted, and my ears were drooping. I watched the sweat drip off Reggie's chin for a little while, and then I said, "Reg, I've got to admit. This sounds just a little bit far-fetched. Are you sure you got the message right?"

"Well, Farfel, you're the one who can answer that one—because the message came through you."

"Say what?" I confess to a note of indignation in my voice.

"At first, I had no idea why I felt like I had to go out and punish all those fornicators, Farf. I was flying blind, y'know. I thought I was just acting on impulse. I wondered, was I crazy?" Reggie said this in an even, reflective tone that almost seemed coherent. "But then, you helped me see the light. It was your simple, ignorant animal revelation—that killing them all, one by one, was the only way to discourage their evil ways. You were like the burning bush, boy. Through you, I've been inspired to purge the rottenness that comes from the human hunger for sex, sex, sex!"

"Reggie, I didn't say that. I've never said anything like that."

"No, of course you haven't. Not in so many words. After all, you're just a fuckin' dumb dog. But I understood. The message came through because you were only an empty vessel."

DAVID BENJAMIN

"Empty?" I said.

"Why else," said Reggie, "would God have enabled you to speak to me? Dogs can't talk. You couldn't talk either, Farfel, until you came to me."

"No, that's not—"

"But God reached down. He gave you the power to speak to me, only me. You are God's begotten messenger, sent down to make me special and spur me on my mission."

"Gee whiz, Reg," I said. "I can see how you might think that talking to me might make you feel, well, special. But trust me, man. I am absolutely not God's messenger. God doesn't work that way."

But Reggie wasn't paying me any attention.

"Thanks to you, I've seen my purpose," said Reggie. "And thanks to you, I also see that I must mend my own ways and carry out my mission carefully, secretly, intelligently—like the Pink Panther. People will follow. A movement will rise. But, first, goddammit, I gotta get organized."

I opened my mouth to continue the argument but then snapped it shut. I was dizzy from all the U-turns. Reggie—especially in a state of acute agitation—wasn't a human that even a border collie could reason with.

Besides, I was a little miffed by the reference to the Pink Panther—who, after all, is a cat.

On our way home that day, Reggie detoured to Fulton Avenue, where he found a luggage wholesaler. He bought a roomy canvas rucksack in a nice neutral khaki brown with no logos or markings. He also picked up a gallon of Clorox and a big box of thirty-gallon extra-strength Hefty bags at Walgreens.

DAVID BENJAMIN

11

"Heaven is by favor; if it were by merit, your dog would go in and you would stay out. Of all the creatures ever made (man) is the most detestable. Of the entire brood, he is the only one ... that possesses malice. He is the only creature that inflicts pain for sport, knowing it to be pain."
—Mark Twain

Two uneventful nights later, I was dozing on my rag rug, and Reggie seemed content to lounge on his La-Z-Boy watching Stephen Colbert. Suddenly, he sat bolt upright and stabbed at the television remote. The TV went dark. Reggie lunged from his chair and grabbed his rucksack, which he now called a "go bag." He had packed it with a change of clothes, a towel, a plastic Johnson & Johnson towelette dispenser, a couple of Hefty bags and his big, ugly, newly-honed pigsticker.

"Gotta go," he said.

"Wait," I said.

He didn't. He was out the door in twenty seconds, slamming it behind him and leaving me trapped like a lapdog inside the empty apartment.

"Curses," I muttered. "Foiled again." Most dogs live their

lives as convicts thrown into a cell for crimes we did not commit.

It was close to four in the morning when Reggie finally threw open the door, slipped inside and dropped the "go bag" onto the floor. Closing the door, he leaned against it, throwing his head back and saying, "Whoo-ee."

I didn't have to guess. Ostensibly, Reggie was spotless, in fresh sweatpants, a clean hoodie and broken-in desert boots. My nose told me a different tale. The rucksack, which lay at my level, overflowed with the mixed fragrance of blood, offal and a hint of brain tissue. These smells seeped through two layers of Hefty bag and virtually drooled off the blade of the hidden knife. Even Reggie reeked.

Before he arrived, he had stripped away his blood-soaked clothes, toweled himself from head to toe and swabbed his face and hands with antiseptic. Any human passing him on the street wouldn't have spared Reggie a second glance. His outward innocuousness was a Klingon shield of invisibility. He roamed the night like an odorless wraith.

But to a dog, Reggie was a walking butcher shop. A film of human gore clung to his every surface, spiced cloyingly by the testosterone and adrenalin that had gushed into his pores while he was slicing and dicing his victim—or, more likely, victims. The ambience of slaughter surrounded Reggie, filled the room and clouded my senses, afflicting me with a clash of anguish and bloodlust.

Bloodlust, yes—because dogs can't help but feel a little (or a lot) turned on by the sickly sweet pungency of fresh-tapped blood—even human blood. Of course, your well-adjusted domestic dog would never even think about eating a person. Or killing one.

Dogs are perpetually puzzled by the alacrity with which humans knock each other off. In canine culture, this sort of intraspecies havoc is almost unthinkable. Unless a dog has been habitually abused, psychologically twisted and conditioned to violate his basic gut-level protective instincts, he can't conceive of attacking a fellow carnivore, especially humans—to whom we owe our singular status in the animal kingdom. The fact that people can kill other people and take actual joy in killing wolves, lions, tigers, crocodiles and other top predators is a conundrum of human nature that a dog in his or her right mind cannot fathom.

I'm not suggesting that we're morally superior to humans. But we occupy a simpler and more pragmatic moral universe. I mean, if dogs started ganging up on people, we'd squander the tenuous trust it has taken us 50,000 years to cultivate, which would leave us all pretty much doomed. Dogs are resilient and we're good fighters, especially in close quarters. Before the Industrial Revolution left us hopelessly behind in the arms race, there was a historical moment when dogs could have ruled the earth. But today—prudently—we accept our status as subordinate citizens if only for the simple reason that we don't none of us have trigger fingers.

I was pondering this while Reggie was in the shower, washing away the residue of death. After he had dressed in boxers, a t-shirt and his ratty plaid flannel robe, he cleaned and bleached his knife in the kitchen sink, leaving only his bloody clothes, tucked in his rucksack beside the door, to stink up the joint. I did my best to ignore its siren song of carnivorous allure.

Reggie settled into his La-Z-Boy and punched in his mother's number.

"Mommy, I've got great news."

What was he going to do? Tell her he'd just diced some innocent woman into bite-size morsels?

"Well, there's a dance."

A what? I perked up my ears.

"Yes, Mom. At school. It's formal, and I was so excited that I asked Antoinette before I realized how much it would cost ... Oh, yes, well, there's my tux rental, and a corsage for Antoinette, and everybody goes out afterwards to a really nice night spot in Manhattan ... Oh, I knew you'd understand, Mommy. Yes, a limo ... Right. Nothing but the best for Antoinette. I'd love for you to meet her ..."

I plumped back onto my rug. Reggie had just committed homicide, and here he was, scamming Mommy with a fake prom.

There are moments when the human storm really creeps me out.

As soon as Reggie finished shaking down his mother, he sank sleepily into his chair. I padded over and said, "Well."

He said, "What?"

I said, "So, you went out and did it again."

"Had to."

I was tempted to quiz Reggie about the body count, but it was way past our bedtime. So I went straight to the point.

"Reggie, please. Tell me again. Why do you do this?"

"I toldja, ya dumb mutt. It's my mission."

Here was my quandary. Dogs don't get missions from God. Nobody does, actually, but dogs know this better than humans. We can't delude ourselves on this point, because our communication with God is still direct. Reggie was right about God not talking to humans. He gave up answering people eons ago because they kept making bigger and bigger demands. He just said one day, "All right. That's enough." The only reason dogs still hear from God is because we never ask for anything. It's not really complicated. Mostly, God whispers little messages that pass unexpectedly through our heads, like "Good dog," or "Bad dog," or "Go lie down." I always interpret that last one as meaning, "Don't try messing around in human affairs." Unfortunately, as a trained police officer, I tend to meddle, which means I hear a few too many "Bad dog" comments popping up in my cortex. But that's no big deal, because nobody's better than God at not holding a grudge.

Once in a while, I'll hear that unmistakable voice from on high in my head saying, "Hey, don't roll in that. It's disgusting." This, frankly, is my only point of disagreement with God because it's glaringly evident that God instilled in all dogs the urge to roll in stinky stuff, especially the rotting, maggot-infested flesh of other animals. When I think objectively about the lure of decomposition, I'm mildly appalled at myself, and I see God's point. But it's hard to resist, especially because—after you've wallowed in a crow-pecked heap of three-week-old roadkill—the lingering ambience tends to be an aphrodisiac for lady dogs.

Anyway, as one of the millions of dogs who heed the occasional word of God, I know for sure that God has long since ceased to send shmucks like Reggie on missions of any sort. All human crusades, as any mixed-breed yellow dog can tell you, are pure delusion.

So, I said, "Reggie, you know, I'm not really sure about this mission of yours."

"Yeah, well, I *am* sure, you dumbass flea circus."

(For the record, I don't have one flea.)

I nodded. "I see. Yes. But you're killing people." I almost said "innocent people" but bit my tongue in the nick of time. Ouch.

"Killing people? No. You don't get it, mutt. People are the fuckin' collateral damage. My mission is to stop sex. People stopped needing sex decades ago. Fucking is obsolete, man. It's barbaric and violent and ugly. We have scientific ways to make babies. But you can't understand this 'cause you're a goddamn dog. Jesus! Why am I even talking to you?"

I sighed and accepted serenely yet another bigoted insult.

"But these people you're killing. They're your own species."

"Species? These filthy creatures, they aren't my species. You said it yourself, Farf. They're a whole separate species. They're sinking back into the swamp. They're reversing evolution and

DAVID BENJAMIN

becoming less than human. I'm superior. I've risen above the gutter where they crawl around and fornicate. I am pure and I am spreading purity, cleansing humanity."

I'd heard the spiel before. I could have spent another hour trying to convince Reggie to stop killing. But Reggie wanted to kill, and he was my master. If I convinced him to stifle his deepest urges, was I placing my needs ahead of his? Was I being disloyal? Was I violating the Code? Here was a dilemma I was too tired to explore. It was almost dawn. I turned away, did the usual three circles and settled back onto my rug.

I was drifting off when a new thought brought me back around. Clearly, I couldn't convince Reggie to abandon his mission. But maybe I could get him to bring me along on his grisly sprees as a sort of wingdog. I was there when he attacked the lovers in DUMBO, and I almost saved the girl. (If only she hadn't turned—like Lot's wife—to look back!).

Perhaps if I accompanied Reggie every time, I could find a way to intervene again. I might distract Reggie, break his rhythm, upset his focus, guide him gently and sympathetically away from his victim. He'd still have his lunatic mission, and his urges would still gnaw away at his psyche. But if I could prevent just one murder ...

As I was thinking about this, I opened an eye to discover that Reggie had extricated himself from his La-Z-Boy. He'd settled down at his computer, and he was tapping away with a satanic glint in his eye.

This, I thought, *could lead to no good*.

12

*"The only creatures that are evolved enough to
convey pure love are dogs and infants."*
—Johnny Depp

I didn't see Reggie's letter to the *Daily News* until he proudly brought a copy home two days after he'd written it. The headline, of course, covered the whole front page. It was superimposed over a blood-curdling photo of a young girl who had been slit open like a striped bass and dropped between two dumpsters in an alley.

Under a small subhead that said, "**LETTER FROM THE BROOKLYN RIPPER**," it read:

"I AM MOSES"

Oh my God, I thought. Putting his harebrained "philosophy" in writing was going to get Reggie into *so* much trouble. I could only hope that this impulsive outpouring would provide NYPD's crack detectives with some clue to catching Reggie before he struck again.

I was desperate to read the *Daily News* but had to wait 'til

Reggie went out. He didn't know I could read. This was a secret I preferred to keep.

It was hours before Reggie left to run an errand. As soon as he was out the door, I wrestled the newspaper to the floor, nosed it open to the story, squinted hard at the tiny type and got a load of what the clever editors at the *Daily News* were calling, with all due pretentiousness, "The Moses Manifesto":

> *You only call me a murderer, the 'Brooklyn Ripper,' because you can only gaze stupidly at a scene of wasted humanity stewing in its own tainted blood. You are ignorant of my purpose, your brains poisoned in puddles of vaginal discharge. I am no more a killer than Moses was a killer when he swept the Red Sea over the corrupt and voluptuary Egyptians whose only purpose was to drag him back into bondage. Humanity today suffers a far worse bondage than the Israelites suffered in slavery. They are the slaves of the lust and degradation, the violence and gross impurity of gratuitous sexual intercourse. Like Moses, I have been sent forth by a vengeful God to set my people free, to liberate all people, especially Woman, whose precious virginity is humanity's greatest treasure and worst tragedy—tragedy because it is always ripped away in its freshest most beautiful youth, torn from each innocent girl bloody and screaming, by the first beast who smells it, can't resist it and will do anything to destroy it.*
>
> *I am chosen for this mission because I am the rare gentleman, perhaps the only one still living—because I have yet to meet another like me, another who truly cherishes the celestial wonder of an unshattered womb—who values the purity of Woman more even than the numberless defiled mass of modern women do. In all my life, I am unsullied by sexual congress, untouched by the muck of subhuman lust. Once I thought my purity a deprivation. I sought the slimy thrill of diving violently into womanhood's seductive, destructive grotto. But I have learned, from the very voice of God, that*

virginity is a heavenly gift that makes my mission possible. Virginity preserved is salvation for all. I could not carry out my purpose had I been soiled by the carnal penetration of sacred Woman.

I have realized that this hard, hard mission, seemingly so cruel because so many sinful fornicators must be sacrificed on the bloody altar of their own rapacity, was forced upon me by the thousands, millions of women everywhere who had lost all self-respect. These women spread their legs and open their soon-diseased and wormy wombs to degenerate men who plant in these human sewers, these pits of decay, the seeds of mankind's self-annihilation, a new generation of genetic atrocities who that will hasten humanity's descent into bestiality. If this despoliation of virtue by the worst and filthiest of harlots and whores and "girls gone wild" is allowed to continue unhindered, all women, whether virgins or grandmothers or slobbering sluts, all will be the prey of rapist mobs while the last gentlemen, who stubbornly revere and defend the sacred virtue of women, will be dragged down in the street, beheaded like livestock, hacked to shreds in their hiding places. The world will descend into screaming, writhing chaos, an apocalypse where naked satyrs roam the ruined streets, stroking their erections and hunting newborn infant girls to impale like corndogs.

This is a revelation—to me—from the God of Noah, Lot, Job, Jesus and Moses. God speaks to me as He did to Moses. I cannot reveal my name, lest the defenders of lust, promiscuity and rape seek me out and abort my Godly mission before it is as complete as one lonely avenger can make it. As was true in Moses' time, and in the Flood, thousands must die before the world can be reborn in purity. If you must call me anything, call me not Ripper because what I have ripped was already torn from pure, young flesh, already sundered from the community of true love and plunged into the great shredder of souls. Call me not murderer but Moses. I am Moses returned,

and the Red Sea I have parted is a sea of contaminated blood. God has sent me my mission. He has placed me here in the most evil city in America, in the Sodom and Gomorrah of our time—of all times. He has told me—reluctantly, sadly, because he expected better from humanity—to go forth again and again, until I am exhausted, to punish, mercilessly and permanently, the legion of fornicators in our midst, to end their evil careers before their contagion spreads and ruins another generation, ruins humanity, ruins life itself.
Yours purely,
Moses

I'd barely finished reading this feverish drivel when Reggie returned home with a grocery bag. He made a dinner of Italian sausage and Rice-a-Roni (one of my favorites, too) and then settled restlessly in his chair, kneading his crotch and re-reading in the *Daily News* his ridiculous—and unfortunately verbose—"manifesto."

I found myself gradually slipping toward the disloyal conviction that my master might be further off his rocker than I had been previously willing to admit.

13

"Dogs are better than human beings because they know but do not tell."
—Emily Dickinson

Reggie seemed to be living a charmed life. Here he was, a killer run amok in New York City, charging willy-nilly around Brooklyn, murdering people on a depressingly regular basis. Yet, as I watched the panicky TV news and picked up snippets of information from the tabloids strewn around the park (Reggie, alas, was not a regular newspaper subscriber), I learned that the police—my trusty NYPD—were miles from ending his rampage.

Although my master had confined himself to a few contiguous neighborhoods in Brooklyn, detectives had not found a clue to Reggie's whereabouts. He had killed with both a knife and a gun, forcing the police to wonder if they were dealing with more than one killer. Most important of all, in my view, there was this: New York harbors probably the highest percentage of freaks and sickos in the entire Western Hemisphere. Police had picked up, grilled and released at least twenty guys who looked like they were a lot more screwed up and deranged than Reggie.

Reggie might well be the most harmless-looking killer in history. Madame Tussauds wouldn't have anything to do with him. He looks like that shlemiel Jared who got famous in Subway commercials, as bland as a low-fat turkey hoagie on homogenized white bread. I think if he up and actually tried to get arrested, waving a bloody knife in the cops' faces, they'd just pinch his pudgy cheek and send him home.

They might even worry about what might happen to him on the streets among the killers—and give him a lift.

• • •

Anyway, he decided to take me along with him the other night.

It was still July, still hot. But when we turned off Bedford Avenue onto Dekalb, there was an invigorating breeze in our faces. At almost one in the morning, nobody paid any attention to Reggie, and—although people tend to be wary of big dogs—I fielded barely a glance.

About thirty minutes later, we turned down one of the brownstone streets near Fort Greene Park, whose name I couldn't make out in the dark. It could have been Cumberland, South Oxford, South Portland or South Elliott. Stone staircases with wrought-iron banisters stretched as far as I could see, and parked cars lined the curbs. In a few hours, people would be scrambling to move the cars before the parking police and street cleaners showed up in tandem. But now, this avenue of old but newly affluent residences was deathly still. I knew we were hunting and I was praying—I could easily picture God, who's a strict Deist, scoffing at my ineffectual supplications—that no prey would appear.

When they did.

The woman, in blue skinny jeans and tank top, was pressed against the fender and hood of what I think was a Kia SUV. A man, with over-coifed hair and spotty facial hair, was kissing her rather sloppily and running his hands up her torso. We stopped. Reggie slipped into concealment behind a sycamore. I stayed in sight of the couple—as if expecting them to unclinch and look around. I perched alertly on my haunches and lolled out my tongue in as friendly a fashion as any German shepherd can manage. My eyes were large and non-judgmental.

Meanwhile, I could hear Reggie. A high-pitched keening from deep in his throat was barely audible to anyone human. But for me, it was fingernails on a blackboard. My hackles stood up involuntarily. I could also hear Reggie's rucksack rustling. He was groping for his gutting knife.

Darn, I thought.

The couple had progressed swiftly to unfastening each other's flies. She was panting heavily and reaching for his you-know-what. He was sort of humming while tugging her jeans—which were really tight— downward.

Reggie peeked around the tree, saw what was going on, and … well, the only word I can think of, but it's an understatement, is *exploded*.

The scream he uttered is something I've never heard from another human. He attacked faster than he seemed normally capable of moving. Covering perhaps thirty yards of narrow, root-heaved slate sidewalk, without tripping—he seemed to be veritably gliding above the ground. He reached the startled lovers in the time it took him to roar the four syllables of "FORNICATOOOOOOOOOOOOORS!"

Reggie's battle cry was still echoing off the brownstones as he plunged that hideous knife into the guy's back and ripped downward with such strength that the gash, as far I could tell, included two or three severed ribs.

"Lord," I said softly, "have mercy," knowing full well that the Lord wanted nothing to do with this atrocity.

I won't describe the rest. Suffice to say that both the guy and the girl, unfortunately, caught with their pants half-down and their privates partly exposed—I mean, what an undignified way to be found, and photographed from twenty different angles, later that morning—were not just dead in a few seconds, but slashed and scored about the face and neck beyond recognition. When Reggie ripped open their abdomens, spilling entrails onto the pavement, I had to turn my head—despite my canine appetites.

Those who say that dogs cannot weep didn't see me that night.

I mourned not just for this luckless couple but because I did nothing to intervene. As Reggie's rage dispersed, as though flowing into the gutter with the blood of the two sudden corpses at his feet, I tried telling myself that I had come along to observe Reggie, to see how he had devolved into this madness, to measure his illness and to consider how I might, somehow, intercede in a way that prevented the next detonation—without, of course, violating the sacred Code of the Dog.

I knew that I was walking a tightrope—which is physically impossible for dogs. But I labored to assure myself that I was at least facing up to my problem, and Reggie's. I wasn't just cowering comfortably at home on my rag rug, denying the inhumanity of my human, as Cupcake would certainly advise me to do. I was there to bear witness.

Either that or I was a passive accomplice.

As he staggered toward me, satiated and weak at the knees, Reggie stripped off his t-shirt and wrapped it around his still-dripping knife. Returning to where I had sat haplessly watching, he took from his rucksack a clean change of clothes, careful not to soil any garment. When he shed his bloodsoaked pants, I put my head between my paws and closed my eyes 'til all the noise and grunting was over.

Reggie was toweling bodily fluids from his arms and face when I sat back up and looked around. It hadn't been a loud murder. Reggie had killed them both before they were able to cry out. Indeed, Reggie had been the noisiest of the three.

But, with all the shouting and shuffling, not a single window had lit up anywhere up and down the row of brownstones. Now, minutes later, there remained not a soul on this street. Whoever called New York the city that never sleeps hasn't been to Fort Greene.

It was a long trek back to our apartment, all the moreso because Reggie was redolent of his crime. To me, with the combined pungency of sweat, blood and offal, he was a reeking neon advertisement for bloody murder. He smelled so richly of the deceased couple that I had to walk slightly ahead of him—upwind after a fashion—lest I get woozy. But none of this was evident to other humans, few of whom we encountered. I was surprised when we saw another couple in a doorway on Dekalb, holding hands and nuzzling affectionately. I feared a fresh rage from Reggie, but he gave them a wide berth and trudged on, sleepy and enervated. I thanked the Lord—with a pang of irony—for their survival.

As we turned onto Bedford Avenue, I ventured to speak.

"You've improved," I said softly.

Reggie shook his head as though waking. "Huh? What?"

"You seem to have gotten better at that," I said.

Reggie stopped, looked down. He smiled crookedly, arching his eyes upward in that way humans have of condescending to small children and dumb animals. "Ya think, dog?"

"Yes," I replied flatly.

"Well, yeah." We started moving.

"However," I began.

"What?" He stopped again, an edge of irritation in his voice.

Cautiously, I said, "Well, you obviously don't want anyone to stop you in the swift completion of your appointed rounds."

"No."

"You waited 'til very late. You chose a really quiet, secluded street. You used the element of surprise. You hid all signs of ... well, your activity. And you left the scene very quickly."

"Yeah, I know all that. What's your point, fuckmutt?"

DAVID BENJAMIN

"No, no," I said. "I shouldn't say anything. You did fine."

Reggie was still annoyed but curious now. "Say anything? Say anything about what?"

"Well, if you don't want to risk getting caught …"

"Course I don't want to get caught, ya goddamn flea factory."

"I know that," I said. "But I am a little concerned."

"Concerned?"

"Well, it just seems like you're still taking some pretty big chances."

"Chances? Whaddya mean by that?"

I had him thinking now. I said, in a conciliatory tone. Reminiscent of past rants, he started up again with "cleansing humanity of the filth and violence of sexual hunger," etc.

I broke in. "Yes, I heard clips from your manifesto on TV. It's very eloquent," I said. "But who are you after, really? Who's the cause of this filth and violence? Who's really to blame? Who's the instigator in all this rampant promiscuity?"

We'd started walking, but Reggie jerked to a halt. He knitted his brow in deep contemplation.

"I mean," I went on, "if you look at it from a dog's point of view, it's pretty clear."

"Whaddya mean by that? I'm not a fuckin' dog."

"True," I said. "But I am—literally. Woof woof."

Reggie was curious. We were still a few blocks from home. Traffic was almost nonexistent. Bedford Avenue, as usual, conveyed an unclean air of menace. Reggie leaned back. "So?" he said.

"So," I said, "my nose is my guide. And when I smell a lady dog in heat, it's like hitting me upside the head with a bag of steelies. I lose all restraint. My equilibrium goes haywire. My head is so full of the girl's sex juices that I can't see anything but that three square inches of pink skin underneath her tail."

"Yeah?" said Reggie. He was fascinated. He had to be, because I was spinning a story that matched his own warped theology.

"At this moment, neither the lady dog nor I have any conscious control of our impulses. We're helpless. Her overpowering fragrance is a physiological function that takes over her body, involuntarily, once or twice a year. My response is programmed into my brain like an automatic sprinkler system reacting to a tongue of flame. Her body is saying, 'Hump me, baby!' and mine is consumed by a lust that permits nothing but immediate sexual congress."

"Really?" said Reggie. "That's what happens? You can't help yourself?"

Well, not quite. To some extent, I can help myself. Any dog can resist, just like humans. But unlike humans, we have no social norms that frown on spontaneous, frantic, barking, squealing public copulation. But I wasn't going to explain this to Reggie.

"No," I lied. "It just sweeps over me and leaves me helpless to resist."

"Wow."

"But my point is: this happens to people, too," I said. "The only difference is that human noses are so weak that the effect of a woman's sexual emanations on a man aren't obvious to the man. They're subtle. They're subconscious. The eventual impact is the same. You lose control. You think you've acted with premeditation, but you haven't. You've been sucked irresistibly into a sexual vortex too powerful to fight. Nor is the woman to blame for whatever happens next. Her body exudes this powerful, invisible aura of desire in spite of what she might think she wants. She is as much the victim of her own chemistry as is the man who throws her down and impales her like a raging bull."

"No kidding?" said Reggie. "Really?"

"Well, don't ask me. Ask any reputable scientist," I said, comfortably aware that Reggie had no acquaintance with any scientist, reputable or otherwise.

"So, you see," I rambled on, "the ultimate source of the

sexual iniquity to which you object—"

"I see!" Reggie exclaimed. "It's the girl! It's always the girl."

"Yes," I said, "because of the unseen sexual magnetism that seeps from every pore and orifice of the female body …"

Reggie had embraced my idiotic theory. "I get it. Girls say they said, 'No.' They say they weren't asking for it. Because they weren't. Or they didn't think they were. But their bodies were asking for it all along, sending out the message: 'Fuck me, fuck me!'"

"Well, I wouldn't exactly put it that way, Reg. But yes, that's about the size of it," I said. "But you see what that means for your mission, don't you?"

Reggie's face fell as he strained for meaning. "No. What?"

"Well, you have to cut off the problem at the source."

"Yeah?"

"What's the source?"

"Girls, right?"

"Girls indeed."

"Oh!" Reggie had it, finally. "So, I shouldn't be killing the guys."

"Well, that seems like the inescapable conclusion," I replied.

"Hm, yeah, you could be right. But …"

"But what?"

I had worked Reggie around to a fifty-percent reduction (in truth, probably more than that) in his victim pool, but now he was quibbling.

"Well, Jesus, Farf, you're just a dumb fuckin' dog," said Reggie. "What kind of an asshole am I if I take advice from a dumb fuckin' dog."

I sighed and said, "Haven't you already?"

"Well, sort of, I got to admit," said Reggie, "that you helped me see the hand of God in my life. But that's not really you, is it, Farf. You're just sort of a tool in God's purpose. He comes to me through you because I'm with you all the time, right?"

I felt a deep weariness in my bones. All I really wanted to do was plop down on my rug and sleep 'til Christmas.

"Look, Reg, I understand your reluctance. I am only a dog," I said. "But this isn't my idea. This is scientific fact that I've learned by eavesdropping on really smart humans, just like you. All I'm really doing here, by telling you this, is synthesizing the ideas you've been expressing all along. Really, Reg."

"Nah," Reggie scoffed.

"No, it's true, Reg," I said. "After all, isn't every dog just a reflection, in every way, of his master?"

Reggie pondered this for a long time as we continued our way home.

Finally, on our doorstep, Reggie said, "I see what you mean."

I looked up receptively, hanging my tongue.

"I mean," said Reggie, "that's what I've been coming around to all along."

We went through the door and headed up the stairs, Reggie still talking as much to himself as to me. "I mean, when I think about how women affect me, I mean the way I just lose my perspective and stare at 'em, and want 'em, and wish I could just grab 'em and pull up their skirts and pull down their panties and just, you now—right there on the street. I mean, like a fuckin' dog ..."

When Reggie put it that way, I felt embarrassed to be a dog.

Reggie shoved his key into the lock and swung open the door.

"I mean, it wasn't me, really. I didn't want to be like that. But women, they make me feel like that. I can't help it. None of us can help it. Even those snotty fratboys and alpha male shitheads. If girls didn't send out all those chemical feelers, those guys might not be such shitheads. Y'know?"

Reggie was on a roll. I didn't bother to interrupt, just went gratefully to the refuge of my rag rug. He talked on, in the same vein, for a half-hour. I had dozed off when he spoke directly to me.

DAVID BENJAMIN

I raised my head. "I'm sorry. What was that?"

"I said, from now on. No more guys," said Reggie. "Just girls. The source of all human corruption. The fountain of sin."

I wanted to sleep, but while Reggie was receptive, I decided to venture a little more counsel.

"The knife," I said, "is pretty messy."

"Say what?"

"I mean," I said, "your method is compromising your mission."

"I don't know what the fuck—"

"It's simple. Open up your rucksack. What do you find?"

Reggie didn't actually open his rucksack. Nor did he answer my question, just glowered at me with his classic "you dumb mutt" stare.

I said, "What's in there is a lot of blood on your clothes and all over your knife. Even after you throw most of that stuff away somewhere, it still has your DNA all over it and, of course, the DNA of the man and woman you killed tonight. It's all evidence against you. Unnecessary evidence."

"Whaddya mean?"

"Reggie, you have that nice new gun in your bedside table. You've used it how many times? Twice?"

"Yeah? So?"

"Well, Reg. It's just so much tidier than the knife. There will be blood, but none of it on you, your clothes, or your gun. You don't have to strip down and change in the street, where people might see you. You can just go bang, bang and walk away."

"I don' know about that," Reggie muttered.

I settled back, leaving Reggie to think about all these deathstyle changes.

As I finally fell asleep that morning, I felt some consolation for the horrible sacrifice of those innocent humans in Brooklyn. Without breaching my loyalty to my master, I had convinced Reggie to restrict his mortal malice to a far smaller demographic than before, and I'd planted in his mind the idea of substituting, for his ugly, silent blade, a noisy weapon more likely to draw attention to him. And it would be traceable—afterward—through ballistic forensics.

14

"Questers of the truth, that's who dogs are, seekers after the invisible scent of another being's authentic core."
—Jeffrey Moussaieff Masson

For a while, my resolution to accompany Reggie on all his nocturnal wanderings didn't work out very well. Despite my blandishments and pleas, he locked me inside the next two times and came back fragrant with gore. He published his second "Moses manifesto" in the *Daily News*. It was a muddled re-hash of the first one he'd written. Its only novel passage posed the hypothesis that "lust," especially of the female variety, degrades embryos:

> *As a result, [he wrote] the union of sperm and egg is dangerously compromised every time a man and woman, drawn whorishly together by animal attraction, rutting like instinct-driven beasts or stuck together like earthworms drenched in slime, engage in the raw impulse of intercourse. Over generations, the chemical corruption that accompanies the very act of conception builds up in the human species, dragging it not forward in evolution but backward toward the cave and the stinking swamp. Non-sexual reproduction,*

in laboratories, without lust, "love" or emotion of any sort, is the only hope for the advancement of the human species.

Admittedly, Reggie's prose was purple and his reasoning ludicrous. But, despite its flaws, the manifesto served Reggie's purpose, escalating the public terror that swelled his ego. I don't think I need to remind any New Yorker of the sense of panic that gripped the city in those days, especially in bucolic Brooklyn.

I was amazed that Reggie could go prowling the streets in the wee hours and still find any people out there, much less the young women he preferred to stalk. I pictured him, lumbering from tree to tree, like a Stephen King clown from Hell, slowly closing in on some harmless barista who'd just finished a graveyard shift and couldn't find a taxi to save her life.

NYPD patrols had doubled in Brooklyn, and then tripled. But Reggie, spotting an NYPD cruiser creeping between the narrow streets with cars parked on both sides, could slip unseen into the shadows, recesses and stairwells that mark the familiar brownstone landscape of Fort Greene, Clinton Hill, Williamsburg and Bedford-Stuyvesant. Reggie and I both knew the territory better than any policeman. Besides, Reggie could just as easily hide in the open, as he shambled along comically, looking for all the world like a big, shaggy English sheepdog, innocuous, sexless, hairy and huggable.

Reggie was steadily refining the methodology in his madness. Inspired by his "mission," he'd become more careful, more efficient and less predictable. He stayed out longer, sometimes five hours, which told me that he was selecting his victims with great care and postponing his *coup de grace* 'til he was absolutely certain that there were no witnesses. He varied the length of time between his adventures. He carried the gun sometimes but usually brought it back unfired and odorless. He came home clean and bloodless (but stinky) despite using his knife. There was an air of purposeful sangfroid in his manner, and his recovery from each episode grew less twitchy and anguished. He waited 'til morning to call his mother, always telling her that he'd had a wonderful date the night before with Antoinette. He described the restaurant where they had dined and told Mommy in mouth-watering detail the dishes they had eaten. He discussed the wine and described the dessert. He would meticulously recite a synopsis of the movie they had attended. Later, he switched to describing Broadway musicals and operas at the Met. Sondheim and Verdi were more appropriate to the refined tastes of Antoinette, and—being far more expensive than movies—they elicited bigger contributions to Reggie's bank account.

I lay there listening to all of Reggie's whoppers, disgusted with my master and queasy in my stomach. But I was powerless to object or interfere. The Code bound me like a straitjacket.

One late summer day, Reggie took me on the usual circuit of Fort Greene Park. The weather had cooled slightly, the humidity was down and the sun felt good on my fur. As I strolled along with Reggie, I resisted all the interesting smells that swept over me on a southerly breeze. I kept my leash slightly slack. Every time a young woman in snug jeans or wearing a summer dress appeared, I watched Reggie's eyes and waited for my chance. It came with a strawberry blonde on a bicycle, bending over her handlebars, exposing copious cleavage and a lavender lace bra that covered almost nothing. As she pedaled toward us, a closer look beneath her skirt revealed that her panties matched her bra.

Her effect on Reggie was galvanic. He wavered, then staggered, as she approached. She showed him, of course, no interest whatsoever. Reggie's grip on the leash went noodly, and I seized the moment, breaking free and sprinting over the hill and down toward Myrtle Avenue like a Scottish deerhound after a stag.

Whoopee. There's nothing—nothing!—like running free

on the grass, in the summer air, with your leash trailing on the ground, while your master's startled voice fades behind you and blends eventually into the hum of the city. This was enough fun that I would have broken free just for the thrill. But I had a job to do that day. Somewhere in the park or nearby, I hoped, I could find Jesse, the little boy with whom I had spoken a month or so before. After seeing him, I realized I should have been more explicit about my problem. I should have told him who Reggie was and what he was doing. I should have said, "Go to your parents, Jesse. Tell them you're scared of Reggie, my master. Tell them he has a gun, that he might be the Brooklyn killer."

Sure. He's just a little kid. Who would believe him, especially if he mentioned that he'd heard it all from a talking dog? But if I could find Jesse again, I might be able to plant in his mind the conviction that this big slob in the park with a dog is a homicidal boogyman. If I did, then Jesse might tell his mom and dad, and they—while scoffing and telling him to stop making up wild stories about strangers—well, they might decide to err on the side of caution and talk to a policeman. Even if it's just a few lighthearted words in passing, it might be just enough to pique the cop's curiosity.

And maybe then, this sheepish-looking shlemiel with the German shepherd might appear, to the next NYPD officer who sees him, just a teensy bit less cuddly and harmless than he seemed before.

So, I ranged across Fort Greene Park sniffing for little Jesse. Technically, by the way, I was within my rights according to the Code. A dog is allowed to say just about anything to anybody because humans, as a rule, don't understand a word that any dog says. So, while a dog cannot perform any canine deed that betrays his or her master, talking is statutorily exempt. Besides, I was off the leash, a condition so rare and intoxicating for an urban dog that no other dog, or even God, could blame me for anything I might do or say while running free.

I hunted the kid for a half-hour without even picking up his day-old scent (humans, who are more odiferous than other humans can imagine, leave a trail in the air that lingers for hours and clings to the ground for as long as three days). Finally, in desperation, I started to approach other people, mainly little kids, to see if they understood me.

Most of them, seeing a big, wild-eyed dog with a black muzzle bearing down on them, steered away. Some, foolishly, started running. Others, when I got close enough to speak, just looked at me blankly, puzzled by what they heard as a lot of low-key growling interspersed with a succession of urfs, arfs, woofs and whining. I was eliciting what seemed like a promising response from a middle-aged woman in a flowing dress, redolent of ginseng incense, with a headband and lots of necklaces, when Reggie sneaked out from behind a tree and grabbed my scruff.

"There you are, you bad boy," he said, wrapping the leash twice around his hand.

"Oh, he's yours?" said the woman.

"Um, sorry," said Reggie sheepishly.

"Oh, no problem. He's a handsome dog."

"Um," said Reggie.

"Lady, please," I shouted. "Can you understand anything I'm saying to you? Anything at all?"

"Amazing," said the woman. "There's something almost human about him. What's his name?"

"Um, Farfel," said Reggie, pulling me away from the woman.

"Well," she said, "bye, Farfel."

"Shit," I said, abandoning all decorum.

I looked back once, and there was surprise on the woman's face—as though that last word had gotten through to her. But I was too far away to say anything more. Anyway, I was probably imagining it.

15

*"If you want sex, have an affair.
If you want a relationship, buy a dog."*
—Julia Burchill

As the weather cooled in September, Reggie seemed to calm. I was hopeful that his lust for blood was a sort of fever. Might it break and pass away as winter approached? Or was I just kidding myself?

I'd been pondering Reggie's thesis on the devolutionary arc of human sex. From a dog's angle, the idea was ridiculous. A dog assigns no values, ethical or aesthetic, to the simple task of copulation. For a dog, sex is a force that never changes and won't go away, like tides and gravity.

I posed this to Reggie. He was watching the Game Show Channel and eating Cheetos out of a huge economy-size bag. I was curled up on my rag rug. He glowered at me and punched the "mute" button ferociously.

"I mean," I said, "it's like the moon making the tide come in. Or gravity. The urge is just part of nature. Animal nature. Human nature. Just nature, Reg. You can't stop it. You don't need to stop it. Nobody can stop it. Really. It just goes on and on."

I thought this a pretty cogent argument. Simple. Clear. Empirically sound.

"What the fuck do you know?" He stood up menacingly. This was a gesture that didn't really work. Reggie's not a scary-looking guy. Cheeto dust trickled down his shirt.

"Well," I began.

"You're just a fuckin' *dawg*."

There it was, all over again. Speciesism. I let it drift to the floor to settle among the orange crumbs.

"True, Reg. Quite true. I lack a certain empathy with the human condition," I said. "But look around. The human condition obviously includes sex. If it did not, there would be no human condition, because there'd be no humans."

"You really don't understand a fuckin' thing, do you?"

"Reggie, come on. Face it. You can't stop something as universal as sex, no matter how hard you try," I said, pressing on. "People like sex. Everybody has sex."

"I don't have sex."

Well, he had me there.

"Emily Dickinson never had sex!" Reggie said a little too loudly. "Emily Dickinson never had babies. Emily Dickinson contributed more to the world than a million women who fucked their brains out and spewed babies like rabbits dropping turds."

Again, Reggie's topsy-turvy logic left me confused and speechless. Reggie seized the opening.

"Look, mutt, all I been saying is I got nothin' against babies. But we don't need sex anymore to make babies. Mankind has outgrown the need for sex but hasn't matured enough to give up sex and evolve to a higher state. Mankind needs motivation. Don'tcha see, Farf? What better motivation than fear? If people start to realize that having sex could get them killed, well, they just might hesitate, put it off, think twice and say, 'Hey, this is a pretty crude way to keep the species going. This is what dogs do, and rats. Pigs fuck, snakes fuck.

Cockroaches fuck like crazy, for Chrissake!' Humans are the peak of evolution. But we're still lowering ourselves to the level of reptiles and bugs."

"Reggie," I said, "people don't just have sex to make babies, you know. That's what separates humans from—"

"I don't think I'm the only one, either," said Reggie, ignoring my point. "I mean, there's thousands of us out there, scorned and pissed on by all those women who only want to fuck the alpha males. Some guys get laid every night; the rest of us could go our whole lives without doing it once."

"Well, you see, there's my point again, Reggie. Those alpha males you hate so much, who are getting lots of sex—they're not making any babies. They're using protection. They're just doing it for fun. Humans have sex for fun, Reggie."

"Yeah, well, some of them do. And the rest of us?" said Reggie. "There are a lot of us, muttfuck. Incels! Millions of us. We're screwed but we can't get laid. And I'm setting the example for them. They'll see what I'm doing. They'll read my manifestos. They'll understand. They'll go out, just like me. They'll hunt down the whores and frat boys. They'll catch them with their pants down, just like me. And pretty soon, all the sluts and their horny boyfriends with their fuckpads and rape drugs and French ticklers, they'll start thinking twice. They'll look over their shoulders. They'll wonder. Is there an incel behind that tree? They'll understand, slowly and surely, that sex isn't fun anymore. And it's not even necessary. And life is simpler, man. No muss. No fuss. No fucking mind games. No heartbreak. Man will ascend to a higher, purer state."

He was still standing there, looking down at me, little flecks of spit on his lower lip. I didn't speak because, well, why should I? He had this cockamamie idea that he could scare the entire male population of the world into either impotence, abstinence or homicide. How does a sentient dog answer something like that?

"What the fuck am I doing?" said Reggie suddenly. He

conked himself in the forehead and smiled at me. "Arguing with a dog. I bet you can't even really talk, you fuckin' mutt. I'm just dreaming this whole stupid conversation."

To show me there were no hard feelings, Reggie came over, tousled my head, rubbed behind my ears and treated me to a handful of Cheetos. I sighed, gobbled my treat and nestled into my rug. As usual, Reggie wasn't remotely receptive to reason. But he was my master, and I couldn't give up hope. Reggie would eventually either mend his ways or get caught. Until then, I had to put my faith in the patience and boundless sympathy I'd learned while lying on the floor at the feet of Dr. Menzies. My job was to watch, listen, bide my time and play as dog-dumb as I could without completely losing my self-respect.

• • •

That day, as we took our long walk to Fort Greene Park, Reggie spotted Gloria and Cupcake. He froze in place. I sat, cocking my head toward Reggie to see what he would do. Cupcake, who was downwind of us, picked up my scent. She barked noncommittally, basically to show off her nose. No bouncing, no wagging. Not even a desultory growl to acknowledge Gloria's recent horrible experience with Reggie. Cupcake wasn't a naturally emotional dog.

I nodded toward Cupcake and urfed once, audible only to Reggie. Gloria finally looked in our direction.

It was a taut moment. Gloria and Reggie were a good hundred yards apart, locking eyes across the playing field. If I'd been Gloria, I would have turned and run, looking for help, barking for the police. But I'm just a dog. I tend to think in straight lines. Humans sometimes don't seem to think at all, and when they do, their minds tend to draw curlicues. So, I wasn't terribly surprised—just alarmed—when sweet, weak, plain Gloria raised her non-leash hand toward us, made a little wave at Reggie, and then, can you believe it? She smiled.

Dear God.

Two minutes later, they were side by side on a bench, Reggie admitting that he had behaved badly.

"Behaved badly?" I said to Cupcake. "He was going to rape and murder her, for Pete's sake!"

"Who's Pete?" asked Cupcake.

"I had no idea you were so ... straitlaced," Gloria was saying. "I was ... I mean, I pushed too hard."

"Well, you caught me by surprise, yeah. But I totally lost my cool," said Reggie. "I mean, Jesus. I hit you, didn't I?"

"But I led you on."

"Oh God," I muttered. "No no no no no."

"What's the trouble, big boy?" said Cupcake.

"Your mistress, Gloria. Does she have no self-esteem whatsoever?"

"Not that I've noticed," said Cupcake. "She's pretty much a doormat for anybody who wants to walk all over her."

"But my master, he'll kill her."

"Yeah, right. That guy's a killer," said Cupcake. She snorted in an unladylike way.

"I'd like to make it up to you," said Reggie. "Prove I can be a gentleman."

"Well," said Gloria. She was hesitant. This was good. Maybe she'd tell him, thanks but no thanks. Shove off, you brute.

"Just a cup of coffee. We can go to Connecticut Muffin. We can leave the dogs outside. Watch them."

"Say no, say no, say no," I urfed.

"Hey, cut it out," said Cupcake. "If they go there, I'll get a muffin. You, too. Guaranteed. Gloria's a soft touch."

"I don't want a damn muff—"

"Well, okay," said Gloria to Reggie.

"Shit," I said.

"Watch your language, big boy," said Cupcake.

She was right. I know I'm losing my cool when I sink to profanity.

DAVID BENJAMIN

And suddenly, they were off to Connecticut Muffin on Myrtle Avenue, dragging Cupcake and me behind. Reggie and Gloria went inside, got coffee and sat down at a table to talk. Cupcake and I were leashed to a bench on the sidewalk. I noticed that a few people passing by were tempted to pet Cupcake, who's cute even when she's not trying. But they tended to veer off when they got a load of me. I rarely get petted by strangers.

"So," said Cupcake, "wanna hump?"

"Pardon?

"You know, big boy. Hump. Couple. The ol' two-backed beast."

"Now?"

"When else?"

"No, listen—"

"What's the trouble? Not up to the job?"

"We have to talk."

"We can talk while we hump. Come on, big boy. Climb on."

"Later!" I said.

Cupcake peered back at me over a shoulder. Suddenly, her eyes grew wide.

"Oh my goodness. I've heard that there were gay dogs, even in Brooklyn. *Especially* in Brooklyn! But you're the first—"

"I'm not gay. I'm just preoccupied."

Cupcake, who had been presenting her comely little moist privates provocatively, turned to face me. "You must be preoccupied something fierce to turn me down, big boy. What's on your mind?"

"We have to do something to keep my master away from Gloria."

"Why should we do that? We're getting muffins out of it already. You see that bag on the table?"

"Look, my master is dangerous."

"Well, he's a guy. They're all dangerous in their own way,"

said Cupcake, cocking her head and showing me a flash of tongue. "I bet you can be pretty dangerous yourself, big boy."

"Oh, for Pete's sake!"

"Who is this Pete?"

"Look, Reggie thinks he's on a mission from God," I said.

"A mission?" asked Cupcake. "To do what?"

"End sex."

"Say what?"

"He wants to stop people from having sex because he thinks sex is causing humanity to go backward."

"Go backward where?"

"To become animals again."

"Well, wouldn't that be an improvement?" said Cupcake. This might have been the first intelligent remark she'd uttered since I met her.

"From our point of view, yes," I said. "But for a human, it's crazy."

"To end sex or become an animal again?" asked Cupcake.

"Both," I said.

"Okay, I'll bite," said Cupcake. "You say your master's crazy? Fine, but what's the big deal? In my experience, most humans are nutty as a Payday bar. Oh, wow. By the way, have you ever tried eating one of those? They get all stuck between your canines, and then, for hours you end up—"

"Look, sorry, C.C., but this is important. Reggie isn't just regular human crazy. He's all the way around the bend. He's crazy enough to kill people. He's been doing it."

"Doing what?" I really did wish Cupcake was just a teensy bit smarter.

"Killing people," I said. "He tried to kill Gloria."

"No, he didn't."

"Yes, he did. I was there."

"You're kidding me."

"No, I'm not."

DAVID BENJAMIN

"You're saying your master tried to kill my mistress?" said Cupcake, sitting down and fixing her gaze on me. "You mean, end her life? Rub her out?"

"Right," I replied. "He attacked her, threw her on the floor, tried to rape her and then pulled a knife on her."

Cupcake rolled her eyes, "Well, if he really did that," she said, "then why is she in there having coffee with him?"

"Well, she's your woman," I said. "You said she's a doormat."

Cupcake had to stop and think.

"Okay," she said, in a different tone. "Tell me what happened."

I told her, in detail as alarming as possible. Cupcake took it all in coolly. I described how I had barked and snarled Gloria from the apartment and sent her fleeing in terror down the stairs.

I asked again if Cupcake could explain why Gloria, after that experience, would willingly get within a thousand yards of the maniac who almost murdered her.

"Well, you see," said Cupcake, "Gloria has a hard time with reality."

"What do you mean?" I asked.

"She tends to tidy it up. She'll change things in her memory so they come out better in the end," said Cupcake. "She probably doesn't remember much about Reggie trying to rape her or hitting her. She probably blames the whole thing on herself. Or you."

"On me?"

"Oh, but don't worry. She's forgiven you. She probably thinks you just got excited by all the fuss. You overreacted."

"Overreacted?"

"Did you?"

"No, I saved her life, for Pete's sake!"

"Okay, that tears it. I've got to know who—"

"Do you read the papers?" I asked.

"Really! Now, that's crude. I'll have you know that I was housebroken at six weeks."

"No no," I said. "The news, C.C. Do you follow the news at all?"

"Well, as much as the next dog."

"Then you've heard of the Brooklyn Ripper?"

"Oh, well, yes. Who hasn't?"

"Well, that's him, babe."

"That's who?"

"Reggie. My master."

"What?" said Cupcake, dropping her jaw. "Your master is the Clinton Hill killer?"

"Yes."

"*That guy* is the criminal mastermind who has the whole New York City police force chasing their tails?

"Yes. That's right."

"Oh, spare me," said Cupcake. "Him?"

"Honest to God."

"I don't believe you. That's ridiculous."

"He calls himself Moses," I said. "He thinks he's like Moses. He's been denied sex, like God denied Moses the Promised Land. Reggie thinks God wants him to end sex by scaring people away from it."

"Ah, come on, big boy. You're pulling my leg."

"No. It's true. He talks about it all the time."

"Well, it's perfectly ridiculous."

"Don't tell me," I said. "Tell him."

"Maybe I would if I believed you. But even if I did, he wouldn't understand a word I say. He's a human," said Cupcake.

"He might," I said. "He understands me."

"Well, now I *know* you're pulling my leg!"

It took a while, but I finally convinced Cupcake that certain people, for reasons unknown to science, can understand dogs. I said Reggie was one of those rare specimens, probably because he's clinically deranged. But I mentioned the little boy, Jesse.

"Well, then, why doesn't anyone understand me?" asked Cupcake.

"Maybe," I said, "it's your French accent."

"I don't have a French accent."

I got Cupcake back around to the news and all the uproar over the Brooklyn Ripper. She knew about the murders but only from brief glimpses on TV. It turned out that because Cupcake had been housebroken so fast, she never learned to read or had much interest. Her consumption of television news was also limited because Gloria mostly watched the Food Channel.

"She's a wonderful cook," said Cupcake, "and—best of all—really messy. I've licked some of Brooklyn's loveliest sauces off our kitchen floor. And Gloria's leftovers are just heaven. I struggle constantly to keep my girlish figure."

This was, I guess, nice for Cupcake, but it scared me. If Gloria was like every other good cook I've known, she loved to show off. She would invite people over to feed them her latest recipe.

I looked through the window of Connecticut Muffin. They'd been talking for a half-hour now. Gloria was probably saying, at that moment, that she's a pretty good chef and would Reggie like to come over sometime for a nice home-cooked meal?

I trembled at the thought.

"What's wrong with you?"

"I was trembling at the thought."

"What thought?"

"Never mind."

"So," said Cupcake, turning away.

"What?" I asked.

"Are we gonna hump, or not?"

"Oh, for Pete's sake."

"Wait! Who is this—"

I'd had another thought.

"Listen," I said. "We're dogs, right?"

"Hey, no flies on you, big boy."

"No, what I mean is, we live by the Code."

"Absolutely," said Cupcake. We were face-to-face again. Cupcake had apparently resigned herself to a non-humping encounter. "The Code is all we have."

I shared Cupcake's reverence for the golden rule of all dogdom, but I didn't agree entirely with her fundamentalism.

"What if your master's crazy?" I said. "What if he's broken all the human codes and turned into a murderer?"

"Wow. You've really convinced yourself that big creampuff is a murderer, haven't you?" said Cupcake.

"Yes! Yes, he is. I've seen him do it. He's a serial killer."

"Who?"

"What?"

"Who's he killing?"

"Well, for one, he went after Gloria. Before that, he attacked lovers, together, men and women," I said. "But lately, I think I managed to convince him only to go after women. You know, reduce the victim pool."

"Ah," said Cupcake. "Human women?"

"Well, yes. Of course."

"He's not killing dogs?"

"No."

"Well, then, it's simple, big boy. You have to stay true to your master."

I knew she was going to say that, but I still felt my stomach turn. "Even if he's so crazy that he's butchering people with a giant knife. Gutting them like fish?"

"People. He's gutting *people* like fish. Not dogs," said Cupcake. She scrunched her muzzle thoughtfully and added, "I guess if he were going after us, then maybe you'd have a way out of the Code. But humans? None of our business."

I stared at Cupcake in consternation. She looked back with icy assurance, and I knew she was right. The Code is the Code.

Suddenly, Reggie was beside me, untying my leash from the bench. He patted Cupcake once on the head. She flung out her tongue and wriggled sensuously. What a flirt.

"We gotta go," he said. "I've got work to do tonight."

Reggie said a quick goodbye to Gloria and tugged me up Myrtle in the direction of Bedford.

"What sort of work?" I asked, trying to sound casual.

"Shut the fuck up, you dumb mutt."

I could feel the Code in my gut, gnawing away at my soul.

16

"The world was conquered through the understanding of dogs; the world exists through the understanding of dogs."
—Friedrich Wilhelm Nietzsche

When Reggie said we had "work to do," it chilled me all the way down to my hocks. I feared another of his nocturnal excursions. So I was relieved, at first, when he sat down at his computer and launched another manifesto.

I didn't have the chance to read it 'til a few (eventful) days later, but his central thesis was the degradation that has already turned women into a less-than-human subspecies of the human race.

This is the main part of what got published in the *Daily News* under a headline that read:

"She-Beasts Must Die!"

Sexuality has become evil because women have seized control of it, twisting men to their lustful will and devilish purposes. Women decide whether or not sex will happen. They control which men get it and which men don't, even though women are flawed, warped, sick and inferior creatures. They are more THING than people. They're like bacteria that take over the body and bend it to their sickness, rotting it from within until it bursts open in a torrent of pus, blood and corruption. There's something fundamentally diseased at the core of the female brain that not only reduces their humanity but steadily, progressively decays it until they are no more human than a dog or a Gila monster. Women can't intelligently choose a proper mate. They are drawn to superficial men with savage and degenerate tendencies, whose minds are sewers of lust, violence and deviancy. In a fair, just world, the choice of mates would be left solely to men of intelligence, rationality and scientific knowledge. There are few of us left, but we must prevail. We cannot allow women to choose their men, because they can't help but choose the wrong mates. This is a choice that will doom the human race, breeding generation upon generation of morons and cretins and narcissist assholes. Sex has given women a disproportionate measure of power over society. Like bacteria run wild, like a plague that threatens to literally wipe out humanity as we know it, women must be stopped before it's too late. They have sunk to the level of beasts, she-beasts who need to be captured, restrained, put in cages and kept in concentration camps. Once men have regained control of our sexuality and the future of the human race, we can select the women who are genetically preferable to breed—by artificial means, without the rutting competition and corruption of intercourse—and propagate the species. Once we have harvested the eggs we need, we can let the brood females die behind the fences, by disease, starvation and by fighting among themselves like the beasts that they are. We have to do this because women have lost their moral capacity and cannot think beyond their depraved emotions and vile sexual impulses.

I am the Moses of this message. My mission to hunt down and snuff out the carriers of the female plague is the first step in cleansing humanity. The women I eliminate are the examples that all other women, and all men must heed, if we are to save ourselves, from women, from the obsolete beast behavior of sexual penetration and from the end of us all.

It's longer than that. The poor editors at the Daily News had to jump Reggie's manifesto twice to fit it all into the newspaper. But this is the main gist, which repeats and repeats 'til you want to track down Reggie, grab him by the throat and force him to just shut up.

Which I was in a position to do if I weren't his loyal dog and "best friend."

After banging away at his manifesto for four hours, Reggie was as wired as I've ever seen him. As he paced the room, seething with hatred, clenching and unclenching, banging his fists on doors, walls and tabletops, I suggested that it might calm him a little to call his mother.

"That BITCH!?" he screamed. "She's one of them. She's the reason for all this shit!"

Well, it was just a thought.

"I gotta get out of here," he said. It was just after midnight. I knew what this meant. My mind strained for some way to forestall the inevitable.

As he was grabbing for his keys, I said, as coolly as I could manage, "Reg, you know, they're out in force. They're looking for you."

"Who? Who? WHO?" Reggie replied, owlishly.

"The police, Reg. The NYPD. You've become public enemy number one."

"I'm not their enemy, those dumb fucks. I'm their friend. I'm their fucking savior!"

"Well, they're still looking for you, Reg. Some of them might feel the way you do, but they still have to enforce the law," I said, "and I was thinking …"

"You? Thinking? That's a laugh. You're a fuckin' dog. Do you *know* you're a fuckin' dog?"

"Yes, I remember every time I scratch behind my ear with my hind foot," I said. "But that's exactly why I can help you."

"Help me? You? Help me what?"

"Well, the police are looking for a killer, stalking the night, armed to the teeth, right?"

Reggie paused in his pacing, looking down at me. I had assumed the standard subservient pose of the good doggie, seated on my haunches, tongue out, eyes cast upward reverently, tail gently swishing back and forth on the floor (collecting lint that I would later have to shake off).

"For any cop in New York, Reg, you'd be a career-maker. You're the collar of the century."

"Really?" I could see Reggie actually swell slightly.

"Oh, yes," I said. "But what they're not looking for, it seems to me, is a sleepy-looking guy whose only reason for being on the street in the wee small hours is that his dog woke him out of a sound sleep because the dog needed to pee."

Reggie thought about this.

"You mean," he said, "I should take you along."

I held my tongue, trying to look agreeable and loyal, letting Reggie compute the notion.

"I think you're right, mutt," said Reggie. "You might be a stupid flea magnet, but you're a good prop. Yeah. Why didn't I think of this before? Okay. Let's go."

And so, we were out together ten minutes later, heading down Bedford toward Williamsburg. I had no idea what I could do to deter Reggie from his godly mission, but I knew that if I were at least present at the crime, I had a chance to intervene.

Or, as my master's loyal pet, I could stand by and watch it all go down without lifting a paw.

A dog's life, trust me, it's a bitch.

・ ・ ・

There's a street with a broad cobbled sidewalk called

Washington Park on the east side of Fort Greene Park. Joggers regularly sprain ankles and shred their menisci there, and every Saturday, there's a wonderfully fragrant farmers' market. At night, under a canopy of trees, it's either spooky or romantic, depending on your point of view. It was there that Reggie spotted a woman, all by herself. She was long-legged in a short skirt with a light fall coat. Hair tumbled down her back, and her scent, as it wafted on the breeze, reminded me of oatmeal and apples sprinkled with spearmint. Something she was wearing was fresh from the dry cleaners. Even from a block away, the redolence of perchloroethylene stung my eyes. She had stopped beneath the faint glow of a streetlight and was rummaging through a roomy handbag. I pricked up my ears to hear what was she was mumbling to herself. Somewhere in the bag was a mobile phone she couldn't find.

Reggie hadn't made a move on her yet, so I figured it was okay to bark. I had opened my mouth to do just that when Reggie silenced me, yanking violently on my choke chain.

"You, dipshit," he said. "Not a peep."

Well, that queered it. Orders from my master. No barking. But the girl was in peril for her life. Reggie had swung his backpack. He was reaching inside for his knife, which he found instantly. The girl, not so lucky, was still hunting for her phone. She had no idea that we were there.

I had another option. While he dug in his bag, Reggie had looped my leash on his wrist. Rising up on my hind legs and lunging straight forward, I snapped Reggie's arm from its hold on the backpack and tore the leash free before he could get a grip on his end. I was off.

Reggie could have shouted, but that would have alerted the girl. He could only stand and watch as I bounded along the cobblestones, straight toward the woman. I thought about knocking her down or running circles around her but saw no point in either option. If I flustered or frightened her without explaining why I was carrying on like a puppy after a Frisbee,

I might just be making Reggie's "mission" that much easier. So, I sprinted right past her, brushing her leg. She jumped slightly and said, "Oh!" I kept going, scanning the street for a police cruiser, peering myopically into shadows, hoping to spot a cop on the beat.

Nothing.

Where were the police who were reputed to be blanketing Clinton Hill?

When I reached a cross street, I paused. I think this was Willoughby Avenue. I looked down the street, hopefully. It was deserted. Nothing stirred. No cop emerged providentially from the double row of parked cars. I looked back. The girl was a murky figure in the distance. I saw no sign of Reggie. This respite would not last.

I lit out for Myrtle Avenue, a major artery that had traffic and activity—and, presumably, cops—all night long. When I got to Myrtle and turned left, along the north side of the park, there I saw—a half block down—a cop. No, two cops, male and female, on the sidewalk, talking quietly, oblivious to the teeming, sinful city around them.

Great, I rushed up to them, wagging, wheezing, trying to look harmless and urgent at the same time.

"Hey, you guys, listen," I said in Dogspeak. They immediately backed away. The male cop, medium-build, dark-skinned with a big belly and a spoiled-tomato scent, spread his legs and guided the woman cop—a beige-colored human with a definite air of cilantro—behind his shoulder. The woman was light on her feet and looked like she could handle herself, but she seemed tolerant of the other cop's misplaced chivalry. They poked their nightsticks in my direction.

I said, "Please. I don't want to hurt anybody, but there's a woman in danger. You need to help her. Right now!"

"You think he bites?" said the male cop.

"Where the hell is his owner?" said the she-cop.

"I don't bite, dammit!" I cried. "I need a cop. To save a woman!"

"Funny-sounding dog," said the she-cop.

"Look, get on the horn," said the he-cop. "Call Animal Control."

I made one more try. "I used to be NYPD! Please! Listen!"

"I'll try to grab his collar," said the he-cop.

"Be careful," said the she-cop. "That dog is huge."

"Oh, don't worry about me. I have a way with dogs," said the he-cop.

"A way with dogs, my ass," I said. "If you did, you'd *listen* to me!"

"C'mere, boy, c'mere. You settle down now. We won't hurt you, boy. Will we, Felicia."

"Oh no, we like you, boy. You're a big, sweet baby, aren't you?"

I took off, heading for the Myrtle Avenue business district—which, of course, at this hour was deader than Hooch. But, in two blocks, I was able to intercept a squad car as it pulled out from a side street. I ran in front of the headlights, and the driver slammed on the brakes. A second later, two cops were out of the car, trying to surround me. They'd obviously received a radio report that I was running loose and possibly rabid. People are basically alarmist when it comes to dogs, especially at night.

I backed away from the two cops, keeping my escape lanes open while struggling to reason with them in Dogspeak, hoping desperately that something I said—just one word—might penetrate their human-biased crania and draw them into conversation. All I wanted was for one of them to stop, turn to the other and utter the words that somebody said every week for eighteen years and 591 episodes of *Lassie*.

"I think he's trying to tell us something."

Trouble is, no human in real life, in the whole history of

dogs, has ever said, "I think he's trying to tell us something." Humans never expect dogs to tell them anything—which is one of the many reasons humans keep screwing things up.

Clearly, there wasn't anybody going to break the *Lassie* embargo that night in Brooklyn. After a few more minutes with the cruiser crew, full of sound and fury signifying bupkes, I heard the unmistakable siren of an Animal Control unit and lit out, heading down the very side street from which the cruiser had emerged. I turned on Willoughby and completed the circuit back to Washington Park. The cobbled street was still as tranquil as a moon crater, not one blue uniform in sight. I saw neither Reggie nor the girl on the cobblestones, so I paused, lifted my nose and drank in the night.

There it was, a tendril of dense scent, wafting into my head like a needle pulling a thread—blood, sputum, offal, feces, and maybe worst of all, a whiff of semen.

I found them just inside Fort Greene Park, invisible behind a snow fence enclosure piled with leaves. She was a heap of blood-soaked flesh and shredded clothing, her face—thank God—twisted away from me. He was naked but for his briefs, quietly tucking his bloodied clothing into his rucksack. He stopped when I arrived.

"You missed all the fun, Farf," said Reggie. Killing, now a habit for him, had settled his nerves and softened his disposition.

"Now, you just sit there, boy. Be good. I'll be ready in a minute."

A moment later, we were again moseying toward Myrtle, a man out for a reluctant walk with his canine protector. A police car finally appeared. It came toward us but barely slowed as it passed. The cruiser continued toward Dekalb, rolling past a mangled body that wouldn't be discovered 'til the dawn's earliest jogger entered the park.

We returned home via Myrtle and Bedford, passing lots of police but encountering none, because—as Reggie had discovered—there's nothing less suspicious than a sleep-deprived New Yorker curbing his best friend at three in the wee hours.

17

"If dogs could talk, perhaps we would find it as hard to get along with them as we do with people."
—Karel Čapek

Reggie had surprised me—actually, I was dumbfounded—with his improved skills as a murderer. He had never done anything particularly well in his life except perhaps mooch off his mom. He was lousy at holding a job because, when he got one, he was chronically confused about the simplest chores—running a cash register, remembering to put eggs and bread on the top of the bag, zipping his pants after bathroom breaks. His punctuality was nonexistent, and his misanthropy so obvious that customers recoiled from him. Bosses seemed to take pleasure in firing him.

But at killing strange women in the dead of night? Well, Reggie had found his *métier*!

And his accomplice. After his triumph in Fort Greene Park, I became the faithful canine companion to every Reggie-the-Ripper stroll around Brooklyn. As the weeks passed, Reggie also developed an uncharacteristic patience. He limited himself to a victim once every five days or so, even a week—long enough for public vigilance to wane just slightly. After a few days, the *Post* or the *Daily News* would inevitably publish a headline saying something like, "Is the Brooklyn killer finished?" or "Has the Horror Ended?"

Reggie loved publicity like that. It tickled his overdeveloped sense of melodrama. He would wait several days, then vamp for another day or two, and then—squish! He dashed the hopes of the terrified city with a fresh outrage that juiced the circulation of the bloodthirsty tabloids.

Here's what never ceased to amaze me. Although Brooklynites from East New York to Bay Ridge were rigid with fear and the streets were a ghost town after sunset, Reggie could always ferret out a target. It might mean three hours of scouring the desolate sidewalks. But he knew that no matter how scary the mean streets, there would always be a few party girls stumbling home on high heels in the darkest hours before the dawn. They would be alone. They would be tired, stoned, disheveled and redolent of hurried, casual coitus. They would arouse in Reggie a fury that clouded his mind and ignited his frenzy. Typically, the woozy girl would think to scream only when Reggie's ghastly blade touched her neck and severed her vocal cords. She would crumple to the pavement, gushing blood and gasping helplessly, like a beached fish, while Reggie slashed her ripe flesh, cursed her iniquity and climaxed in his cargo pants.

The odors that accompanied these performances left me dizzy, nauseous and horny.

I made efforts to intervene, but they were puny, ineffectual, futile. As long as I was Reggie's ward, as long as my leash was wrapped on his hand or tied to a nearby banister, I was impotent to save these girls' lives and confounded by my conflicting vows, one governed by the Code of the Dog, the other rendered unto the NYPD to "serve and protect" the very New Yorkers I was helping Reggie dismember.

Murder took on a grim sameness. After the last ounce of blood had pulsed from the luckless woman on the sidewalk,

Reggie would calmly disrobe, right over her, stripping nude and carefully removing a fresh change of clothes from his rucksack. He could afford to take his time and linger because the streets were more eerily empty than any normal night—thanks to Reggie. Each time, he meticulously doused his bloody knife in bleach from a plastic bottle, wiping it spotless and dry with an unbloodied part of his soiled shirt. A puddle of Clorox became one of his "trademarks," but it proved a useless clue to finding him. Then he would stuff the evidence into the rucksack and take out a pristine ensemble of anonymous purchases from thrift stores—gym pants, sweatshirt, a cheap windbreaker and high-top, silent-running Converse All Stars. He would dress slowly and calmly, looking down often at the new corpse, his face glowing with pride and triumph. The last item would be a pair of disposable latex gloves. Then, rucksack on his back, he would hide the body, but not very well, in the dooryard of a basement apartment, perhaps behind a row of garbage cans. The poor girl's remains would be visible with the first light of day, and a renewed cry of anguish would resound across the great metropolis.

Juiced by an overdose of homicidal adrenalin, Reggie would stay up those mornings, unable to sleep. He turned on the local news show, waiting for his handiwork to be discovered and proclaimed. He would make a fist then, thrust it forward, and say, "Yessss!"

And call his mom.

"Oh, mom! Did you see the news? ... Yes, another one ... I know. Isn't it awful? ... No, no, don't worry about me. This maniac is only killing women, after all. I worry about you, Mommy! ... No, I don't agree, Mommy. Sure, he's over here in Brooklyn. But there's no reason he couldn't suddenly decide to target Manhattan ... Because he has a mission, Mommy ... Oh, I know. It doesn't make sense to people like you and me, but there seems to be a method to his madness ..."

I listened to Reggie and wondered. He could, at one

moment, succumb to a violent distemper that left innocent girls in mangled heaps among rubbish and rats. The next moment, he could talk about his very own criminal depredations as though someone else was responsible, as though he understood how deviant he had become. From one instant to the next, Reggie was two creatures. One was a shy and awkward mama's boy, barely functional in society. The other was a vampire, calculating, efficient, maniacal and deadly.

But messy.

One late morning, after Reggie had finished talking with Mommy, I asked, "Reg, I'm curious."

Reggie now was usually mellow after a murder, ready for conversation and tolerant of my lowly canine status.

"What about, Farf?"

"Well, you've used your gun a few times. But you seem to prefer the knife."

Reggie didn't look at me. He didn't even open his eyes. "Uh-huh," he said. "What's your point?"

I reminded him that the gun was neater and quicker. He wouldn't need to change his clothes after a murder.

Of course, I had an ulterior motive. As long as Reggie used that hideous knife, he could kill silently, drawing no notice. The gun was loud. Even one shot would ring out like an alarm in the silent hours of early morning. Eventually, one such shot might expose Reggie before he could tug me around a corner and vacate the scene of his crime.

Reggie sat forward and clasped his hands. He looked at me condescendingly.

"Ah, Farfel, you're a mere dog, driven by primitive instinct, insensitive to finer, deeper, more intricate emotions."

This was no time to dispute Reggie's deep-seated speciesism. I humored him.

"Yes, I guess that's true."

"A gun is so sudden. It's too fast and it's too ... removed," said Reggie. "Shooting one of those whores is like I'm looking at dirty videos and jerking off. There's no touching. No body heat. No physical contact."

Reggie's eyes went dreamy. "But when I wield my gleaming blade? Well, Jesus, Farfel, I guess that's as close as I'll ever get to the actual intercourse that has been denied me by the heartless conspiracy of women. I can feel the knife go inside the bitch. I'm penetrating her. I go in and out, in and out, up and down, all over her body. All that blood that comes out—it's her orgasm, boy. Her last climax. The knife is intimate, close, wet, exciting. I open her up, here, there, wherever I want—and I'm inside, man. Inside the bitch, and nobody else will ever be inside her again."

"I see," I said, sorry that I had asked. I wanted to rinse my ears with Listerine.

"Hey, man, it's not like I'm not open-minded about guns," said Reggie. "Sometimes blowing the bitch's brains out really is a better option. Depends on the circumstances. Hey, how 'bout if I use the gun next time, Farf, just to please you?"

"Hey, don't do me any favors," I said. "I wouldn't want to give you any ideas."

"Ideas." Reggie laughed mirthlessly. "Ideas from a fuckin' dog? That's a good one, Farf."

"Uh-huh."

• • •

For a while after the murder in Fort Greene Park, Reggie steered away from there. I was grateful. There are probably more dog owners per block in the gentrified areas of Brooklyn than anywhere in the five boroughs, and the mecca for all these dog owners—who have few open-space options—is Fort Greene Park. On a Saturday morning, with the farmers' market operating on the park's edge, it's rampant with dogs, many running loose and greeting their leashed compatriots while owners blissfully pat and rub whatever pooch comes within range. On days like this, I talk with ten, twenty other dogs, keeping abreast of canine doings from Bed-Stuy to Prospect Heights. I find out who's having puppies, getting spayed, being adopted and added to the local dogverse and, of course, all the diseased, unwanted and luckless mutts being "put down."

(I hate that phrase, of course. People are killed, murdered, executed. Dogs are euthanized by euphemism.)

After Reggie's homicidal tendencies became an unfortunate habit, I spread the word among dogs in Fort Greene Park. Cupcake had been the first, but by mid-October, pretty much every pup in Clinton Hill, Fort Greene and beyond knew that my master was the Ripper. A lot of good it did. All a human ever hears is a lot of arf arf arf. If our benighted bipeds had only paid us a smidgeon of attention, countless lives might have been saved.

On that front, one night, I had an astounding breakthrough. Until I didn't.

It was just past midnight, and we were walking—stalking, really. I felt Reggie relax his grip, and I was able to break free. He shouted "Hey!" at me but didn't give chase. By that stage in our relationship, he knew I would eventually tire of my freedom (and weary of dodging Animal Control). I'd come trotting back with my tail held high.

The Code says I have to come back.

We'd been on Dekalb Avenue, coincidentally kiddy-corner from the police precinct on Classon. I didn't even think of running into the station and trying to report Reggie to the NYPD. Instead, I lit out down Classon for several blocks, screeching to a halt when I saw two cops leaning over a homeless guy who had set up shop with a discarded mattress and a dirty blanket in the doorway of a defunct bodega. The store's windows had been long since boarded up, and the homeless guy was doing no one any harm. But these two cops seemed determined to roust him and make his already lousy life a little more wretched.

Partly to distract them, partly out of pure, idiot hopefulness, I approached the two cops. They were a typical male-female pairing. He was coffee-colored and tall, with a scent that blended Old Spice, saddle soap and burnt butter. The lady cop was white and smaller, with a Japanese-spaniel face, protuberant chest and ambience of Dove, L'Oreal and marinara. The homeless guy, of course, reeked of so many sources that his fragrance exploded in my nose and momentarily stunned my senses.

Cautiously, beginning with an urf and a whiny growl, I interrupted the male cop's abusive monolog as he stood over the bum.

"Excuse me," I said, enunciating as clearly as I could manage.

"Hey, Phil," said the lady cop, "looks like that dog slipped his owner. See the leash?"

"Oh," said Phil, the male cop, glancing at me. "Yeah, looks like it."

Since I didn't pose an evident threat, the cops returned their attention to the homeless guy, demanding that he get up and go along with them. The homeless guy, reasonably, was insisting that he couldn't leave his "stuff" unguarded in the doorway. Somebody would steal it. He was right.

I thought about stepping in and arguing the homeless guy's case but quickly realized that if the cops weren't listening to him, they were far less likely to take advice from a stray German shepherd. So I went straight to my main message. After all, Reggie might catch up to me any second.

"I know the killer," I said with crisp and strident clarity. "He's my master. His name is Reggie. He's the one murdering all those women."

The cops ignored me. I repeated every word.

"The goddamn dog isn't going away," said Phil. "Maybe we should call Animal Control?"

"I don't know, Phil," said the lady cop. "He looks pretty clean and well-fed. His owner'll probably show up."

"Yeah, well, fine. But I wish to Christ he'd shut up."

Of course, shutting up was the last thing on my agenda. "You have to listen to me. Please!" I barked. "I know the killer. He's my master."

"Really? That psycho is your master?"

This question came from neither of the cops. The homeless guy had suddenly turned to me and spoken.

My eyes widened. My tail involuntarily started wagging.

The male cop grabbed the homeless guy by the shoulder. The homeless guy tore free and said, "Hey, come on! I'm not doin' nothin'. I'm a law-abiding derelict. Why don't you just leave me alone?"

The cop went on about why he couldn't leave the homeless guy alone. Then he activated his radio. He started ordering some sort of vehicle to haul the "bum" away.

This gave the homeless guy a chance to talk to me again. I couldn't believe my ears.

"Hey, fella. I'm Luther," he said. "What's your name, boy?"

"You can understand what I'm saying?" I asked.

"Yeah," said Luther. "It's a gift. What's your name?"

"Um, Farfel."

"So, Farfel," he said. "You said you know who the Ripper is. Is that true?"

"Yes, it's true. He's my master. His name is Reggie Stockwell. We live over on —"

"Officer!" Luther had turned toward the police again. "Listen, Officer. You'll never believe this."

Phil, the male cop, broke off from a radio conversation and glared at Luther. "Believe what?"

"This dog here, he belongs to the Brooklyn Ripper. That guy who's been killing women all over the neighborhood, man."

"The dog?" said the lady cop. "Belongs to the Ripper?"

"Yeah, yeah! This is his dog! Right here!"

"And how," said the lady cop, "do you know this, Sherlock?"

"He told me."

"Who told you?"

"The dog. Right here. His name is Farfel."

"Farfel? The dog? Told you?"

"Yeah, lady. He said so. He said to me, 'My master is the Ripper.' Right out loud."

"The dog told you? How?"

"How? Whaddya mean, how? The dog just talked to me. In plain English. I heard him."

"Jesus, this drunken scumbag is worse than I thought," said Phil. "We better put him on the bus to Bellevue."

"Aw, c'mon, officer. Gimme a fuckin' break. I'm not nuts. I just understand dogs. I mean, I got a way with dogs, honest. Christ. It's a gift."

"The bus is on the way, Phil," said the lady cop. "You think I should call Animal Control."

"Well, I don't see any owner."

"Okay, I'll call."

That was my cue. I took off. Luther yelled at me, "Hey, don't go! Hey! Where—"

I didn't slow down 'til I was past the Sisters of Mercy convent on Willoughby. I knew the spot without looking around because the nuns had a rare female ginkgo tree. Even when she wasn't in heat in the fall, she exuded an armpit rankness that provided a beacon for every quadruped in the vicinity.

As I slowed down and trotted in the general direction where I'd left Reggie, I felt the irony of it all. On one hand, I could be understood by the rare, gifted human. But this phenomenon included only little kids, psychopathic killers and, apparently, bums. I was a voice crying out to a voiceless constituency.

I found Reggie by and by, peering hungrily through a wrought-iron fence into the campus of Pratt Institute. This little college is a green oasis among brownstones, its buildings ranging from Victorian to postmodern, its grounds scattered with student sculptures, its students—especially the artsy young women—trailing pheromones like scarlet streamers.

I could feel Reggie's hunger. Somewhere, faintly, a clock struck two. In the distance, around a corner came a woman, perhaps twenty years old, swinging her purse and chattering on a cell phone. She didn't see us.

I trembled with dread.

18

*"I wonder if other dogs think poodles are
members of a weird religious cult."*
—Rita Rudner

A few days later, after Reggie's murder near Pratt had blown over, we were back at Fort Greene Park. Fall had arrived but the sun was out, taking the edge off a cool day. The park was colorful with turning leaves. Reggie spotted Gloria and Cupcake and lurched to a halt, tugging at my choke chain. Obediently, I sat down.

Being a good doggie is a drag.

I sniffed the air and caught Cupcake's scent. It was always a little off because Gloria had an unfortunate habit of spraying Cupcake with a cheap cologne that was the house brand of a dollar store in the Fulton Street mall. It made Cupcake smell like an aging hooker.

Nevertheless, I was eager to talk to Cupcake. So, I said to Reggie, "You gonna say hello?"

"Hello," said Reggie.

"Not to me, Reg," I replied patiently. "Gloria. You haven't seen her in a couple of weeks."

"Eh, I dunno," he muttered. He shuffled his feet, tucked in

his chin and gazed surreptitiously at Gloria across the soccer pitch.

"Come on, Reg. She's nice."

"I smell a rat," he said.

"What do you mean by that?" I know how rats smell. One quick sniff told me that the closest rat, a pregnant female gnawing an orange rind, was halfway up the block on South Elliott.

"I mean, she's a woman. One of *them*. Sweet on the outside, beast inside."

"Beast? Gloria?" I said. "She's afraid of her own shadow."

"Yeah, so it seems," said Reggie. "Those are the worst ones."

"Jeez, Reggie, you talk like you actually know something about women."

"I know *everything* about women!"

Here was the lunatic Reggie seeping to the surface. Hoping to sublimate the monster, I said, "Well then, Reg, since you do know everything about women, you know she can't do you any harm if you just say hello to her in a public park."

"Eh, maybe."

"Besides, look there. She's seen you. She's waving."

"Shit."

"Let's go, Reg. A few minutes of social repartée isn't going to kill you."

"Well, yeah. I guess."

And so, we began to shuffle across the soccer pitch in Gloria's direction. She responded by hastening to meet us halfway.

"I was hoping to see you," Gloria said to Reggie.

"Oh yeah? Why?" Reggie's voice was suspicious.

"Hello, C.C.," I said to Cupcake.

"Hey there, big boy. Is that an erection I see?"

I wasn't the least bit tumescent. I said, "You probably do. This park is full of horny dogs."

"Boy, you really are hard-to-get," said Cupcake. "Do they have Viagra for dogs?"

"Listen, I need to talk, okay? Not hump," I said.

"Well, I don't know what's wrong with you," said Cupcake, "but I can do both at the same time."

"It's been so long since I've seen you here," said Gloria to Reggie.

"Well, I've been busy," said Reggie. Maybe the understatement of the year.

"I was sort of hoping we could go and have coffee again. That was nice the other day," said Gloria.

"Can't today," said Reggie brusquely. "Gotta be somewhere."

I got the feeling Reggie was going to cut this short, so I focused on Cupcake.

"C.C., please, just listen."

"Fine. What?"

"You remember, I told you Reggie is the killer. The Ripper who's been attacking all those women in Brooklyn."

"Reggie? Who's Reggie?"

"My *master*!"

"Oh yeah, that's right. I have a hard time remembering human names. They all sound so much alike."

"Right. Well, Reggie's the one who's been killing those women."

"What women?"

"The women who've been getting killed."

"They have?"

"Yes, all over Brooklyn! Don't you remember? I told you. Weeks ago!"

"Human women?"

"Yes."

"Oh." She shrugged, indicating her indifference to the business of humans among humans. Life would be so much simpler if I could be so callous.

DAVID BENJAMIN

"Okay, C.C., here's the thing."

"The thing? Oh, good. I'll turn around. You shove it in."

Cupcake had a one-track mind. I told her that the thing she wanted was not the thing I was talking about. I decided I had to shock her into paying attention.

"I used to be a cop," I said.

"Say what?"

"I used to be a cop," I repeated more slowly.

"You, a cop?"

"Yes, I worked in the canine unit with a police sergeant named Marilyn."

"Marilyn, huh? Was he nice?"

"She. Yes, she was nice."

"You don't look like a cop. You look sweet."

"Thanks, C.C. But my point is that I still have many of the attitudes and feelings I had when I was in the NYPD."

"Say what?"

"I mean, I still think like a cop. I see the world from a police officer's perspective."

"Well, I guess that's natural, big boy. Once a flatfoot, always a flatfoot."

"What I'm saying, C.C., is that, from a cop's point of view, someone going around killing innocent women in the middle of the night is a bad thing."

"Well, sure. They might only be humans, but what the fuck, right? They deserve to live."

"I'm glad you feel that way," I said. Meanwhile, I could hear Reggie trying to disengage from Gloria.

"If it wasn't for humans, where would dogs be?" said Cupcake.

"I'm glad you agree with me," I replied, "because I'm torn between my duty as a dog and my duty as a cop."

Cupcake sat suddenly, twisting her head. Her eyes darkened. "What do you mean by that?"

"Well, I mean, as a cop, I find it harder and harder—"

"Aren't you more like an ex-cop?" Cupcake said.

"Well, like you said, once a flatfoot ..."

"No, wait a minute," said Cupcake. "I can see what you're getting at here, big boy. I'm not some dumb, drooling, born-yesterday Weimaraner, you know."

"Hey, I never said—"

"You can't break the Code, fella," said Cupcake.

"Well, depending on what I decide to do, C.C., I wouldn't be breaking it, not exactly ..."

"Cop, ex-cop, or no cop at all, you're a dog, bro. D. O. G. *You cannot break the Code.* You can't even question the Code. Think, you big galoot. Where would we be without the Code? They'd be hunting us down, setting out traps, ripping off our pelts and collecting bounties. They'd be turning us into fucking fur coats!"

"I understand," I muttered. "I realize—"

"The hell you do," snapped Cupcake. "I listen, you know."

"Listen?"

"Yes! You've been looking for a way out of the Code ever since I met you. I should probably report you."

"To whom?"

We sat there, looking at each other. Cupcake was ticked off. I was just frustrated.

Gloria, to whom I was tuned with one ear, was trying to extend some sort of invitation to Reggie. Not a good idea. What could I do about it? Fortunately, Reggie seemed loath to accept. If he did, though, Gloria would be in deep doo-doo.

"Cupcake," I appealed, "your own mistress is in danger. This guy goes around killing women. Honest to God."

"Women. Humans."

"He might decide to kill Gloria."

"So?" Cupcake was unmoved.

"Well, for Pete's sake, Cupcake, if my master set out to murder Gloria, and I knew about it ahead of time, don't you think I should save her? If I could protect Gloria from a

DAVID BENJAMIN

horrible, bloody death, wouldn't that merit one little exception from your damn Code?"

"An exception?"

"Yes."

"To the Code?"

"Yes."

"Lemme ask you something," said Cupcake.

"Of course. What?"

"Gloria. Is she a dog?"

"No."

"Then, no."

"No?"

"She doesn't count."

"But he might kill her."

"Your master?"

"Yes!"

"Him? That giant dough ball?"

"Yes, him."

"Kill Gloria?"

"Yes, C.C., I told you. He's the one who—"

"No way."

"What?"

"He's not a killer, big boy," said Cupcake, twisting one side of her mouth into a weird canine grin. "You're just telling me all this stuff to get into my pants."

"You don't have pants. You're a dog!"

"So," said Cupcake, with a coquettish little wriggle, "you finally noticed?"

Reggie was yanking my leash.

"Come on, moron. We're outa here."

As we departed the park, I turned once to look at Cupcake. She saw me and lifted her tail just so, to remind me of what I'd just missed out on.

I had an erection all the way home.

19

"A hound will die for you, but never lie to you."
—George R.R. Martin

Reggie took me out on another of his ghastly excursions two nights later. He found his quarry at St. Joseph's College, in front of the McEntegart Hall Library on Clinton Avenue. Of course, the library was closed. The whole campus was closed, the streets were deserted. It was two in the morning, and there was a maniac stalking Brooklyn.

But in front of the library, inside a brick-walled circular walkway, there's an array of metal tables and chairs anchored to a concrete floor. As we approached this little terrace, I couldn't believe my eyes, because there, at one of those tables, for no sane reason on earth, a boy and girl were huddled against the wee-hour chill and nuzzling each other like *Lady and the Tramp*. She was on his lap, her hand inside his coat. While exploring her mouth with his tongue, he was massaging her groin and fumbling with the snap on her jeans.

"Look at them," Reggie whispered. "He's gonna bend the evil bitch right over that fucking table."

Reggie always imagined men bending women over large, inanimate objects.

"Reggie, they're kids in love."

"You shut the fuck up, mutt. Not a sound out of you."

Moving quicker than I could think, Reggie knotted my leash to a railing. From there, I could see what happened next to that unsuspecting pair of young lovers. And smell it? Whoo-ee.

Among all the outrages Reggie committed in my presence, I think this murder was the hardest for me because he had tied me directly downwind.

As Reggie wielded his knife—with such efficiency that neither girl nor boy was able to utter a peep before being forever silenced, and with such gusto that chunks of the victims landed thirty feet from the scene of the crime—I drank in the rich, tempting fragrance of human *sashimi*. For an instinctive predator, it was the front of the line at a buffet. For man's best friend, it was a nightmare of red death.

This ordeal set my soul at war with my senses. Dizzied by bloodlust and wracked with horrified remorse, I cast about for some sort of relief from my mixed feelings. Desperately, I pushed my muzzle into a leaf-covered patch of earth beneath the nearest tree, inhaling whatever smells I could find. I smothered the smells of Reggie's fresh-killed quarry with the pungency of leaf litter, pooch-pee, a hint of squirrel scat, a frisson of banana peel and, for some reason, a strong pong of 10W-40 motor oil.

I stayed that way, my nose buried and my eyes closed, breathing shallowly, feeling clammy and lightheaded 'til I felt sure I wouldn't be overcome. All this took perhaps sixty seconds, but it seemed like an hour. When I looked up, Reggie was finished. He was taking off a shirt so blood-soaked that no one could have guessed its original color.

Afterward, I said, "My God, Reggie, you barely left that boy's head attached. I thought you'd sworn off attacking men. I thought women were the big problem."

"Collateral damage," said Reggie breezily. "He was a

witness. I can't have witnesses. Besides, he was ruined before I got to him, turned into a seething victim of lust by that she-beast temptress who put him under the spell of her ravenous vagina."

I recognized another of my character flaws right then. Ever since I'd learned it, I loved the language of Shakespeare, Chaucer and King James. Here I was, walking away from a murder scene that would have made Jack the Ripper reconsider his career path, and yet I couldn't help but admire the poetic sonorousness of the phrase "ravenous vagina."

Was there something wrong with me?

This question haunted me that morning and the next day. I worried that I might have subconsciously developed some perverse esteem for Reggie's worst self. Did I actually admire his almost lupine skill at tracking his prey, dragging her down and ripping her open? Did my primordial instincts as a tooth-and-claw wilderness hunter make me unfit to interfere with his crimes? Was I an ex-cop, or was I, deep down, a willing co-predator?

My questions were partly answered, in the negative, the next day when, atop the hill in Fort Greene Park, I saw the little boy, Jesse, chasing a squirrel. I pulled my trusty slack-and-jerk trick on Reggie, yanking my leash deftly from his grip. Reggie was just articulating an irritated "Hey!" when I rounded the foot of the hill, galloping beyond his sight. I climbed then, on the Washington Park side so I could approach Jesse from the crest of the hill. As I hurried to intercept him, I kept an eye out for his mother. She had to be nearby. Knowing mothers, especially the young helicopter moms in gentrified Brooklyn, I knew the sight of me, an overgrown police dog with a face as black as Yaphet Kotto, could incite a fit of screaming panic. I also knew there were armed people in this park. I didn't want to be shot.

It was an altogether touchy moment.

I spotted Jesse and slowed to a dogtrot, as benign-looking

as I could manage. I located the mother on a bench about twenty yards uphill, immersed in her cell phone. If dogs ever pass humans on the evolutionary scale, it'll be because all those people staring at their itty-bitty screens won't see us as we saunter by, right under their noses, and take over.

In a moment, I was close enough to Jesse that he could hear me panting. He gave up the squirrel, which had climbed a tree. He turned.

"Hey, Jesse," I said softly.

His face beamed. "Hey, you're that dog."

"How are you, Jesse?"

"Oh, I'm fine," he said. "Wow, you really can talk!"

"We all can, Jesse. It's no big deal."

"Really?"

"Oh yes," I said. "The big deal is that you can understand me, Jesse."

"Wow. Hey, Farfel, I gotta show you to my mom," said Jesse. "I told her I met this dog who talks, and she thinks I'm just makin' it up."

"Wait, no. Listen," I said. "Not yet, okay?"

I was on deadline here. Reggie was climbing the hill as we spoke. If his mother saw this huge dog looming over her little boy, I might not squeeze in another syllable. I had seconds, maybe, to get my message across.

"Yeah, but Mom doesn't think—"

"I know, Jesse. But you can't win that battle. Grownups like your mom don't understand dogs because they don't believe dogs can say anything worth understanding. They're deaf to us."

"Yeah, but—"

"Jesse, please. I'll meet your mom, that's fine. But first, there's something really important I have to tell you."

Jesse looked curious but a little confused. What was he, nine years old?

"Have you heard about the killings, people being killed, here in Brooklyn?"

Jesse's eyes bugged. "Oh, the Ripper?" he exclaimed.

"Yes, the Ripper."

If a dog could blush! I mean, really. Here I was, going around with a master whom the whole darn world knew as the Ripper. I could die of embarrassment.

I pressed on. "Well, I know who he is."

"Who who is?"

Great. A dumb question. If this kid couldn't catch my drift, I'd lost my only line of communication.

"I know who the Ripper is, Jesse. I know the man who's killing all those people."

Jesse's eyes told me that he had caught on.

"Wow. You mean, you know the Ripper?"

"That's right, Jesse," I said. "I know who he is, and I need your help to stop him."

"Me?"

"Yes."

"Aw, c'mon. I'm just a little kid. I'm only eight. This guy, the Ripper. He's huge. That's what they say!"

"Well, he's pretty big," I said. "But listen—"

"How big?"

"Oh, I don't know exactly. Maybe six-four."

"Oh! Wow! He's, like, a giant!"

"Listen, Jesse—"

"HEY!" It was Reggie's voice. He'd spotted me. I could feel his feet pounding the earth. His scent was already reaching my nose.

Suddenly, "Oh my GOD!" A woman's voice, shrill with terror. Jesse's mother. of course. The jig was up.

I had seconds. They were both sprinting toward me, Reggie afraid I'd rat him out, the mother horrified that I was going to eat her child whole.

DAVID BENJAMIN

"Jesse, his name is Reggie. Reggie Stockwell. He's—"

That was all I managed. "You goddamn moron dog!"

Reggie was all over me. He seized my choke chain and cut off my wind, wrapping the leash twice around his hand. Jerked backward, I sat down abruptly.

A second later, the mother had swooped in and smothered Jesse in her arms. She glared accusingly at me, then at Reggie. She shouted, "What's WRONG with you? You can't let a monster like that run free! I should call the POLICE!"

"Excuse me, ma'am," Reggie was speaking but barely loud enough to hear.

"This is a PUBLIC PARK, you know! PUBLIC! For PEOPLE!"

"I know, ma'am. He doesn't bite. He's a good—"

"That THING shouldn't even be here on a LEASH! Look at him!"

I was tempted to actually growl at the woman—which was completely antithetical to my NYPD training. She was the sort of innocent civilian I was sworn to serve and protect. But the virulence of her bigotry was almost unbearable. I hadn't lifted a whisker to harm her precious little Jesse, and there I was, sitting obediently, my tongue flopped out all pink and cute from the side of my mouth. I was giving this shrieking harridan my very best big brown soulful-eyes look, and all she could do was spew animalist hysteria.

"This beast. This rabid monster! He could have KILLED my son. KILLED him!"

"Oh, no, ma'am, no. He's gentle, really."

Suddenly, Reggie was yanking my chain and poking a finger at my face. "Look what you've done, you big mutt. You scared the little boy. You got his mother all upset. Why can't you behave? Huh?"

And he was dragging me away. The mother kept screaming. We moved fast. I tried to turn, but Reggie kept a tight leash. Then, as we descended down the hill, I heard Jesse say, in as fearless a voice as I've ever heard, "Bye, Farfel."

That was my consolation from an ugly scene. And that I'd managed to confide Reggie's name to the kid. But had he heard me? Did he understand? Would he tell his mother? Better he should go straight to a cop and tell the cop. But would the cop believe him? Would anybody believe him?

A murder tip from a talking dog?

Fat chance.

20

"When a man's best friend is his dog, that dog has a problem."
—Edward Abbey

At first, it was just a rustling and clomping in the hallway. Reggie couldn't hear it, but he didn't have a dog's ears. To me, the noises were both audible and mysterious. Reggie's door was a portal normally ignored by all the world, but these footsteps seemed headed straight toward us.

I heard snatches of half-whispered conversation, including one voice saying "don't know why," and another muttering, "fucking task force," followed by a couple of words from the first speaker. I think they were "goose chase."

Then the door banged, and the first voice, stentorian and stern, came through the door. It filled me with hope and exultation. It said, "Mr. Stockwell? Police."

Police! Had they tracked Reggie down?

Reggie was galvanized, launched from his La-Z-Boy and jittering with emotion—whether fear or excitement, I couldn't discern, because I was equally electrified.

Was my long nightmare finally over?

Spinning in a full circle, Reggie flapped his arms. He went

pink (how do humans do that?). He stage-whispered, "What should I do?"

"It's the police, Reggie. You've got to open the door."

"I know that, moron," Reggie hissed at me.

The voice spoke again, impatiently. As a former NYPD officer, I knew that the lightning strike, even in a routine inquiry, was standard police procedure.

"Mr. Stockwell. Open up. This is the police."

After another spin and a little more flapping, Reggie lunged toward the door. He grabbed the knob and froze there. He stared at the door. His lips moved silently. Then he said, under his breath, "Cool, Reg. Be cool."

I was behind him, bouncing eagerly on my front feet. My tail wagged out of control, swinging in ragged figure-eights and thumping against a nearby table leg.

"Mr. Stockwell!"

Reggie snapped open both bolts, almost in a panic, and opened the door 'til the chain-lock stopped it. I heard the first voice.

"Reginald Stockwell?"

"Reggie," replied Reggie.

The voice softened. "Hello, Reggie. May we come in for a moment?"

"You have ID?"

"Sure."

I couldn't see the shield and ID from the floor, but Reggie said, "Okay." He closed the door to unhook the chain. As he did so, he said to me, "You behave, dipshit."

I sat, not saying a word, projecting Lassie-like obedience.

The door swung open, revealing two plainclothes detectives. They strolled inside in the authoritative style that has long since typified the seasoned NYPD investigator. I was proud.

The voice I'd heard from the hallway spoke to Reggie. It belonged to a burly man of perhaps forty-five years, slightly thick in the waist. His face was broad, clean-shaven and droopy around the edges, like an English mastiff. His eyes were sad but alert. He wore a brown Men's Wearhouse suit that was at least five years old but clean and pressed. His scent was a mixture of Dial soap and cheap tobacco, with hints of sage, bacon and shoe polish. He said, "Mr. Stockwell. I'm Detective Sergeant Driscoll. This is my partner, Detective De Mars."

Detective De Mars was younger and slimmer with more of a fox terrier aspect, his blue suit more dapper but nonetheless off-the-rack. His tie had a Picasso motif. Judging from his scent, which had a lot more pollen and a whiff of Bermuda grass muted by Lavoris, I guessed that he lived either in the eastern part of Queens or Staten Island. His mouth affected a knowing smirk but suggested a measure of trepidation. He was, I could tell, not long off the beat.

Driscoll closed the door, faced Reggie and laid out the situation.

"We're sorry to bother you, Mr. Stockwell. But we're following up on a tip. It's probably nothing."

Classic, I thought. Treat the suspect respectfully. Call him "Mister." Put him at ease by downplaying the suspicions that brought the police force into his living room.

I was having a hard time containing myself. I was so glad to see cops finally on Reggie's trail, possibly sparing me the moral crisis of dealing personally with his transgressions, that I was flinging my tongue every which way. My tail wagged so hard that my hips rocked and rolled, and my feet were losing their grip.

"Hi, guys," I blurted out in Dogspeak. "How ya doin'?"

Reggie understood—and ignored—me. He said. "Would you gentlemen like to sit down? Can I get you something? Coffee wouldn't take but a few minutes."

Very cool, I thought. Reggie was keeping his composure. But, of course, both detectives were men. In an all-male setting, Reggie verged on normalcy.

All this suavity from Reggie was the last thing I wanted. Impetuously, I said to Detective Driscoll, "Boy, am I glad you guys showed up."

Reggie turned just enough to glare at me.

"Quiet, boy."

"Nice dog," said Detective De Mars.

"Yeah," said Reggie. "But stupid. Really stupid."

De Mars seemed amused at the noises I was making. "He looks pretty smart to me," he said.

"Yes!" I said, still in Dogspeak but sticking to words of one syllable in hopes of getting through. "I used to be on the job. NYPD K-9. I worked with Marilyn Kane. Maybe you know her?"

"He barks funny," said De Mars.

"Yeah," said Reggie, "he has sort of a speech defect." Then he grabbed my collar. "Now, you settle down, boy. Or I'll have to lock you in the bathroom."

I sighed. I sat. The cops hadn't understood a word. They were, after all, only human. All I could do now was depend on their cop-sense and Reggie's natural transparency.

"Hey, sorry about the dog," said Reggie.

"Oh no," said Driscoll. "In this neighborhood, with what's been goin' on around here lately, havin' a dog nearby is a helluva good idea."

"So, fellas," said Reggie, "can I get you that coffee?"

Fellas? I thought.

"No, no. We won't be long."

"We just have a few questions," De Mars added.

"Okay then," said Reggie. "But let's get comfortable."

Quickly, he pulled a chair past me and placed it beside his La-Z-Boy. He sat on the ottoman and gestured the detectives to take a load off. They did, each on the edge of his seat.

"So, shoot," said Reggie, spreading his hands expansively. I'd never seen him so gregarious. Why didn't he act this way with Gloria?

"Well," said Driscoll, "we were wondering. Five nights ago … That would be the 16th, right, Phil?"

"Well, the morning of the 17th, actually," said De Mars.

"That's right, the 17th," said Driscoll. "Mr. Stockwell, that morning, where were you at about 3 a.m.?"

"*Three* a.m.?" asked Reggie.

"Yes, 3 a.m.," said Driscoll, with a note of impatience.

I knew the answer, of course. I banged my tail on the floor and urfed significantly.

No one paid me any attention. A dog with crime-stopping information is a voice barking in the forest primeval as mighty oaks, unheard, topple all around him.

"Well, gee, Detective, I was where everybody else is at that hour. Here in bed, asleep."

"I see," said Driscoll, all business. "Do you have any witnesses who could verify your whereabouts?"

Reggie smiled, reached out and patted my head condescendingly. "Well, just Farfel here." He took my chin in his hand and lifted my face. "That's where we were, weren't we, boy? Right here. Sleeping like babies."

"No, Reggie, no," I replied through Reggie's grip on my mouth. "We were over in Clinton Hill, at St. Jos—"

"No one besides the dog?" said Driscoll, cutting me off. Humans have no manners at all when it comes to dogs.

"No. Sorry," said Reggie, grinning at the detectives and pinching me painfully. "I didn't get lucky that night. Or any night this month. Sorry."

Or any night in your whole pathetic life, I thought.

Reggie was laughing coolly and naturally. The cops smiled cordially.

The atmosphere was cozier than I had hoped when the police walked in.

"Well, you're right, Mr. Stockwell—"

"Oh, come on, Detective, call me Reggie."

"Oh. Yes, well, Reggie. You're right," said Driscoll, a little despondently. "At 3 a.m., everybody is home in bed. I often wish I could say that about myself."

Suddenly, to my surprise, Reggie seized the initiative.

"Listen, I know it's none of my business, but what's this all about? What brings you here, to me, of all people?"

Driscoll looked to De Mars, who spoke to Reggie. "It's just routine, Mr. St—, er, Reggie."

Reggie pressed. "It's about the murders, isn't it? The killings over around Clinton Hill, right?"

Neither detective responded, but their body language leaked the answer.

"This crazy fucker has to be a guy just about like me, I bet," said Reggie. "Single white male. About my age. Hey, I've seen a lot of episodes of *Criminal Minds*. I fit the profile, right? And you guys have to follow up every possibility."

Driscoll and De Mars exchanged glances.

Reggie rolled on. "And I don't blame you guys one bit. You've got to catch this freak. He's a total wacko, right? I mean, wow, talk about Jack the Ripper, y'know? I'm scared every time I take Farfel out for a walk."

"Well," Driscoll finally answered, "we're doing our best to catch him."

"But it's not exactly our case," said De Mars.

"Really?" said Reggie.

"Yes, that's right," said Driscoll. I sensed a little reluctance in his voice, but he had been drawn in by Reggie's—well, what was this? Charm?

Reggie said, "Yeah, I read in the *Daily News* that the whole police force is pitchin' in on this case."

"Yes," said Driscoll. "Detective De Mars and I usually handle property crimes out of the 88th Precinct. They've got us following up on tips."

"And you got a tip about me?"

"Not really," De Mars started to say. Driscoll cut him off with a sharp look.

"Like we said, it's routine," said Driscoll.

Reggie stood up. "Hey, guys, I understand," he said. "Listen, if it'll be any help, why don't you search the place? You have my permission. Drawers, closets, fridge, whatever."

I couldn't keep my ears from standing at attention. Reggie was literally begging to be nabbed. I thought of the gun beside his bed, his "go bag" with a change of clothes and a roll of garbage bags. That big ugly knife was in the bureau, probably with enough bloody DNA to tie him to at least three murders.

What was Reggie thinking?

"Oh no," said Driscoll, also standing up.

"No, no! Search the place, dammit," I cried out, startling everyone (including myself).

"Farfel! Pipe down," said Reggie. "Silly mutt."

"That won't be necessary," Driscoll went on.

"Hey, fellas, I know the whole department is working this case 24/7, chasing down every little lead you get, right?" said Reggie. "And my only witness for that night is this big dumb dog. So, if you toss my apartment, you can cross me off your list, once and for all, so you can devote your time to the real killer. So, please, go ahead. Search away. I don't mind. I want to help you guys."

He was asking for it! All these cops had to do was look around. Reggie's incriminating rucksack was sitting beside the door in what the police call "plain sight!"

"Oh no, Mr. Stockwell, I mean, Reggie. We appreciate your cooperation. God knows we could stand a few more helpful citizens like you. But we never intended to toss anything. We just had a few questions. We've asked them. You've answered."

De Mars added, "Yeah, I think we're done here."

Oh my God, I thought. But I held my tongue. It was clear that objections from the furry family pet would fall on deaf ears. I might as well have been a goldfish.

Quickly, Detectives Driscoll and De Mars bade Reggie an apologetic farewell, promising to never bother him again as they edged their way out the door. While Reggie stood motionless, peering through the peephole, I could hear the detectives shuffling away and talking wearily.

"I told you." This was Driscoll's voice. "Another fuckin' bum steer."

"So," replied De Mars, "was that supposed to be the dog? The one that talked to the kid?"

"Jesus, Phil, you don't actually believe …"

They faded away.

Suddenly, Reggie was all over me. Laughing and whooping, he grabbed me by the scruff, rubbed my ears, mussed my coat and hugged me.

"Was that great!" he exclaimed. "Wow! What a feeling! What a coup! Way to go, Farfel!"

"Way to go?" I asked.

"You were gonna rat me out, weren't you?"

"Well," I began.

"Hey, that's okay, ya dumb fuckin' mutt. You couldn't tattle if you tried. I know that now. But Jesus Christ! You had me worried for a minute there. I mean, holy shit, I thought, what if somehow these fuckin' police could understand this fuckin' police dog, right? What if there's some sort of dog/police secret code, y'know?"

"Reggie, dogs and police can't—"

"Can't understand a fuckin' thing! I know. But Jesus, talk about suspense. That was great. I think I was actually turned on, Farf! And you know what?"

My shoulders sagged. "What?" I muttered.

"I think all that, like, tension—it saved my ass. I was juiced, man. I mean, if I wasn't so keyed up, I might've cracked, y'know?"

"Wait," I said. "You mean if I'd kept my mouth shut, you might've confessed."

He thought for a moment, backing up and sitting on the edge of his La-Z-Boy.

"Yeah, maybe," said Reggie. "Shit, I don't know."

He reached out and gripped my chin. His eyes shone with excitement. "When you started talking to the cops? I mean, holy shit, that was it, baby. I didn't know what I was gonna do. But then, both of 'em just stared at you like morons. Didn't have any idea what you were saying. And I knew I was home free. They had nothin', man. They weren't even homicide cops, f'Chrissake. They were a couple of fuckin' errand boys!"

"Yes, well …"

"So, I told 'em, 'Search the joint.' And what if they had?"

I said, "Well, they would have found the knife, the gun—"

"Yeah, right! Everything!" said Reggie. "I thought about that even when I was tellin' 'em to search. They would've found all of my gear, along with my writings about what I've done and what I still have to do. They would've thrown me in jail, denied of the chance to exact revenge on my enemies. I can't imagine a hell darker than that."

"So," I asked, cocking my head, "why did you do it? Why did you risk the search?"

"Because I knew they wouldn't—No! No, wait a fuckin' minute here." Reggie paused. He slid back in his La-Z-Boy. "No, I had no idea what they would do. They might've searched. But I was so excited by the moment, by the presence right here of the force that could destroy me. I couldn't resist. I couldn't *not* take the risk, Farfel. I had to know what would happen. I had to go all the way."

Somehow, I understood this. Reggie had transposed his existence to the fringe of human civilization, where only daring escapades and extreme feelings gave any satisfaction. I didn't bother to explain this.

"And when they said no, whoa!" Reggie crowed. "Wow! Holy shit! What a feeling! What a high!"

He laughed, spread his arms and bounced off the back of his chair.

I didn't share Reggie's exhilaration. I headed for my rug.

DAVID BENJAMIN

"All thanks to you, you fuckin' traitor," said Reggie.

This stung worse than anything Reggie had ever said to me. Technically, I wasn't a traitor. I hadn't broken the Code, not truly. But I had gone to the brink. If, by some miracle, either detective had understood me, I would have committed the greatest crime known to dogdom.

I looked up from my little nest on the rug. Reggie was squirming in place, grinning and jittering.

"I was just trying to save you from yourself," I said, rationalizing my near-betrayal.

Reggie sat up, gazing at me reflectively. "I think you already have," he said. "You clarified my purpose in life."

"What do you mean?"

"You threw me into the fire, Farfel. You tested my faith. You showed me that I could face danger. I could look my nemesis in the eye and not back down. You showed me that my cause is true and good. It has to be, because otherwise, I would have crumbled. If I was just a common crook, if I was the fucked-up whack job that those cops think they're looking for, they would've caught me. They would've seen through me. They would've searched and found everything. But they trusted me, man. They believed in me because I believe in me!"

"Really?" I said. "Ya think?"

"Yes. They saw my purity of purpose. Thanks to you, Farfel."

"Please, don't thank me," I said.

Reggie was going to say something more, but the phone rang.

21

"Dogs are wise. They crawl away into a quiet corner and lick their wounds and do not rejoin the world until they are whole once more."
—Agatha Christie

Reggie was on the phone with Mom. I listened with one ear but found myself distracted by his scent. It had changed. That familiar mélange of sweat, chicken and lubricating oil had faded into an entirely new ambience that my nose interpreted as rotten apricots marinating in chlorine.

What had changed Reggie's very odor? Murder? Tension? His conquest of the two detectives?

"Wait. What are you saying, Mom? Marriage?"

I pricked up my ears. Who was getting married?

"But who?" said Reggie, his voice trembling. "Why?"

Reggie's mother getting married? It couldn't be. I crept a little closer to Reggie, hanging on every word, frustrated to get only half the conversation.

"Neal what?" said Reggie. "Neal Vander Voort?"

That's a name? I thought.

Reggie was wondering the same. "What the hell kind of name is that? Dutch? ... Really ... All the way back to the founding of New York City? You're kidding? Really?"

That's right, I thought. *New York was New Amsterdam. The oldest families in the city were Dutch. Peter Minuit and all that. So, was he rich?*

"So," asked Reggie, "he must be rich."

There was a pause while Reggie's mother talked. Then a series of spoken fragments as they went back and forth, Reggie's voice rising with each exchange.

"Numisma-what? ... Oh, rare coins. Well, that's money, right? So he must ... No? ... A small business? How small? ... Oh ... Well, what about his family? I mean, with a name like Vander Voort!"

For a while, Reggie listened. Then: "A nice living? What the hell is a nice living?"

By this time, I'd figured out that Neal Vander Voort was not rich and that Reggie was taking his impecuniousness as a personal affront.

"Mom, listen, you can't marry this jerk ... No, it's not just a matter of supporting you. You have to think about me. I'm your son. I'd love to get a job and be independent. You know that, Mom. But I'm building a career here. Architecture is a terrifically demanding field, and Pratt is expensive ... Yes, Mom, that's my point. Don't you see? I'm tapped out, and I know I'm draining your resources, too ... No, Mom, no. It's not just school. If it was just school, but there's rent here. I mean, I'm living in a crummy dump of an apartment surrounded by stewbums and niggers and welfare cheats ... Yes, Mom. I'm sorry, Mom. 'Black people,' okay? ... Right, well, the point I'm trying to make—I mean, besides all my living expenses, there's this goddamn dog who eats like a horse ..."

I growled under my breath. I do not eat like anything but a refined and weight-conscious—but full-grown—German shepherd.

"Mom, look." Reggie's spiel went on. "I don't like it any more than you do, but you have a responsibility. I mean, your first responsibility is your own flesh and blood, Mom. That's me. I need your help. Without you, what do I do? Get a shitty cashier's job at Walgreens or flip Whoppers for the rest of my life at Wendy's?"

Burger King, I thought.

Reggie went on. "Give up on my career? I should tell Antoinette, so long, sweetheart, I'm heading for a dead end, and I won't drag you down with me? Tell her she's too good for me?"

He stopped for a moment. His mother had broken in, pausing his tirade.

"My point!" he suddenly shouted into the phone. "My point is responsibility. Your responsibility, Mom! You're a young divorcée, Mom. Attractive, with a little bit of money. You're a catch, Mom. You can have any eligible bachelor in New York. And what do you do? You pick a coin collector who doesn't have two nickels to rub together? Mom, you owe it to me, to yourself, to marry a guy with money. I need it. You need it. This isn't a matter of—what?"

His mother's voice came to me faintly. "Reggie. I don't care about money. I love Neal."

"Love!" said Reggie. "Bullshit, Mom. Love is bullshit. Love is just a word this son of a bitch is using on you so he can screw your brains out, turn you into a sex slave and get all your money. And where does that leave me?"

Reggie broke off, pulled the phone from his ear and stared at it. He spoke again. "Mom? ... Shit!"

She had obviously hung up. If I were she, I would have done so sooner. And changed my number.

I said, "Smooth, big guy."

"Shut the fuck up."

"You should call her back."

"What the fuck for?"

"To apologize."

"She should be apologizing to me."

"To you? Why on earth should she?"

"Why? *Why?* Because she went behind my back and got herself engaged to this asshole who can't do either of us any good."

"But she loves the guy."

Reggie just sneered.

"Besides," he said a moment later.

"Besides what?"

"Well, I don't care. She does. She feels bad when we argue, but I don't give a shit. She'll want to make up with me."

Reggie was right. The next morning, a greeting card from Mom arrived by express mail. The card contained a check.

"See?" said Reggie, flapping the check under my nose.

"Yes, well," I replied, backing away from Reggie. "She's still going to marry Neal."

Reggie's face darkened. "Because she's a slut and a whore."

"Reggie, come on. She's your mother."

But Reggie was on his way to the computer, his mind racing, his fingers twitching.

22

*"Dogs love their friends and bite their enemies,
quite unlike people, who are incapable of pure love
and always have to mix love and hate."*
—Sigmund Freud

The "manifesto" that Reggie spun after the fight with his mother over her engagement was shorter than previous editions, and it wandered less. The *Daily News* printed it under the headline:

Ripper to Mommy:
'YOU'RE NEXT!'

Reggie brought home the usual stack of newspapers, so I was able to read it the same day it appeared. The editors of the *Daily News* didn't really get the point, but then, they hadn't been privy to Reggie's conversation with Mommy. Here's the whole thing:

All women are whores, by nature and by upbringing. Every woman, driven by a hunger for security or by the wet lust that leaks from her body and smells like dead fish, sells herself to men whose only sexual impulse is to rape, possess and destroy. There is no sex without rape, possession and destruction. As all women are groveling, degenerate whores, all men are murderers. They yearn secretly, subconsciously, to kill the women they rape, contemptuous of them because they gave in so eagerly, so disgustingly, to being raped and raped and raped again, screaming for more even as their flesh is ripped open and their beauty is battered into purple pulp. Women ask to be raped, beg for it and crawl at the feet of their rapists because degradation is their only defense. Rape and whoredom protect them from the violent death they deserve. Women's ultimate defense is motherhood. It covers the stain of their willing rape by the savage, murderous race of alpha males. But women, even shrouded and sanctified by motherhood, remain whores.

Every mom is the biggest, sluttiest, cheapest whore there can be because she has sold herself in slavery to the murderer who buys her as cheaply as he can and then mounts her proudly on his petard to kill her slowly, to punish her for being so cheap, so easy, so willing to live and die as a whore. Every mother dies a whore, murdered by her master, because every penis is a knife plunging not once—swiftly and mercifully, killing her instantly—but entering her body countless times, over and over again, murdering her by tiny degrees, penetrating her womb until she bleeds out her life for the man who raped her and the sons whose deepest, rawest, truest desire is to rape her, too, and bleed her dry, and pound her submissive face into jelly.

My knife is mercy for all the whores who have sold themselves and shamed their children. My knife accomplishes in a beautiful, generous, forgiving instant what will otherwise take years, decades, eons. My holy intervention spares women the lifetime of whorish, creeping, licking, stinking degradation that is otherwise their destiny on this filthy and desolate earth. I bestow the only freedom that any mother will ever know— freedom from the thankless, hideous horror of life itself.

For a while after I read this and recovered from the bleak depression it caused, I wondered if Reggie was planning to murder his own mother. But his impulsiveness was balanced by his cunning. The police would read his rant, connect it to Mom's murder, and they'd have Reggie locked up within hours. Reggie couldn't risk that.

Actually, I don't think Reggie was even thinking about his mother by the time he finished composing his manifesto. His anger at Mom for falling in love with Neal Vander Voort, who was probably a perfectly nice guy, grew into a demented rage that had little to do with her. In Reggie's heart, Mom was the one untouchable woman. On one side of his weird brain, Mom was his ideal, the last pure female, the living incarnation of the Virgin. On the other side of his brain, she was the fallen woman, Eve, the temptress and whore. She represented Reggie's epitome of what the world does to reduce every woman to sluthood, sex slavery and, well, all that stuff he raves about. He loved his mother absolutely—really, he worshipped her—on the good side of his brain. On the dark side, he despised and scorned her. But there was a pragmatic sliver between those two halves of his brain that said to him: You can't kill her. You depend on her. Because she loves you as much as you've always loved her, she gives you anything you ask for. Besides mere sustenance, you depend on her for the only healthy emotions you feel. If she is gone, you cannot survive, nor can you continue your crusade. Her death will lead your pursuers to you, just as surely as if you left a bloody trail from her corpse to your La-Z-Boy.

Mom—alone among all the women in New York City and despite the tabloid headlines—was safe. I wish I could have said the same for that beautiful woman the following night in front of the big church on Lafayette Avenue.

23

*"Yesterday I was a dog. Today I'm a dog.
Tomorrow I'll probably still be a dog.
Sigh! There's so little hope for advancement."*

—Snoopy

Until the clash with his mother and the ugly manifesto that followed, I had really, honestly harbored hopes for Reggie. The cooler weather of autumn had seemed to calm him. As we enjoyed an uneventful week or so, I thought that maybe his fever of carnal retribution might have broken. I thought he might slip into some sort of dormancy. He might even fulfill the fantasy he kept spinning for his mother and enroll in college. Or just get a job.

But that all fell apart the night after the *Daily News* spilled what got to be known as the "Mommy Manifesto." Reggie paced and talked to himself all day, unable to rest, exultant over his splash in the newspapers but frustrated by the idea that he had done nothing lately to deserve his celebrity. I tried to soothe him, but every word seemed to fuel his fury. My heart sank when he threw on his coat and grabbed my leash.

For more than two hours on a blustery September night, we stalked the sidewalks of Brooklyn. We ranged toward

Flushing Avenue and once around Commodore Perry Park before steering back into Fort Greene. We saw not one fellow pedestrian. Cold and fear had driven even the drunk, drugged and homeless into hiding. The exception to our solitude was the occasional prowl car. When Reggie spotted one, he steered me to the curb and made a show of nagging me to "do my business" (which I'd done long before). The police would slow long enough to look us over but then pull away. We looked like a giant Pillsbury doughboy and his faithful canine companion Rin Tin Tin—the unlikeliest mass murderers in all of Brooklyn.

I could have raised my voice and shouted the truth. But the unimaginative police in their patrol cars wouldn't have understood or heard me. Their windows were rolled up against the chill.

By the time we reached Lafayette Avenue, strolling back toward Bedford, it was near three on the stillest, emptiest, darkest morning I could remember. I looked up once for stars, but the sky was a gray shroud crowding the treetops. The silence was eerie. Now and then, far off toward Flatbush Avenue, a siren would wail faintly and then fade. The only sounds nearby came from us—Reggie's shoes rustling the dead leaves that strewed the slate-panel sidewalk and an occasional clink from my choke chain.

In this so-deep quiet, it wasn't surprising that we heard her before we saw her. There was a great church ahead of us, across the street. We'd passed it often. I know its name, but I'm reluctant to reveal it lest I associate a house of God with Reggie's evil rampage. If you really want to know, it was in all the newspapers, on all the websites, immortalized on YouTube. Look it up there if you must, but don't blame God or his innocent tabernacle. He doesn't get involved in these things anymore—hasn't uttered a word to anyone two-legged for thousands of years. Long ago, he sincerely tried to correct the human depravity he had set loose but discovered that it exceeded even his worst imaginings. His heart was broken a thousand times. So, he finally accepted that this was how he had made Man. People were bound by their nature to either ignore his advice entirely or twist it beyond recognition. So he wisely, sadly withdrew, waiting and hoping, patiently marking the few gradual signs of humanity's advancement.

• • •

There's a dense, black shadow in the church's deeply arched doorways. From that darkness came a faint sound of sobbing. Unmistakably, the voice was a woman's, and it was young.

Heaven only knows what she was crying about. I thought later that a boyfriend or lover must have hurt her. They had argued, perhaps, and he had left her there. I've seen those quarrels once in a while on the street. They're always young. Usually, one marches away angrily. The other, left behind, fumes or cries. And waits. Usually, time and distance—not much—cools their anger enough that they look around, see each other and reunite, perhaps cautiously, sometimes with an air of embarrassment. After that, I never know. Humans are unpredictable. Mostly, I think, they kiss and make up. Sometimes the fight starts up again.

This fight must have been a big one because there was no sign of the male.

As we got closer, my nose informed me that, yes, a man had left the scene, perhaps fifteen minutes before. Reggie sensed this, too, by instinct. His only thought was to punish her for knowing that man, for loving him and for losing him. The man had ruined her, and Reggie would complete her ruin. If the man finally, belatedly, regretted the fight and hurried back to her, there would be nothing for him to salvage.

The girl, whom I could finally make out, sat huddled on the church steps, crying softly. In her voice, I could hear a shiver that bespoke the cold.

Reggie shivered also but with eager expectation. Even as he

knotted my leash to a chain-link fence, I heard his rucksack—the "go bag"—slipping from his shoulders. As he crossed the street toward the girl, he was digging into the bag with his right hand.

I lifted my ears and listened. When Reggie bent to her, his voice was gentle and sympathetic.

"Are you okay?"

The startled girl stood abruptly and took several steps toward the sidewalk. I saw her in the glow of a streetlight. Her face, framed by fawn-colored hair and a wool cloche, was beautiful even though damp from crying and flushed with emotion. In my nose, faintly, the floury sweetness of her makeup combined with the salt tang of her tears.

"Oh no. I'm. I'm," I heard her say.

"Is there anything?" Reggie said. I saw the knife in his hand then. She didn't see it. I couldn't just let this happen.

I barked.

The girl lurched at the sound, looking up, peering across the street.

I barked again as Reggie's knife crossed her throat. When I saw the blood pouring down her coat, splashing on the church steps in huge drops, I slumped, looked away and lay down. I put my face between my paws and waited.

It was a half-hour before Reggie, dressed in fresh clothes but stinking, as usual, of semen and sudden death, stood over me, glowing with accomplishment. I looked across the street. The blood on the steps was hard to discern in the wee-hour gloom. A streak on the pavement told me that Reggie had dragged her into bushes beside the church, where he had also stripped and changed.

"Thanks, dipshit," said Reggie. "If you hadn't barked, I might've had trouble with her."

This wasn't true. But Reggie, who knew how I felt about his ravages, enjoyed reminding me of my helpless complicity.

We had walked barely two blocks beyond the church when

a police cruiser came up behind us. The cop in the passenger seat rolled down his windows.

"Excuse me, sir."

Reggie led me over to the police car.

"Hi," he said.

"Pretty late to be out here," said the cop. His face was blank, his eyes hard.

"Oh, you're tellin' me," said Reggie. "The poor dog has a case of the trots that just won't stop. He wakes me up out of a sound sleep and drags me outside at—Jesus, what time is it, anyway?"

The cop's face relaxed. He read his watch. "Half past three."

"Oh, damn," said Reggie. "And I've gotta be in to work early tomorrow. And I need to make time to get the dog into the vet's. God knows what's goin' on in his bowels."

"Well, okay, um," said the cop. "Just make sure you clean up after—"

"Oh, don't worry about that," said Reggie. He patted his backpack. "I made sure to carry all the equipment I needed for that. I hate to think of people steppin' in what ol' Rex here leaves behind."

Rex? I thought

"Uh-huh," said the cop, rolling up his window. There's nothing like the mention of diarrhea to swiftly end a conversation.

The police car departed. I hadn't tried to say a word. *What's the point?* I thought.

But as we got home, I came to a heightened appreciation of my role in Reggie's horrible spree. With me as his incontinent canine cover, he could go out at any time of night, spend hours searching for a victim and get away with it. I had to consider some sort of intervention. I had to start earnestly thinking beyond the Code.

But what becomes of a dog who breaks the Code?

. . .

I was still fretting over this dilemma two mornings later when Reggie and I encountered Gloria and Cupcake in the park. Reggie, fresh from reading about the Lafayette Street murder in the papers, was full of piss and vinegar. He felt so good that he lingered with Gloria, making small talk, lamenting the weather, almost flirting.

This gave me a chance to pose my crisis to Cupcake.

Yes, I grant that despite being a poodle, Cupcake is no mental giant (I suspected a stain of cocker spaniel contamination somewhere in her pedigree). But I regarded her a good sounding board on ethical issues because she's so dogmatic.

"Hey, C.C., how's it hangin'?" I said casually.

"That's a question I should ask you, big boy. You want to stick it in me?"

I sighed. As usual, diverting Cupcake's one-track mind would be a chore.

"Not right now," I said. "Listen, do you know that little boy, Jesse, who comes to the park with his mother?"

"You mean that kid who understands Dogspeak?"

I perked up. "Oh, you know! Have you talked with him, too?"

"Not a word," said Cupcake, righteously. "And you shouldn't either, ya big lug. It's not natural."

"Well, gosh," I said. "Reggie understands me, too."

"Are you trying to suggest that your master is natural?"

"Well, no," I said. "You've got a point, C.C."

"Damn right I do," she said. "Now, you ready to hump?"

I ignored this and said, "Anyway, I told Jesse."

Cupcake had been in the process of presenting her pudenda. She paused and turned.

"Say what?" she said.

"I told Jesse, the little boy."

"Told him *what*?" Her voice was accusatory.

"About Reggie."

"You told that kid about what your master's been doing?"

"That's right, C.C."

"Jesus, Mary and St. Bernard!" said Cupcake, glowering at me and baring her canines. "You ratted out a human to another human?"

"Well, it didn't work. Apparently, somehow, Jesse reported what I had told him, and the cops came to our house to question Reggie. But I could tell they were just going through the motions. They didn't believe Jesse. And they went away. They didn't even search the place."

Cupcake shook her head and let her tail hang. "I don't know about you, big boy."

"What do you mean by that?"

"What I mean, ya big lug, is that you're skating close to the edge."

"I'm just trying to do what's right, C.C."

"What's right for you, Farfel, is to be a dog. Quit talking to humans. Act like a dog. Think like a dog. Obey like a damn dog."

"Easy for you to say, C.C. Your master is not a murderer."

"That doesn't matter, and you know it," Cupcake insisted. "Your master is your master. You understand the concept of 'master,' don'tcha?"

"Even if my master's a murderer?"

"Even if, dumbbell. There are no exceptions. Nothing gets you out of the Code."

"Yes, well," I said, "I'm beginning to have second thoughts about the almighty Code."

"Don't even say that," said Cupcake. "You know what happens if we violate the Code?"

"I know, I know," I began.

Cupcake, a hard growl deep in her throat, said, "No, I don't think you do, big boy, because without the Code, you're nothing. I'm nothing. Dogs are nothing because we cease to be dogs. We lose the trust of the humans and they toss us out into the snow and the mud and the herds of ravening cats."

"Ravening cats?"

"We'll have no comfy cushions, no dog dish on the kitchen floor, no vet visits and grooming salons. Nothing, big boy. We revert to the wild. We sink back to the barbarity of the Stone Age. Worse, we become wolves, scouring the woods for scraps, eating carrion and spitting out the maggots, tearing at each other and killing our weaker brethren because it's every wolf for himself all over again, big boy. You'll be fine, maybe. But I'll be lunch for some big fucking pitbull."

"Well," I said, trying to lighten the mood, "I'd protect you."

"The hell you would. You and the pitbull would be fighting over my body, like wolves with a roadkill raccoon," snarled Cupcake. "Listen, you know what wolves are? They're an endangered species. Is that what you want? And there are states right now issuing licenses for humans to hunt wolves. Is that what you want? Roving gangs of NRA rednecks chasing you through the swamp, aiming AK-47s and grenade launchers at your ass? You break the Code, big boy, and that's what you get. Hunters! Coming after you. Leghold traps and poisoned hamburger!"

"But he's a murderer," I whispered. Reggie hadn't been listening to Cupcake and me. We were speaking in dog English. But he looked down at me suspiciously.

"Murderer. You keep saying that," said Cupcake, her voice suggesting both doubt and denial. "So, who's he murdering?"

"Well, two nights ago—"

"Haven't we been through this before?"

"Listen to me, C.C. Two nights ago—"

"He's murdering people, right?"

"Well, he's concentrating now on women."

"Human women?"

"Right."

"Not dogs?"

"No."

"Well then."

"But," I said, "even if he's only killing humans, it's barbaric."

"No."

"No?"

"As long as people just murder other people, that's good old human nature," said Cupcake. "If *we* start murdering people, *that's* barbaric. And that's the end of canine civilization as we know it."

"But—"

"That's why we have the Code," she said with finality. "That's why we have to stay absolutely faithful to the Code."

"Hey!" said Reggie suddenly. "Shut up, mutt. We gotta go."

Just as suddenly, Reggie said goodbye to Gloria and hustled me toward Dekalb Avenue. Gloria didn't seem bothered by the brusque departure.

"See you again soon, Reggie," she crooned.

All the way home, Cupcake's words bounced around my head, fighting with my doubts. Nothing was resolved.

24

"Dogs never bite me. Just humans"
—Marilyn Monroe

To chase or not to chase?

That's the question that has haunted me since my earliest puppyhood. If there is a great unresolved—intractable—controversy in the world of dogs, this is it. Of course, it's inherent in canine genetics that we are hunters. The sight of a fellow furry creature foraging in the leaf litter or burying a nut sends a sudden surge of adrenalin through every sentient, self-respecting dog. But I believe—and I share this conviction with my NYPD mentor, Scout—that dogs have evolved into rational beings capable of making choices and regulating the power of instinct.

Once, I nearly choked to death on my collar while trying—impulsively—to chase a gopher. After the little rodent had disappeared down its hole, Scout asked me, "What was your point?"

Well, I was a puppy. I didn't know that a dog could have a point for anything I might do. I was fully captive to my id. I simply looked confused. Scout nipped me paternally and then settled pedagogically onto his haunches. He noted my quarry, who had been frolicking on a distant patch of lawn, was evidently captive of its own id. It was gopher mating season.

"They do their foreplay out on the grass, but they mate underground. And when they're ready, they're in a hurry," said Scout. "So, you see, even though it looked like he was dizzy with lust, that gopher never ventured more than six feet from his burrow."

Scout continued to teach. "How far away was the gopher from you?"

Dogs measure distance in "wolves," the body length of a wolf minus the tail, which, in human terms, is about sixty-four inches. So, I told Scout, "Hm, well, about ten wolves."

"Right," he said. "And you're going to cover ten wolves—dragging Marilyn—while that gopher's zipping six feet to his hole?"

I had no response, of course. Rationally, a domestic dog, of any breed, has little or no chance to catch almost any creature it chases before the quick little sucker scoots down its burrow or up a tree.

I offered Scout one justification. "But it's fun," I said.

Scout had heard this alibi before. "It's fun because it's running," he said. "So run, but run for the joy of running, not to act out some primordial desire to overtake some innocent herbivore and crush it in your jaws."

Scout was right. Even when wild dogs run free as certified carnivores, we don't chase anything alone. We operate in groups and use both cunning and teamwork to bring down quarry that outweighs us by hundreds of pounds—elk and wildebeests, not bunnies and groundhogs.

The whole notion of urban dogs chasing chipmunks, gophers, squirrels and—for some demented reason—cars, is not just silly, Scout explained to me. It's beneath a serious dog's dignity.

Of course, dignity is not a concept I've ever been able to get across to some of dogdom's dumber breeds, your Corgis, your French bulldogs and your hopelessly moronic Dobermans. But the debate rages on even among Labs, spaniels and various terriers. One of my obedience classmates, a shorthair named Igor, said to me, "Look, chasing is tradition. If I ever caught a squirrel, I wouldn't know what the hell to do with it. And while I was trying to figure it out, the damn thing might scratch my eyes out. Did you ever look close at the claws on those little bastards? But the point ..."

(You see. Dogs think about points!)

"... is the chase itself. A dog's gotta chase what a dog's gotta chase. If we stop chasing, are we still dogs at all?"

Igor's position was powerful and convincing, but I opted for Scout and dignity. I've gotten to a point now where, when I see a squirrel—and Brooklyn's crawling with them—I watch it instinctively. Sometimes, I even try to make eye contact and scare the little nutcracker. But I feel no thrill, no urge to attack, just a saliva rush, a stiffness in my tail and a tingle in my hind legs.

But I digress.

I was getting around to a troubling moment of drama the other night.

It was the most wee among the wee hours, Reggie leading me around the cold, deserted streets, peering into every shadow and kneading his crotch while I just tried to fight off a chronic case of the creeps. We were a little way down the familiar slate sidewalks of South Portland Avenue, heading toward Fulton. Up the street, a girl emerged from one of the brownstones, skipping nimbly down the steps.

I had an instant flashback to the weeping girl on the church steps on Lafayette Avenue and felt a wave of desperation. The young woman was twentyish, underdressed for the weather in a light blue sweater, black slacks and a bright red wool scarf. Riffling in the autumn breeze, her mane of sorrel hair evoked a well-groomed afghan hound. The breeze also wafted to me a suite of interesting aromas—a hint of merlot mixed with that surprisingly good brie from Trader Joe's and cheap French bread. She also gave off a strong tang of bodily fluids which, I was grateful, Reggie was too nasally retarded to smell. She was carrying books, so she must have been a student from Pratt, St. Francis, St Joseph, LIU or ... well, there are so many schools in the neighborhood. My nose told me that she was probably fresh from a tryst with a guy who had a persistent acne issue (malignant skin oils mixed with benzoyl peroxide pimple remedies have a pungency that clings to every surface, carries for miles and makes my eyes water).

Reggie was immediately galvanized at the sight of the girl. I sucked in my breath, ready to bark her to safety.

I wondered why was she coming out at this hour while fear stalked the streets.

Judging by her haste, I guessed that spending the entire night with Mr. Blackhead was the last thing she wanted to do. But also, her armful of books suggested that she had a big test in the morning. I guessed that she was hurrying back to her dorm to study all the way up'til class or—more likely—die right here by Reggie's hand.

Remembering my attempted mischief at the church on Lafayette, Reggie read my mind.

"Bark, you dumb fuck," he whispered, "and I'll kill you."

I had to obey. I ground my molars and exposed my canines, hoping ridiculously that the girl might peer through the dark, see my bared fangs and run away in terror. But we were still twenty yards away and concealed by the shadow of a tree.

She hadn't noticed us, but she was clearly nervous to be out so late, so alone. She turned hurriedly away from us.

Reggie looked around, scanning the street and peering back toward Fort Greene Park for signs of police activity.

There were no cops in sight, anywhere. Reggie began stalking,

She was moving fast. In response, Reggie picked up his

pace, eager to stage a ghastly scene that I was loath to witness and, what's worse, smell. His hand was on his knife. Within a minute, with Fulton Street still far away, she was barely twenty feet ahead of us. Reggie, in gumshoes, was as quiet as death on the hoof.

And then, as we passed a tree, my nose caught the acidic pong of a squirrel turd among the leaves—and it hit me.

Suddenly, before Reggie could react or resist, I launched into a fit of non-barking noise, growling, whinging, clawing at the sidewalk and slobbering like a Newfoundland. I yanked Reggie off-balance, off the sidewalk, between two parked cars and into the street. I strained mightily at the leash, now breathless because I had tightened the choke chain to suffocation level.

But it was working. All the fuss and frenzy, with Reggie suddenly shouting at me, "What the fuck are you doing, ya goddamn moron dog?" In the corner of my eye, as I dragged Reggie toward a towering sycamore on the opposite curb, I saw the girl turn, put her hand over her mouth and gape at our struggle. Seconds later, as I pulled Reggie laboriously away from her, she was sprinting in the other direction, making little involuntary canine-frequency peeps that no other human could hear. Just as I was about to pass out from choke-chain suffocation, I relaxed so abruptly that Reggie lurched forward, tripped over me and fell in the street.

"You fucking—ouch! Jesus."

Looking up toward the tree, I said, with a note of disappointment, "Oops, got away."

Reggie was livid, his jowls purple, his eyes bulging from their orbits like blisters on a dead sunbather.

"What the fuck was that?"

"Squirrel," I said matter-of-factly.

"What?"

"I saw a squirrel," I said blandly. "Dogs chase squirrels. It went up that tree."

Reggie was roaring. "Squirrel? I don't see no fuckin' squirrel."

"It went around to the back side of the tree. That's what squirrels do."

Reggie stood up, brushing street dirt off his pants. He was seething with frustration. Before he could launch into a rage and start beating on me, I volunteered an explanation.

"Okay, Reggie, you're not a dog."

"No shit, Fido."

"No, wait, listen," I said. "Dogs, you see, we've got squirrel radar that humans can't even imagine. I mean, sometimes, when the wind is right, I can smell one of those little excrescences a mile away. I can stick my tongue and taste its body odor in the air. I tell ya, Reggie, we really hate 'em. It's the sacred mission of every dog on earth to catch and kill every squirrel he sees. We can't help the urge. It goes back to Pleistocene times. It's in our blood. It's our genes, our deepest psychic need! We smell a squirrel, we go crazy. We lose all control."

Reggie's face went from furious to fuddled. "Really?"

"Sorry, Reg," I said, lowering my eyes and tucking my tail. "I couldn't help myself."

Of course, this was all poppycock. There was no squirrel. I had no urge. But my mock confession calmed Reggie strangely.

"Really? Squirrels?" said Reggie. "I never knew."

Reggie started us back toward the park, shuffling along thoughtfully. Finally, he said, "Thanks."

"Thanks," I asked, "for what?"

He didn't answer for a while. Then, as we were heading up Dekalb, Reggie patted me on the head, scratched an ear and said, "Boy, oh boy, do I know how you feel."

This, of course, brought back my case of the creeps. It stuck with me all the way home.

. . .

Over the next few days, I monitored the news as thoroughly as I could, hoping to see reports of a disturbance involving a frightened girl and a snarling dog on South Portland Street. But I didn't get my hopes up.

After all, at the most, what the girl saw was a big slob with a dog doing walkies—the same sight the police see when they drive past us. Besides that, she wasn't supposed to be where she was when I scared her away. Admitting that she was there—outside on the streets after midnight on the turf of the Brooklyn Ripper—and explaining why she was there and whom she was with might have gotten the girl in trouble with her school, her parents or the police.

25

"If a dog will not come to you after having looked you in the face, you should go home and examine your conscience."
—Woodrow Wilson

The term "serial killer" kept popping into my head as Reggie walked me along Myrtle Avenue on a sunny Saturday morning. It was Shabbat, and the Orthodox Jews of the neighborhood, on their way to temple, were streaming along the sidewalks. The men were all in black satin and gabardine, many wearing *shtreimel*, doughnut-shaped fur hats made of marten, sable or gray fox. The hats captivated me because the scents that lingered faintly in each kind of fur are distinctive and, to my city-bred nose, exotic. I could only guess which, among the three woodland predators, was which.

I tried to distract my darker thoughts by picturing myself rolling in a great heap of *shtreimel*, absorbing into my own coat an incongruous mélange of wildlife fragrances.

This diversion didn't work. Here I was, side-by-side with a serial killer, shlepping down the street past crowds of unsuspecting Hasidim. It rankled me to admit it to myself, but there it was. Reggie was killing people serially—people who had done him no offense whatsoever except to have normal human sex lives, which, of course, Reggie could not manage.

I had rationalized Reggie's gruesome excursions in every way possible, even telling myself that he was not, in the strict, clinical sense of the term, a serial killer. According to the usual definition, his profile wasn't typical. I had heard Marilyn talking with other cops and even Dr. Menzies about the psychology of murderers like Ted Bundy. Classic serial killers tend to stick to one favorite weapon. They prefer one sex over the other and even choose victims according to body type, hair color, age and other specific criteria. They tend toward ritualism and, most characteristically, they "escalate." Their crimes grow closer and closer together. Reggie followed parts of the pattern, but he deviated and never escalated. His periods of inactivity led me to hope that he might just quit killing after a while, grow tired of the fear and tension and blood. But after a few days—a week at most—he would start up again, usually because something set him off. Like Mom's new beau.

Worse than reconciling myself to Reggie's horrible reality was the awareness that I couldn't do anything to stop him. I was caught in an ethical trap, from which—as Cupcake regularly reminded me—there was no escape. A few times I had managed, clumsily, to deter or distract Reggie—each time feeling guilty because I figured I was committing at least a venial sin against the ironclad Code. But I could not, dared not, interfere directly in Reggie's blood-soaked handiwork. He was master. I was pet. The lines were clear and ineradicable.

However, as a dog on a leash, I enjoyed one imperative that did not violate my oath of loyalty. The Code mentions nothing about being true to the tether. The unwritten law of dogdom, dating back centuries to the very Dawn of Man, is that if someone puts a rope around your throat, it is your canine prerogative—your duty, as it were—to break free and run gladsome through the grass, the wind in your whiskers and your hapless master in lumbering pursuit.

Which is what I did again that Shabbat when Reggie paused a moment and relaxed his grip. With a little leap of my front paws and a powerful push from my haunches, I snapped the leash from his hand and was around the nearest corner before I heard Reggie, far behind, shout, "Hey! Goddammit!"

Ha ha. Free as a bird. Of course, there's no grass to gallop through in this stretch of Brooklyn. I was sprinting on stained and sticky pavement between tenements, some occupied, others derelict. Up ahead, a brick wall on one side, a chain-link fence on the other. On the next corner, the profile of a church steeple against the morning sun. I kept running, a wondrous feeling of liberation—from the leash and the serial murderer who held it—on an unseasonably warm autumn day.

I didn't slow until I heard a human voice, crisp and liquid, in my right ear.

"Whoo-ee!"

I slowed to a trot, turning my head toward the sound.

The voice said, "Hey, boy. Where's the fire?"

I stopped and looked through the chain-link fence. It guarded a grass-edged parking area behind the church. In a notch formed by two rear walls of the church, I saw him, a homeless man in a makeshift shelter of plastic sheeting and cardboard bedding. He was sitting on a ragged mattress, drinking from a paper cup. I said, "Are you talking to me?"

This would sound to him like nonsense, but I had long since decided not to talk down to humans despite their linguistic handicap.

So, I was surprised when he replied, "I never forget a face. Your name is Farfel, right?"

I recognized him then, mainly by his voice. Weeks before, I had seen him arguing with a couple of police officers. "Luther?" I said.

"That's right," he said. "So, where's Reggie?"

Remarkable. He remembered not only me but my master's name.

DAVID BENJAMIN

"Well, he's—" I looked back. Reggie was rounding the far corner, red-faced, galumphing. "Not far behind," I said.

"Come on," said Luther. "Slip through the fence there."

The gate, missing a hinge, hung crookedly, providing a triangle wide enough for a dog, or even a thin person, to slip into the churchyard. With one more look at Reggie's progress, I ducked through the gap. I approached Luther a little gingerly.

"Hey, don't worry, boy. C'mere. I'll throw a blanket over you."

I quickly crept up close to Luther and lay down. The blanket he tossed over me was perfumed with the smells of the street, from spoiled fruit to spilled whiskey and several species of urine. I was tempted to go whole-dog and roll around in it luxuriously. Instead, I hunkered down underneath and froze as Reggie's thundering footsteps approached and halted.

Then Luther's voice.

"Was that your dog?"

"Yeah." Reggie barely got this out between gasps. "He's—"

Luther said, "He came right through here but headed that way."

"Oh. *Gasp*. Okay. *Gasp*. Thanks."

Reggie's feet started up again, fading into the distance.

Luther lifted the richly aromatic blanket.

"He's the Ripper?" he asked.

"Yes," I said, a little embarrassed.

"Doesn't look it."

"I know," I said.

"Looks sort of like Mr. Potato Head."

"Yes," I said, "I guess he does. And he uses me as camouflage."

"Really?" said Luther thoughtfully. "Must be smarter than he looks."

"I guess that's another one of his camouflages," I said.

"You running away from him?"

"No," I said. "I'll go back to him in a few minutes. I just needed a break."

"I can understand that. But why not just ditch him? You obviously don't approve of what he's doing."

"I can't," I said. "It's against the rules. You have to stick by your master, no matter what."

"Yeah," said Luther. "I see that. Yeah."

"You do?" I asked. "Most humans, they don't really get it."

"Oh, I know." Luther's voice was a little sad, I thought. He sipped at whatever was in the paper cup. I drank in a lungful of air, tasting every molecule of the cup's contents. It wasn't coffee. "People aren't much on loyalty. But dogs, it's one of your secret powers, isn't it?"

"We'd be nothing without it."

"Well, I wish everyone felt that way, Farfel."

We sat together for a while then. I hadn't gotten a good look at his face in the dark when we'd met the first time. Now I had a chance to study him with my admittedly weak eyes.

It had always seemed to me that all homeless men, eventually, tend to look like either bloodhounds or briards. But with a lank frame of gray hair and beard surrounding his gaunt face, he reminded me more of an Irish wolfhound, complete with the unlikely gentleness of eyes and mouth typical of the breed. His accent was more Harlem than Donegal, but it was a voice that suggested a good education in far better times.

Of course, he smelled like the bottom of a dumpster behind a dive bar. But, to a dog, this was cause for love at first sniff. I drank in his odors and felt strangely at home.

Finally, looking around, I said, "This spot is better than the storefront you had before."

"Indeed. The good vicar knows I'm here, but so far, he hasn't bothered me. The church is a mighty fortress against the elements. I'm mostly out of the wind here and off the street. This'll be a pretty harsh hideout, though, when winter settles in."

I couldn't imagine being a human, without a coat of fur,

living outdoors through a New York winter. I told Luther so.

"Well, when it gets really bitter, there are places to go. They'll put you up for a few nights. But I don't fancy the company. The ones who aren't dangerously weird tend to be thieves. You have to guard your stuff every second."

"It's a dog-eat-dog world," I said.

Luther laughed at that. "You got that right, boy!"

It was a huge pleasure for me, conversing with a grownup human with whom I didn't have to be careful of every word I said. Before I knew it, at least a half-hour had passed. I had to get back to Reggie before he did something ghastly in broad daylight.

"Listen, I have to go."

"Well, drop in any time, Farfel."

"Thanks," I said. I rose to leave but paused halfway up. "Can you do me a favor?"

"If I can."

"Well, I know the police probably wouldn't take you much more seriously than they would a dog, if they could understand what I'm saying."

"Yeah." He smiled ruefully. "To them, I'm a crazy old derelict."

"Right. But, next time you run into the cops, can you try again? Tell them that the murderer is Reggie Stockwell?"

I told Luther where we lived. I said, "Maybe if they hear it often enough—"

Luther's face screwed into a forlorn scowl. "I don't know, Farfel. I don't exactly go out of my way to socialize with the *gendarmerie*," he said. "And when we do cross paths, well, they tend to be unreceptive."

I remembered my cop days on patrol and the cold hostility I felt emanating from the great city's huddled masses. I recalled the fear, too. A crazy bum could burst from a dark hole, swinging a shank so suddenly that you couldn't get out of the way. The NYPD and New York's homeless community observed, at best, a taut and trustless truce.

"I know how it is," I said. "I was one of them once."

"One of what?"

"I was a police dog," I said. "I've been known to roust the occasional mendicant."

Luther smiled at that. "I think I'll have to hang a shingle up there on the fence. It'll read: 'The Occasional Mendicant.'"

"I'm sorry for that," I said. "I was barely a puppy in those days. I didn't realize—"

"Not a problem, Farfel," said Luther, rubbing behind my ears. "We've looked at life from both sides now, the two of us. I'll tell you what."

I pricked up my ears.

"Most days, it's all I can do to score my meds in the daytime and stay dry through the night. I don't exactly scour the streets looking for a friendly cop on the beat. I steer clear. But for you, Farfel, first cop I see who isn't waving a stick in my face and accusing me of being drunk and disorderly, I'll tell him your whole story."

"He won't believe a word."

"From a crazy old bum?"

"Who talks to dogs."

"Even crazier."

I lifted onto four legs, ready to leave.

"Nothing ventured," I said, "nothing gained."

"One thing, Farfel."

"Yes?"

"Doesn't it sort of break your loyalty oath, you asking me to rat out your master to the cops?"

My shoulders sank a little as though weighted down by the question. "Well, if you're the one who's ratting out Reggie instead of me ..."

I let it hang there.

Luther's smile was sympathetic. "Still nags at your conscience, don't it?"

DAVID BENJAMIN

I didn't have to answer.

"So long," I said, heading for the opening in the fence.

"Don't be a stranger now," said Luther. "And keep your tail up."

I caught up to Reggie near Connecticut Muffin. He scolded me for running off, scratched absently between my eyes and gave me half his muffin. He could be a pretty good master sometimes.

26

"No matter how close we are to another person, few human relationships are as free from strife, disagreement, and frustration as is the relationship you have with a good dog. Few human beings give of themselves to another as a dog gives of itself. I also suspect that we cherish dogs because their unblemished souls make us wish—consciously or unconsciously—that we were as innocent as they are."
—Dean Koontz

I understand why he did it, but I wish Reggie had not killed one of his victims at Pratt Institute. I didn't want him to spoil the place for me. Now, I can't go back there without thinking of that poor girl, half-naked and mangled, sprawled on cold cement in utmost indignity.

For instance, I caught a serious case of the heeby-jeebies today as we walked past Pratt on route to Fort Greene Park. For the first time in my memory, the gates were locked. Guards were everywhere, checking people in and out, frisking innocent, bewildered students. Art students! The dimmest, sweetest, most romantic and unworldly inhabitants of all academia.

He did it last night. I watched it all, step by bloody step. When I think back, it unreels in my mind in slow motion, prolonging my horror, magnifying Reggie's cruelty.

She was leaning next to a doorway, smoking a cigarette. That explains why she was outside at three in the morning, probably taking a break from studying all night. She stepped outside her dormitory and lit up. And why not? She was on her own campus, an intellectual island in a nice part of Brooklyn. Clinton Hill had gentrified a generation ago. She wasn't some party girl out wandering the streets. She was home, at her dorm, taking a well-deserved nicotine break before going back inside to work on her mid-term project, probably some buttressed and cantilevered architectural scale-model dream built of pasteboard, balsa wood, Testors paint and rubber cement.

I thought about all this unfairness as Reggie tied my leash tight to a railing and clamped my mouth once, warning me to silence.

Reggie approached her in an indolent shuffle that mimicked half the shy, ungainly male students on the campus. She saw him in the corner of her eye, sized him up swiftly and returned her attention to her Virginia Slim. He looked no more dangerous than one of the student sculptures scattered around the grounds.

When he exploded upon her, seized her throat and dragged her into a stairwell, she had barely a second to utter a single, muffled, smoky syllable. In an archway between two staircases, he filleted her from end to end. He stood over her body as he undressed. Smeared red and naked, he ejaculated into his bloody shirt—careful not to spill any DNA—then put on fresh togs and returned to me. I reeled with the scent of fresh blood. I salivated involuntarily and felt the ancient urge to feed on fresh prey. Then, as usual, I suppressed the primordial instinct that would turn me back into a nomadic wolf with no place among humans.

Did Reggie have a place among humans?

A silly question. Of course he did. Humans kill one another more prolifically than any other species preys on its own. Reggie's bloodlust, magnified by its wastefulness, made him quintessentially human. Were he a dog, he would not have abandoned his kill. He would have eaten his fill and buried the girl's carcass for later consumption.

You think that's gross? Turn on PBS and catch a few episodes of *Nature*, especially the ones with hyenas and wolverines.

• • •

Next day, by the time we passed Pratt, she had been removed—thank goodness—from the stairwell, zipped into a body bag, trucked to a medical examiner for autopsy. Seen from Willoughby Avenue, the campus seemed deserted. Classes had almost certainly been canceled. Some students had probably fled. Others were holed up in their rooms, peeking out windows at their despoiled oasis.

Reggie walked with a bounce in his step. Murdering girls always cheered him up. When we got to Fort Greene Park, I sensed in him an air of expectancy. He led me around restlessly, impatient whenever I peed on a tree, grumbling over my bowel movement and then almost soiling his hands as he hastily bagged it.

He almost leapt at the sight of Gloria and Cupcake atop the hill near the Prison Ship Martyrs' Monument. Then he dragged me up the hill.

While Cupcake and I went through the obligatory process of sniffing under each other's tails, touching noses and mumbling a few desultory greetings in dog-English, Reggie was dithering and muttering, barely audible. Gloria had to lean in to hear what he was saying.

I mean, Reggie is just pathetic with the opposite sex (except his mother or when he's murdering them). If he just saw women as people rather than some sort of alien species possessed by forces beyond the human mind's capacity to understand ...

Well, never mind. If he were able to converse normally with a girl, would he be a serial killer?

Besides, he seemed actually eager to see Gloria. After a minute or two, he even managed to kick his voice into audible range, at which he noted that the weather wasn't too cold, "especially this close to Halloween."

This led to Gloria reminiscing about her Halloweens back in smalltown Wisconsin and Reggie responding along the same general lines. Halloween being kid stuff, Reggie fell easily into the discussion. Gloria noted that her building was secure, denying her the pleasure of trick-or-treaters at her door. She said this used to make her sad and homesick, but she remedied that by making sure she had something social—a party or dinner guests—on Halloween.

"I'm a pretty good cook," she said.

"I bet you are," said Reggie.

"Oh, no," I said to Cupcake.

"What's wrong? Can't get it up?"

"No," I said. "She's going to ask him over for dinner."

"So what?" said Cupcake. "You wanna hump?"

"Maybe you'd like to see what I can do," said Gloria.

"Do?" asked Reggie.

"Quiet!" I snapped at Cupcake. "I'm listening."

"So, you don't wanna hump?"

"In the kitchen," said Gloria, helpfully.

"Oh," said Reggie. "You mean cooking."

"Yes," said Gloria. "I make a mean chicken cacciatore."

"Oh," said Reggie.

"Why is she doing this?" I said. "He attacked her. Doesn't she remember? He almost killed her. Is she crazy?"

"You really don't understand women, do you, big boy?" said Cupcake.

"So, would you like to try it?" said Gloria.

"Try what?" asked Reggie.

"Is this guy as dumb as he sounds?" asked Cupcake.

"Hush!" I said.

"My chicken cacciatore, silly," said Gloria coquettishly. She didn't give up easily.

"Oh," said Reggie.

"My God, she's doing it. She's inviting him to dinner," I said.

"Of course she is," said Cupcake. "She's lonely, desperate and, worst of all, she's human. She actually feels guilty that he attacked her. She's convinced herself that she led him on."

"Led him on?" I said, astounded.

"Hush," said Cupcake.

"So, what do you think?" said Gloria.

"Think?" said Mr. Monosyllable.

"A nice, quiet Halloween. No kids banging on the door. Homemade cacciatore. Maybe a nice Chianti?"

"Oh," said Reggie.

Gloria waited. She crossed her arms.

"How's it feel having a moron for a master?" Cupcake growled.

"I wish he *were* a moron," I said. "And only a moron."

"You want me to, like," said Reggie haltingly, "come over?"

"Yes."

"To your place?"

"Yes."

"To, like, eat?"

"Yes, for dinner, Reggie. I'd like that. Wouldn't you?"

"On Halloween?"

"Yes."

"Um."

"She shouldn't be doing this," I said. "This is so wrong."

"Oh, come on, big boy. This is a big opportunity for Gloria. Men aren't exactly beating a path to her door, y'know."

"You don't understand," I said.

"Okay," said Reggie, barely above a whisper.

DAVID BENJAMIN

"You'll come?" said Gloria.

"Uh-huh."

"Oh, that's great," said Gloria. She tried to kiss Reggie chastely on the cheek, but he recoiled. She kissed air but was unfazed. "Should we wear costumes?"

"Costumes?"

"He's going to kill her," I said.

"Kill her?"

"He's a serial killer," I said. "You know that, C.C. I keep telling you!"

"Oh, you're just an alarmist."

"Alarmist? Alarmist? You should see what he did to that poor girl over at Pratt last night."

"He killed a Pratt girl?"

"Killed? He impaled her on a ten-inch hunting knife and cut her to shreds."

"Well, she probably had it coming. It's my experience that Pratt girls are ... prats! Tee hee."

"C.C., will you please take this seriously?"

"I am serious, big boy. Seriously horny. How 'bout it? You hard yet?"

She was turning to present her hindquarters, but I maneuvered around to face her again.

"Do you hear what I'm telling you?" I asked imploringly. "My master is a murderer. We have to do something to stop him from killing Gloria."

"Whaddya mean, 'we,' dark face? He's your master."

"You can stop him. You'll be there when she's serving him dinner."

"Me?" said Cupcake, incredulous.

"Yes, if he doesn't bring me along—"

"Look at me."

I looked at Cupcake.

"I weigh twenty pounds, after a heavy meal," said Cupcake.

"So?"

"So, look at your master."

I looked at Reggie, all 250 flabby pounds of him. I sighed.

"So," I said, "you're not going to do anything to protect your mistress?"

It's generally conceded that dogs cannot smile. Poodles, however, have developed the art of sneering. Cupcake sneered.

"Darn it, C.C.," I implored. "This is a matter of life and death."

After another sneer, Cupcake replied, "Okay, Farfel. Tell you what. If ol' lardass up there looks like he's fixing to kill Gloria, I'll bark sharply and nip him on the ankle."

"You really don't believe me, do you?" I said.

"I should believe that this yutz is a homicidal fiend, murdering women all over Brooklyn and yet able to cleverly elude the entire New York police force?"

"So, you don't believe me?"

"Would you, really?"

I checked out Reggie, who was scratching his ass. I noticed the little white flecks of saliva in the corners of his mouth.

"Well," I said.

"Besides, even if he is the Brooklyn Ripper, what could you do? He's the boss. He goes, you follow."

"Yeah, right. The Code," I sighed, exasperated.

"Yes! The Code," replied Cupcake heatedly. "We're dogs, ya big dope. The Code is all we have. Without it, we're on the streets, fighting rats for bread crusts and wondering if there's any nourishment in fly larvae."

Here was the same-old same-old from Cupcake. I tried another angle. "But look, C.C., Gloria's my friend and your mistress. Is it wrong for me to protect a friend?"

"Against your master's wishes?"

"Yes. Wouldn't it be—"

"Okay, let's say your master wants to kill your friend," said Cupcake.

"Yes, what if—"

"As a dog, your duty is simple. You help him," said Cupcake. "You hold her down."

I shook my ears violently, wishing I hadn't heard that. As calmly as I could manage, I replied. "All right, then. We're at your house. I'm holding Gloria down. Reggie is whipping out his knife. And what are you doing all this time?"

"Barking sharply—from a safe distance."

There was no reasoning with Cupcake.

"You're an idiot," I said disgustedly.

"Oh," said Cupcake, feigning indignation. "Just when I was getting all warm and juicy and picturing you, clamped to my haunches."

"C.C., I don't want to hump you. Not now."

"You never wanna hump me. What am I, ugly?"

"Ugly? No, You're perfectly lovely."

"Okay, so you're gay? Why are the good-looking ones always—"

"C.C., we've already been through this. I'm preoccupied, not gay. I have a master who's running amok with a knife all over Brooklyn."

"Well, I'd have to see that to believe it," insisted Cupcake. "Even though he's ridiculously shy and dumber than a Pomeranian, he seems like a nice, harmless guy."

"You have no idea," I said.

. . .

Later, on our way home, I put it straight to Reggie. "Are you really going on a date with Gloria?"

"She invited me over for dinner on Halloween."

"Yes, I heard. You're going to go?"

"Why not?"

"Are you going to kill her, Reggie?"

"Kill her? Kill Gloria?"

"Yes. Like all the others. Like you tried to kill her on your last date!"

Reggie thought about this for a moment. "Well, no. Things were different then."

"Different?"

"Well, I didn't know Gloria very well," said Reggie. "I thought she was like other women."

"Like other women?"

"Yes, deceitful and slutty, obsessed with brutal alpha male gorillas."

"She's not?"

"No, she's rare and special. She sees that fornication is the harbinger of the end of all things. She understands. She's chaste and pure."

"What about the last time?" I said, trying to bring Reggie back down to earth. The last thing I wanted was for Reggie to keep that date. "Didn't she kiss you then? That's not so chaste and pure."

"I've realized that was a pure kiss. Like a nun's kiss."

I had no answer for this. I've been petted by a nun or two, but they didn't try to kiss me—and I don't think they're supposed to kiss anybody. But I had a bad feeling. Reggie used to say that his mother was the only woman on earth worth saving. The only pure woman. But Mom had defiled herself with this new boyfriend, Neal Vander Voort, the numismatist.

Was Gloria nudging Mom off the lonely pedestal of the Madonna? And what would happen to Gloria when she turns out not as "pure" as he expects her to be? Nobody's that good.

Well, I knew what would happen. I knew I'd probably be tied up close by, watching it happen. My skin crawled.

• • •

After our walk, I was hoping that Reggie would call Mom, talk things through, make up with her. But he ignored the phone and slumped in front of the television, apparently exhausted from the rigors of a ten-minute conversation with Gloria.

The TV, of all things, got me thinking that there might be a way out of my dilemma. We were watching a news show on MSNBC when a public service announcement came on for the ASPCA. Some mournful folk singer was crooning lugubriously in the background while a female voice-over solicited viewers to contribute $19 a month. Meanwhile, the screen ran close-up after close-up of wretched-looking dogs and cats incarcerated in shelters. They were bandaged, scabbed, scarred and mangled. Every one looked scared to death. I knew the feeling. I had worked the streets long enough to have encountered lots of dogs who'd gotten kicked around, staked out, eye-gouged and starved by their masters.

More important, I knew Marilyn, my trainer, whose self-hating husband, Randy, tuned her up at least once a week. There were mornings when she came to my kennel bruised or limping, sometimes with a scab on her head or an ugly red mark on her cheek. Worst of all was a look of bewildered betrayal in her eyes, like a dog who tried to do good, who wagged and heeled and fetched and waited all day to take a leak but still got flogged with a rolled-up magazine. For no reason—just because she was there, within swinging range, available for a beating.

On those mornings, Marilyn—although she was as tough a cop as I ever knew—looked like an innocent, loving, stomped-on puppy. It broke my heart. And I wished, every time, that she would just leave the son of a bitch. Humans, after all, had such a thing as divorce.

That's when it hit me.

Every one of these pathetic dogs in the ASPCA ad was alone, left to die, locked up in a kennel and probably just waiting there for the Big Needle. Their masters had divorced them.

If people could divorce people for cruelty, and cruel people could divorce their dogs, why can't a dog—faced with extreme cruelty—divorce his master? It dawned on me that the Code of the Dog might be a two-way street. According to rules that go back to the beginning of time, I knew that dogs owe everything to their masters. But in return, dogs have always lapped up the milk of human kindness. If there is no kindness at all on the human side, how can any of the rules apply?

This question took hold of me and kept me restless all night long.

Until Reggie began killing, I had been a Code fundamentalist like Cupcake. I understood how thin the line is between pampered pethood and feral ostracism. But, as I pondered those crushed, terrified mutts and tabbies on TV, I recognized them as martyrs to the Code. Each had been betrayed by a Code-flouting master who thought he owed his pet not a shred of humaneness.

The epiphany that hit me in the wee hours that morning while Reggie snored away in his La-Z-Boy in front of the jabbering TV was that not even God meant for dogs to be so loyal. God tested Job to the very limit of human endurance, yes. But then, God gave even Job a break. Did God intend canine endurance to exceed the patience, forbearance and saintliness of Job?

I doubted this because, after all, I know God as well as the next dog. I know that he has accepted all dogs into his kingdom, regardless of what we do in our few short years on earth. We're unstained by original sin. We can't transgress in life because our every action is decreed either by our God-given instincts or by the training of our masters. Dogs die knowing that they face no reckoning in the afterlife.

In a flash of insight that woke me from a shallow sleep, I knew that God would take me in even if I broke the Code. I knew this because of those sad dogs wasting away in that kennel on TV. They had followed the Code while their masters had violated every sacred precept of human morality. Those pets, waiting for the execution that would end their pain and numb their heartache, had a God-given right to slip the Code. They deserved to save themselves, but they didn't. They stuck by their masters, beyond all good sense, and went on suffering.

On the other hand, except for verbal abuse, Reggie had barely laid a hand on me. Between us two, he was sticking to his part of the human/dog bargain. I had to work out in my mind—and it kept me restless 'til Reggie woke the next morning—whether the sort of extreme cruelty that abrogates the Code of the Dog extends beyond the dog.

Does the dog have the prerogative to oppose extreme cruelty even if it doesn't affect him (or her) personally?

I wasn't worried about whether God would honor my decision. I knew he would. He doesn't judge dogs any more than he judges people. The question was: Could I live with my own conscience?

27

"Living with a dog is messy—like living with an idealist."
—H.L. Mencken

Somehow, the prospect of a date with Gloria, more than a week away, had whet Reggie's appetite for blood. He blathered away as though he wanted to purge all of Brooklyn of fallen women before he sat down for chicken cacciatore with the borough's only unsoiled virgin.

But he was frustrated. Our expedition the next night came up empty. He dragged me from Bed-Stuy across the width of Clinton Hill, all the way around Fort Greene Park and over to Flushing Avenue, past the Brooklyn Navy Yard, and even into DUMBO. The closest we got to Reggie's quarry was a drunk couple on Navy Street. They were trying to keep each other from bashing into trees and collapsing onto the sidewalk. Reggie, of course, thought they were intoxicated with lust. He speeded us up to overtake them. I did my best to slow him down, plunging my nose into every smelly spot that seemed even remotely interesting.

They were less than a block away. Reggie was yanking brutally on my choke chain when a police cruiser swept around the corner of what I think was York Street. As the police lights twirled and two cops swarmed from the cruiser to intercept the staggering couple, Reggie uttered an oath and took a quick detour.

Our only other human encounter came the next night when a similar police car pulled up beside us. One of the officers stepped out and asked Reggie what we were doing out at this hour, and didn't we know there's a serial killer prowling these streets? Reggie, as usual, blamed it on me, accusing me of diarrhea and enlisting the policeman's sympathy over his obligation to risk his life in the wee hours because of a pooch with the runs.

To which I muttered, "Come on, Reggie. You're laying it on a little thick."

The cop heard but didn't understand and said, "Your dog barks funny."

"He has a speech impediment," said Reggie.

"Harelip?" asked the cop. He reached down and tousled the fur behind my ears. Felt good.

"Sort of," said Reggie.

"Thanks," I said.

"Don't mention it," said Reggie.

"Don't mention what?" said the cop.

"He was talking to me," I said in Dogspeak, very slowly, enunciating every syllable, in hopes that something would get through to the police officer. As a result, both Reggie and the cop just stared at me, the cop looking pitiful, Reggie looking smug.

"Yeah, well," I said. "A pox on both your houses."

On the way home, Reggie said, "You're pathetic. You don't like what I'm doing. So what do you do? You try to communicate with cops. Cops, of all people, the dumbest fucks on the face of the earth. They don't understand a fuckin' word, and you end up banging your dumb fuckin' head against the wall."

I couldn't really explain the Code to Reggie. Between people and dogs, it's unspoken. Humans and canines are supposed to know—and cooperate—implicitly. Unfortunately, while dogs make constant and strenuous efforts to ensure that every other dog adheres strictly to the Code, humans aren't nearly as scrupulous among one another—which is why you get those lugubrious public service commercials showing a lot of bandaged dogs and skeletal cats on Death Row.

"The most pathetic thing about you, y'know—ya stupid mutt—is that, as long as I got you taggin' along with me, I'm the least suspicious guy in all of Brooklyn," said Reggie. "I'm just a regular fella takin' the air with my faithful dog companion, Farfel. You want me to stop cleansing the world of degenerate whores, and you're the best fuckin' reason I don't have to stop. Hah."

Reggie continued, but I tuned him out, scanning the streets for signs of human activity. Cars passed occasionally, almost half of them police vehicles. The patrols had increased, and I wondered whether Reggie could have carried out his mission even if he found a target.

On the TV news that day, I'd heard a report that the NYPD was making progress on the Brooklyn Ripper case. The report made me pass gas in exasperation because I knew it was just cover-your-ass p.r. (pardon my language). After all, I had personally left messages for the Ripper Task Force with Jesse, the little boy, and Luther, the bum. My outreach had led to nothing but Reggie outfoxing Detectives Driscoll and De Mars. If those two palookas were New York's finest, Reggie was right about the IQ of the NYPD. He was destined never to be caught.

My tail was dragging when we got back to the apartment. My little rag rug never felt so good.

• • •

Reggie burned off some of his energy the next day by drafting another of his manifestos. I could tell what he was doing because he tends to be a vocal writer.

"Thousands!" he shouted suddenly, turning on a heel and glaring at me. I cowered, trying to indicate to Reggie that I'd just as soon he did not think out loud. This didn't work.

"Thousands of police! Blind! Blind to me because I am Moses, chosen by God! Died, you know! Never reached the Promised Land."

Thanks to Reggie, I was beginning to understand why God is so withdrawn. He benevolently allowed humans to set up dozens and dozens—hundreds!—of religions, each faith seemingly designed by humans themselves to reconcile their primeval savagery with the civilizing power of their magnificent brains. But God's chosen creatures had perverted every religion into a machine of vindictiveness and death. Here was Reggie, my master, an advanced specimen of the human race, graduate of a parochial education (I won't reveal the denomination—I mean, what's the difference, really? They're all equally grisly), twisting the example of Moses into a justification for serial slaughter against blameless strangers.

Reggie ranged across our living room, his face buried in the New Testament. As he bumped into furniture and tripped on the rug, he roared out his favorite passage from Galatians which, by this time, I pretty much knew by heart.

"For the flesh lusteth against the Spirit," Reggie growled, *"and the Spirit against the flesh: and these are contrary the one to the other: so that ye cannot do the things that ye would!"*

Reggie stopped and pointed at me. "Y'see?!" he shouted.

I rolled my eyes and rolled over.

Reggie went on pacing and reciting. *"But if ye be led of the Spirit, ye are not under the law."*

He stopped again. "Ya hear that?" he said. "Hey, turn over and look at me, ya fuckin' cur."

I obeyed. He yelled. "I'm led of the Spirit."

"So you say," I replied.

"I'm not under anybody's law!"

"Uh-huh," I muttered. I'd long since given up on challenging

Reggie's interpretation of Galatians 5:18.

"Now!" Reggie was reading his favorite lines now. *"The works of the flesh are manifest, which are* these: *Adultery! Fornication! Uncleanness! Lasciviousness!"*

He always breaks off here. Paul's epistle goes on to mention idolatry, witchcraft, hatred, wrath, drunkenness and other sins—many of which Reggie committed regularly. But, as every clergyman's dog knows, the Bible is a veritable Babel of selective exegesis.

"You fear me! Hah!" roared Reggie to his invisible audience. My ears hurt. "Despise me! Go ahead. Hate and despise me! This is my motivation. You lend me strength. Your hate fuels my mission!"

A few more laps of our cramped living room. Then he halted above me, looming up there while I buried my chin between my paws.

"You're right, Farfel!"

I hadn't said a word. I swear. Honest to God. Who was probably listening in, shaking his head sadly, maybe brushing a tear from the corner of his eye. That's if he actually had an eye. God isn't really all that corporeal.

"You see why I have to continue. You're not so dumb, Farf. I'm sorry I said that. You know that I face greater and greater danger every night. More cops. Every night, they're desperate to catch me. But I am more desperate, truly desperate. Desperate unto death. But I cannot fear death. I fear nothing. I could die. I should die. What is there to live for? Right, Farf?"

He glared at me as though I, too, had nothing to live for. I kept my peace but tried to say, with my eyes, no, Reg, I'd rather just go on living, thanks.

He didn't register my silent dissent, but it didn't matter, because his mind had taken another U-turn, lost control and just started spinning wildly.

He lunged toward his desk, fired up his computer, and began whaling away at his innocent, abused keyboard.

DAVID BENJAMIN

The headline, two days later in the *Daily News*, read simply:

"Thou Shalt Kill..."

The transcript below isn't the whole manifesto, but it's as much as I could scan and remember before Reggie snatched the newspaper away from me and flung it into the trash. He didn't know I could read, but I know he suspected. And I preferred to keep him in the dark on this score. Anyway, as you can see, he was evolving from an inchoate obsession toward a utopian scheme for a sex-free society:

We are suicidal fools to let women continue to copulate and breed the rotten fruit of their indiscriminate loins. Rational men of intelligence must assert their superiority and make all the choices. The failed concept of "women's rights" is rushing all of mankind backward to the Stone Age. As the conspiracy of depraved women choose their mates like bitches in heat, all of society slips backward. In each descending generation, we turn little by little into creatures little better than dogs, reptiles, hermaphrodite worms slithering in the muck. The only power women have over society—but it is the greatest power we now know—is sex. Fornication. Lasciviousness. No lower animal on earth is more wanton and depraved than the human female. Women are a deadly infection. Women deserve no more "rights" than we would give to an outbreak of Ebola.

All I ever wanted was to love women and, in turn, be loved by them back. Their behavior towards me has not only earned my hatred. It has proven their absolute iniquity as creatures of God. I am a victim in all of this, but I am rising above it, as Moses climbed the mountain to receive the Commandments. The First Commandment is Thou Shalt Kill the Women. The second is Thou Shalt Gather Their Eggs to Preserve Mankind. The Third Commandment: Thou Shalt Destroy Newborn

Females, except the few who would be caged and fed until puberty for egg-harvesting purposes—and then killed. Like Moses, I am the messenger of good and the vessel of divine purpose. Like Moses, I have suffered horribly—denied the love of women whom I thought, for most of my life, to be my destiny and my right. To love and be loved. But that false and wicked dream has passed, unfulfilled and unfulfillable because love has been subsumed through all the world by the lust of she-beasts, who are the Golden Calf. Now, I am reconciled to suffering. But not to surrender or even to death. I will be fulfilled by striking back, again and again, until my executions of the wicked are understood, until all rational men will join in ridding the planet of the curse and doom of carnal sex. And it will be beautiful. Finally, at long last, I will come down from the mountain to the gratitude of humanity, and together we will destroy the Golden Cow, with its great festering all-consuming womb.

Reggie actually goes on from there, with more description of the womb and the things that come out of it and the stuff it sucks in, like a giant Dyson vacuum cleaner. But the editors trimmed this part substantially because—incredibly—there are things too gross for even the *Daily News*.

The day the manifesto hit the front page, it triggered a new wave of panic, with many New Yorkers accusing the NYPD of incompetence. I knew better, of course. I'd seen the nightly patrols in Brooklyn. I knew that bumbling detectives like Driscoll and De Mars had been re-assigned from their regular duties. I had witnessed vast areas of police responsibility diverted to the pursuit of the Brooklyn Ripper. I couldn't blame the police for not seeing Reggie as he hid in plain sight, strolled the streets, and flaunted me, his trusty German shepherd, as proof of his innocence. The cops were looking high and low for a lean, hungry predator skulking in the shadows, not a sleepy-eyed slob walking his watchdog and looking, for all the world, like one of Al Capp's shmoos.

That day, Reggie's mother called, worried sick because Reggie was living right there, in the hunting grounds of the Brooklyn Ripper. I heard Reggie answer and heard him snarl viciously at his mother. He had yet to forgive her dalliance with the petit-bourgeois Vander Voort. I stood and trotted over to Reggie, wagging and lolling, to indicate my affection for Mom. I thought my attitude might encourage him to talk things out with her.

No dice. He cut her off in the midst of asking if he needed any money.

That afternoon a messenger arrived with another monetary peace offering from Mom. As Reggie opened the envelope and found the check there, it occurred to me that Cupcake might be right about human women. They seem to respond to insult and injury by feeling guilty, begging and bribing their way to forgiveness, and then trying twice as hard to be insulted and injured all over again.

If Reggie'd had any real principles, he would have torn up his mother's check. Instead, we took a walk to the bank and he deposited the dough.

And never called his mother to thank her.

On the way back home, I struck up a conversation in a tone as cool and Menzies-like as I could manage.

"Well, just a few days 'til the big date."

"What big date?"

"You and Gloria. Chicken cacciatore."

"That's not a big date," Reggie insisted.

"Well, you don't go out with girls very often."

"I don't go out with girls at all, dickhead."

"Well, that's true."

"I would have before. But now I know better. I know women. I know what they are."

This was well-trampled ground. So I said, "Well, it might

not be a big deal to you. But I think it's pretty important to Gloria."

"It should be."

"It should?"

"Well, this is a test for her, isn't it? A kind of final exam."

"A test?" I asked warily. "Final?"

Reggie stopped, looked around to see if anyone was watching. We were heading up Willoughby toward Franklin. The street was quiet, except for some schoolchildren a block away. Reggie bent over, facing me. "I have seen her purity, Farfel. You're a fuckin' dog. You wouldn't know purity if it fucked you up the ass. But I've sensed it in Gloria, in her eyes, in her gentle and demure manner. Even in her choice of pets. That poodle is a perfect little lady."

I resisted the urge to gag. If Reggie knew Cupcake the way I knew Cupcake.

"If you know all that already, Reg," I said. "If you know she's pure, then what's to test? Gloria sounds perfect."

"Oh no no no. You wouldn't understand. You have no idea how rare feminine purity is," said Reggie.

Dogs are used to this sort of insulting condescension. "I guess I'm just a dumb beast," I said.

Reggie sensed no sarcasm. "I cannot allow any doubt in my mind about Gloria," he said. "Y'see, dog, I've only seen her offsite."

Reggie's logic was escaping me. It did this often. "Offsite?"

"I consented to this so-called date because I want to see where Gloria lives, to see her in familiar surroundings," said Reggie. "I want to verify my offsite observations."

"I see," I said. Of course, I didn't see a thing.

"At home, she'll let her guard down. I can peer through her façade to the real, inner Gloria."

Peer? I thought. *Or cut?*

"What if," I suggested, "she fails?"

"Oh, I'm not really worried about that. She won't fail. I know her."

"But didn't she fail before?" I said. "When she came to your apartment, you tried to—"

"We were not natural. We'd been drinking," said Reggie. "Besides, that was a different me."

"It was?"

"Yes, I was impetuous then. I didn't understand my power. I hadn't yet seen my mission as I do now. I didn't realize that my calling is not just to erase the evil of sex from our midst, but to seek out—and struggle mightily to save—the last, perishing remnants of feminine goodness."

"Purity."

"Purity," said Reggie.

"You thought your mother was pure," I said.

Reggie's face darkened. He gave my choke chain a vicious tug and started back up Willoughby. "I was wrong," he said.

"But that's what I'm talking about, Reg. What if you're wrong again? About Gloria?" I said. "If she's not as pure as you think, what happens to her?"

"Nothing happens to her, ya dumb fuck. 'Cause I'm not wrong. I've seen into her heart."

"So, you've got x-ray vision."

"No, I have inspiration. If you weren't the stupidest cur on the face of the earth, you would've figured that out by now."

A few hours ago, I was smarter than Benji. Now I was back to idiot status.

"Well," I said, "I was just thinking."

"That's a laugh. You? Thinking?"

I parried this jab and persevered. "It just occurs to me that, before Gloria's big test, which could be a pretty big deal for both of you, wouldn't it be good to get to know her a little better before—"

"What the fuck're you talkin' about?"

"You know, maybe you should put off the date a while.

Hang around the park with her, take her for coffee a few more times. Get familiar. Maybe even hold hands across the table."

My goal was to keep their meetings in public, where Gloria could fail Reggie's lunatic test without getting hacked to shreds.

"I'm familiar, dipshit. More familiar than you can possibly imagine from down there at dog turd level. I'm familiar with all women and their evil nympho ways. And I'm familiar with the difference between those women and Gloria. Ya understand, ya fuckin' flea factory?"

"Yes, I get it."

"The fuck ya do."

I didn't answer. Just shuddered from head to toe to shake the bad karma from my fur.

But it clung all the way home and into the days beyond.

28

"All his life he tried to be a good person. Many times, however, he failed. For after all, he was only human. He wasn't a dog."
—Charles M. Schulz

For the next few days, I found myself wishing, guiltily, for Reggie to go out and attack some stranger. I could feel his tension building. He had built Gloria into a virgin goddess and invested her with expectations so unrealistic that they amounted to a death warrant.

I grew even more anxious on Halloween morning, the day of their date, when I awoke from a dognap (similar to a catnap but better because it features rabbit chasing) and saw him in his La-Z-Boy reading his Bible again.

Reggie caught my eye. "I'm reading about Moses."

"Who else?" I replied warily.

"They call me Moses in the newspapers."

"You call *yourself* Moses in the newspapers," I said.

"Yeah, well, anyway, that's not exactly right," said Reggie. "I'm more like an angel. Of death."

"An angel?"

"Here, listen." Reggie read from a passage I later identified as Exodus, Chapter 12: "And it came to pass, that at midnight the Lord smote all the firstborn in the land of Egypt," Reggie quoted, "from the firstborn of Pharaoh that sat on his throne to the firstborn of the captive that was in the dungeon; and all the firstborn of cattle. And Pharaoh rose up in the night, he, and all his servants and all the Egyptians; and there was a great cry in Egypt, for there was not a house where there was not one dead."

Reggie looked up from the Bible with that familiar lunatic glint in his eye. "You see," he said, "it wasn't actually God who came down and smote the fuckin' Egyptians. I mean, he's God, right? He doesn't do wet work, like some kind of hoodlum. He sends down angels. Like me. To punish evildoers."

"But," I began.

"In those days, Egyptians were the biggest evil on earth. Now, it's sluts and whores and college girls and mothers who say they're not whores, but they're the worst of all the whores. Y'see?"

"Reggie, that's what *you* see. Not me. You have kind of a unique outlook."

This went right past Reggie. He said, "Hey, get a load of this part right here: 'for there was not a house where there was not one dead.' That's why I was sent."

"Sent?"

"Yeah, man."

"You were *sent*? By God?"

"Well, maybe not by God, directly. I mean, I never talked to him like Moses did. It's more like a feeling deep inside. You know, intuition."

"Or indigestion?"

He ignored that. "Because, y'see, when I'm done, when more and more rational men see what I'm doing and join me as angels of death, there won't be a house where some woman isn't dead."

"Yes, but—"

"Except for the angels."

Here was a twist that caught me off guard. I wrinkled the skin between my eyes and cocked my head sidewise.

"What angels?"

"The angels will be spared," said Reggie. "Just like Passover."

"What?" I said. "You're Jewish now?"

Reggie scowled. "This isn't about religion, ya dipshit bone-licker. It's about moral regeneration. It's about—"

"Oh, I get it," I said. "You're talking about Gloria. She's one of your angels? She'll be passed over?"

"She's an angel of life."

"Ah, right," I said. "And you're ..."

"The angel of death."

I shook my head. "You're sure about that?"

"I feel it, man. Deep inside."

"Right. Deep inside," I said. "But, I mean, are you sure about Gloria's angel status? I thought you had a few lingering doubts. I mean, what if—"

"Gloria will be spared. She's pure and she's good. I know this, too. I feel it."

Reggie's sense of "feel" invariably gave me the head-to-tail willies. I looked closely at him. His eyes were glazed. His hands were squeezing the arms of his La-Z-Boy so hard that I feared for the upholstery. His legs squirmed back and forth, and his toes dug at the floor. I decided that prolonging the conversation would only send him further toward the brink. I circled back down and pretended to sleep.

Of course, all this talk about "intuition" had nothing to do with God. Reggie had bought into the example of screwups like Moses. What Reggie did not know is that Moses was among the first of God's bumbling protégés who, over the years, convinced God that consorting with elderly elephants and matching wits with kangaroos was more worthwhile than trying to have an intelligent conversation with any of the humans he'd created. God had despaired of sending "messages" to people before the first draft of Lamentations was finished. Most of the so-called "prophets" in the Old Testament were just making stuff up.

Dogs know this because God gives us the occasional wink to let us know he's got our back. But humans? They've been on their own since Ezekiel.

. . .

Anyway, the big day had arrived. On the afternoon of Halloween, Reggie burst from the apartment. When he returned an hour later, he had a rather nice bouquet of flowers, a bottle of Australian merlot and a Whitman sampler. The aromas of chocolate, caramel, peanut butter and raspberry cream combined with the distinct scents of rose, alstroemeria, narcissus and baby's breath assaulted my senses. As I battled olfactory overload, I realized that Reggie's hopes were as high as that lifeless new tower in Lower Manhattan, and I feared for Gloria.

Reggie snapped on my leash and said, "You're coming along."

I was, to say the least, ambivalent about this excursion. I wanted to be there out of curiosity, if nothing else. But I knew I'd be thrust into a test of character that few pets ever face. If Gloria somehow failed to live up to the fantasy Reggie had concocted out of pent-up virginity and Biblical gibberish, her life would be in profound peril.

And I knew she would probably fail. As far as I could tell, she was a nice, normal (somewhat homely) girl with the same expectations of love, romance and sex appeal that most human beings (and dogs, too!) feel. If she expressed any of those healthy feelings, she was a plucked turkey on Reggie's butcher block. And I would have to make the biggest decision of my life.

As we left the apartment, I was preoccupied with these thoughts and impaired by the powerful fragrances of flowers and candy. The noseprints of Detectives Driscoll and De

Mars, wafting subtly up the stairwell, completely eluded my usually keen nostrils. If I'd only sniffed them out, I could have barked, alerting the detectives of our whereabouts.

But Reggie spotted the bulls before I smelled them. They were two floors below. Reggie turned on me fiercely, ordering me to silence. I had to obey. He turned us around and rushed to the little-used, pee-smelling back staircase. Just my luck, the usual resident bums who crashed there had gone out for an evening of dumpster foraging. If they'd been sprawled as usual on the stairs, the hassle of climbing over them—while they cursed at us and hollered that we should stay off their turf—might have alerted Driscoll and De Mars.

Alas, our coast was clear. We crept out of the building like a wisp of smoke drifting into Bedford-Stuyvesant. I could have sworn that I heard Detective Driscoll, four floors up, knocking on the door and saying, "Reggie? Mr. Stockwell? NYPD."

But I probably imagined that. My ears are good, but not four-stories good.

I wondered about the two detectives. Why had they returned? Maybe Luther had somehow gotten word to them. Luther was regularly rousted by patrolmen, so he had plenty of police contact. If he had managed to reveal that Reggie was the killer—while not mentioning that he got the tip from a talking dog—the police might have been obliged to follow up. With the whole city up in arms about the Brooklyn Ripper, every clue—even the testimony of a dipso in a bodega doorway—had to be pursued. And if detectives like Driscoll and De Mars had heard, for the second time, Reggie's name connected to the killings, they would have pricked up their ears.

But I could not imagine that they were even vaguely suspicious of Reggie. How could they be? Their only "witnesses" were a little kid, a bum and a loquacious German shepherd.

Nonetheless, there they were, rapping on Reggie's door

while he dragged me off to Gloria's apartment to commit God-knows-what fresh horror. For a brief self-piteous moment, I thought, *Why me? What had I done to deserve a master like Reggie?*

But, as we headed down Bedford toward Greene Avenue, I shook this off. It's not in the nature of a shepherd to look at the dark side of life. We're a naturally sunny breed.

I noticed that, besides all the fragrant goodies Reggie was carrying, he was wearing the rucksack he had come to call his "go bag."

Keeping it casual, I said, "Hey, Reg. Why the rucksack tonight?"

Reggie cast me a steely glance. "Just in case, mutt."

"In case," I asked gently, "of what?"

"In case, cheesedick, is all you need to know."

Gloria lived on a lovely block of Washington Avenue not far from an Italian restaurant—called Locanda—that I loved to pass because it gave off great perfume. On the way, we passed a few Halloween celebrants. Kids were trick-or-treating, young couples in elaborate costumes, already loud and tipsy, bound for parties. One woman—dressed as a French chambermaid in high heels, mesh stockings and push-up brassiere—distracted Reggie so badly that I had to plant my feet on his chest and bark in his face.

"Hey, Jesus Christ!" He shoved me down. "Get away from me with your fuckin' dog breath!"

"You're welcome," I said.

We were in front of Gloria's brownstone within twenty minutes. Reggie checked his watch. We were on time.

When Gloria let us in and treated me to a thorough, luxurious ear-and-head rub (women's hands are their sexiest feature), I was heartened by her outfit. She was wearing a modest pink blouse with a high frilled collar, a necklace of (artificial) pewter-black pearls, camel slacks and a black cardigan. As usual, she gave off a delicate fragrance of Light

Blue, with a Pantene chaser. Nothing slutty. No French maid. She had passed Reggie's first test.

Reggie and Gloria went through the ice-breaking rituals that represent the human version of sniffing under each other's tails. Reggie opened the merlot. Gloria brought a tray of corn chips, veggie sticks and sour cream dip. I gave the dip a quick sniff and recognized Lipton's onion soup mix, an old reliable. Then they sat on the couch, two feet apart, and started talking about the weather, Halloween, the kids on the street. Small talk so tiny you needed a jeweler's loupe.

Cupcake made the usual humping overture, which I ignored.

"They don't do that," said Cupcake.

"Don't do what?" I said rather absently. I was focused on Reggie and Gloria, vigilant for any inadvertent word or gesture from Gloria that might loose Reggie's demons.

"Humans. They don't just give right in to the urge and start humping."

"Well, humans have protocols for sexual intercourse. I mean, usually."

"I guess that's why," said Cupcake.

"Why what?"

"Why they're widely regarded as the superior species."

"Wait a minute," I said. "I don't do that either. Does that make me a superior species?"

"Well, you're definitely a superior dog, big boy," replied Cupcake. "So, you ready yet?"

"Ready for what?"

"Humping."

I stopped listening to Cupcake and tuned back in to Reggie, who was talking about video games he used to love as a kid, *World of Warcraft* foremost among them. Gloria was doing a wonderful job of pretending to be interested. She was too good at this, actually. Her submissiveness troubled and confused me.

DAVID BENJAMIN

"Gloria?" I turned on Cupcake. "You think Gloria is a superior species. A woman who gets beat up, almost raped and murdered by my crazy master. And then she shrugs off all that terror and invites him to an intimate home-cooked meal? What the hell is so superior about that?"

"Don't be silly, big boy. I'm the first one to admit that Gloria's one of the runts in the human litter. But she's still a person. And people are the top species."

"Top?"

"Tip-top, toots. Wanna hump?"

"No, we're talking here, "I said. "What makes humans so darn superior, C.C.?"

"Really? You're seriously asking why humans are better than us?"

Cupcake was a true believer. In her whole life, she had never doubted the dog-human hierarchy. For that matter, in most cases, neither did I. But Cupcake clung to the faith because she lacked the energy to question any of the conditions of comfortable, indoor-living, couch-lounging, bed-sleeping urban dogdom.

"Yes, tell me," I said. "What's so special about these creatures?"

Cupcake sighed indulgently and said. "Well, for one, they're bipedal."

"And slower than us."

She went on. "Opposable thumbs. And brain power. They invent things. They build things."

"They build guns, prisons, kennels, religions, nuclear weapons and gas chambers. They build up mighty arsenals and intricate rationales for wiping every living thing off the face of the earth."

"Oh, come on, gloomy. They built the Eiffel Tower. They built Hoover Dam, Hollywood and Disneyland. Lighten up, big boy."

We went on like this for a while, bickering out of habit

but enjoying each other's repartee. Meanwhile, the evening continued placidly for Gloria and Reggie, who moved from the living area to the dining room. Cupcake followed them to hang around the table and gobble up fallen tidbits. I lingered on Gloria's living room carpet. It was a comfy place to brood.

An hour and a half later, I'd begun to think that my dread was ill-founded. Gloria's demure and attentive manner had lulled Reggie into quiescence. He grew more polite as the evening continued. He launched none of his usual rants. He talked about interests he hadn't mentioned to me in a year and even listened to Gloria—for five, ten minutes at a stretch. He laughed at her unfunny jokes. He complimented her mediocre cooking. He even excused himself when he belched.

This was rare Reggie. I began to suspect that Gloria had some sort of occult gift for curing werewolves and pacifying dragons. I lost all doubt in her powers when she put on soft music and coaxed Reggie into an awkward box step in the uncarpeted space between her living and dining rooms.

After a song or two of bad dancing, they returned—holding hands—to Gloria's sofa. She made a quick trip to the kitchen for a fresh bottle of wine. They toasted each other. Reggie said, "This is a really nice evening, Gloria."

"Oh, I'm just having the best time, Reggie," said Gloria.

"And you were worried he was going to do something crazy," said Cupcake.

I wasn't quite ready to relax. "The night is still young, C.C."

"Gloomy gus."

Gloria put her hands on her tummy. She said, "Oof. I think I ate too much. Reggie, you wouldn't mind if I change into something a little more comfortable, would you?"

"Does this mean I can take off my shoes?" asked Reggie.

"Take off anything you want," said Gloria a little too suggestively for my taste.

"Uh-oh," I said.

"What do you mean, uh-oh?" asked Cupcake.

DAVID BENJAMIN

"Well, I'm afraid that when Gloria says 'comfortable,' Reggie has no idea what she means."

"Well, I do," said Cupcake. "I like to watch humans humping. It's so strange and unnatural. All those arms and knees and slobbering on each other's faces, and their feet keep getting in the way. Makes me glad I'm a dog."

"So," I said, "Gloria has lots of sex?"

"What? Gloria?" spluttered Cupcake.

"So," I said, "not so much?"

"Gloria's gotten laid a grand total of once since I've been here," said Cupcake. "But it was fun—and loud. She started screaming. On the other hand, it was all over in, like, a minute and a half. I hope this time—"

"You'd just better hope there is no this time," I snapped back.

"Don't be a wet blanket, big boy. I've been looking forward to the show."

I didn't bother to argue the point with Cupcake. I had told her repeatedly about Reggie, and she either didn't understand or couldn't take me seriously. Poodle or not, the trouble with Cupcake was sheer dumbness. She had precious little experience in life. She had never once run free without a leash—and if she had the opportunity, she probably wouldn't take advantage. She'd just sit there. She had never had to break a rule or even think about the rules. She had never improvised, fended for herself or struck out in an unfamiliar direction. She barely knew what a direction was. She went where she was led. Looking at Cupcake at that moment, I realized that the fundamental force binding every dog, thoughtlessly, to the Code was absence of imagination.

Millions of us huddle in animal shelters, beaten and betrayed, awaiting the quietus of a bare needle, because we don't think beyond an inflexible, inadequate Code. We live and die, often prematurely, by an idealistic mantra that serves only those of us living in the best of homes, the coziest of worlds, the safest of neighborhoods. If we had been so passive and doctrinaire in Paleolithic times, we never would have evolved beyond dire wolves and cavedogs. Once, dogs had the sort of quick wits and resourcefulness that made them virtually equal to humans, capable of guiding them and schooling them in the ways of a harsh and remorseless world. But that, I guess, was long ago. Domestication has killed within most of us—certainly in Cupcake—our innate intellectual powers.

Gloria went into her bedroom. Reggie reached down to scratch behind my ear and said, "See? Didn't I tell ya, mutt? She's perfect."

"Reggie, she's a really nice lady. Really nice," I said. "But you shouldn't expect—I mean, think ... I mean, nobody's perfect."

I was babbling, and Reggie ignored me. Cupcake said, "I wish you wouldn't talk to your human all the time. It's creepy."

"He understands what I'm saying."

"That guy?" said Cupcake. "Shit, big boy. That guy doesn't understand the difference between ass and elbow."

I was going to disagree, but Gloria emerged from her bedroom, clamping my mouth shut so hard that my back teeth hurt.

"Oh my God."

Gloria had changed all right. Into a red silk robe unsecured in the front, revealing a red lace bra and matching panties. Her garter belt connected to black nylon stockings straight out of Frederick's of Hollywood. She was lipsticked, mascara'd, rouged, perfumed and, from my angle, a lot curvier without clothing than she looked when she was dressed.

I shuddered involuntarily. Cupcake, the idiot, proceeded to wag her tail off.

"This is not good," I whispered.

"Whoa, you kidding? This is great," said Cupcake.

"Jesus."

"So?" Gloria said to Reggie as she framed herself in the doorway of her boudoir.

DAVID BENJAMIN

Reggie turned and gaped.

Gloria said, "Too much?"

"Um," said Reggie, almost dropping his wine glass, then setting it down gingerly on the coffee table.

Gloria shifted a hip, revealing more of herself. "Do you like what you see?" she said.

No answer. Reggie didn't move. But I could feel his eyes searching the room for his rucksack.

29

"Dogs are minor angels."
—Jonathan Carroll

Gloria clearly had no talent for reading people. Reggie was clenching every part of his body. His fisted-up knuckles were white. His face was red. His lips were turning purple. His body odor turned instantly rank. He stood up, glaring at Gloria, radiating mortal disillusionment.

"Ew," said Cupcake. "What's that smell?"

But Gloria was still flirting.

"It's been a long time," she said in a tone that I think was supposed to sound sultry.

This, at least, gave Reggie pause. "Long time?"

"Yes," said Gloria. "Since ... you know?"

Reggie's brow furrowed. His mouth unpurpled and hung open several inches. "Since what?"

"Since, you know ... I've made love," admitted Gloria. She slipped her negligee off a shoulder and advanced a step on Reggie.

No, no, no, I thought. *Don't do that.*

"This is getting good," said Cupcake. I actually growled at her.

"You've ... what?" asked Reggie.

"Made love, Reggie," said Gloria. "After all, I'm not exactly a virgin."

I hung my head. Could she have possibly come up with a worse line?

"You're not?"

Gloria smiled mischievously, tossing her hair and blushing. "Oh, Reggie. You couldn't think that. After the way you behaved the last time."

"Last time?" Reggie seemed befuddled and inert. But I knew this passive respite couldn't last.

"Yes, you just about ... well, assaulted me. You remember?"

"You said you're not ..."

"No," said Gloria, moving toward Reggie in a sort of strip club sashay. She lowered her negligee so that she was bare from neck to cleavage.

"... an angel?"

"Angel?" Gloria laughed once. "Oh, hardly! Reggie, I can be a pretty bad girl if I put my mind to it."

Despite my feelings about profanity, I said, "Oh, shit."

As though on cue, Gloria shed her diaphanous robe and stepped within reach of Reggie. All that covered her now were a low-cut lacy bra, the matching thong and garter belt, stockings and a pair of silly black high-heel slippers with furry straps. She had also kept her necklace on.

I understood that humans need clothing because they don't have a built-in fur coat like most dogs do. But I had always been fascinated with the huge effort and expense humans pour into using clothes for more than just warmth. Gloria was obviously planning to engage in unfettered hanky-panky. So, for practical purposes, she should have been naked. But what she chose to wear was, in a human context, better than naked. Her slightly ridiculous costume suggested an eroticism more lurid than outright nudity. Her filaments of silk and satin simultaneously concealed and enhanced her sexuality. And she had sprinkled her lingerie with scents that heightened the pungency of her own fluids.

Speaking of scents, Reggie could barely smell any of them. But they made me lightheaded and, I'm afraid, slowed my wits.

"Ooh, this is gonna be fun," whispered Cupcake.

"Hush, you idiot bitch."

"Bitch?"

Gloria was inches from Reggie. She ran her eyes, almost palpably, down his body and back up to his eyes. She leaned toward him. Her dampness filled my nostrils. I could sense that Reggie's body was responding to her, swelling with the sort of natural hunger that healthy humans ought to feel in a situation like this.

But Reggie was no healthy human.

"Reggie, please," Gloria said breathily, "touch me."

Reggie lurched a step backward. I saw the flush of horror and anger rush upward from his neck to his ears.

"*TOUCH* you?" he roared.

When he slapped her, it was so sudden that I uttered an involuntary yip and staggered backward. Cupcake dove under a chair. Gloria tottered off her heels, lost one slipper entirely and stumbled onto the coffee table. Wine glasses hit the floor and smashed. The bottle toppled and began glugging wine onto the floor.

Reggie crossed the room in a single stride, reaching his "go bag" and rummaging inside clumsily, furiously.

"Touch you? Touch a fucking slut whore bitch cunt?"

Gloria was dazed by Reggie's blow. Her momentum had carried her to the floor between coffee table and sofa, her legs splayed. She was reaching to touch the already darkening bruise on her cheek when Reggie dropped the rucksack and raised his gun, that awful, ugly 9mm automatic. Glowering down at the fallen woman, he chambered a round.

That unmistakable brass-on-steel click awakened Gloria

from her stupor. She closed her legs, in an absurd gesture of modesty, and looked piercingly at Reggie.

"What are you doing?"

"Doing? You filthy temptress. What does it look like I'm doing?"

Gloria didn't answer. Instead, she gathered herself and found a seat on the sofa. Considering her dilemma, I thought this performance extraordinarily cool.

Meanwhile, I was on my feet, several feet to Reggie's left, farther from Gloria. Cupcake stayed under the chair, her nose and eyes visible. I inched stealthily toward Reggie.

"Well, Reggie, I don't understand what's wrong," Gloria finally said, in a voice that sounded calm, but I heard a tremor. "It looks like you're going to shoot me. But, well, you could also make love to me. You seem to be ready for either one."

She was right. I could tell, too. The gun barrel wasn't the only thing pointing at Gloria. Cupcake squirmed forward to sneak a peek. What an idiot.

Reggie uttered a sort of squeak and shook the gun—in both trembling hands—at Gloria.

"You filthy slut! You temptress! You Jezebel!"

"Jezebel?" said Cupcake from under the chair.

"I would never!" shouted Reggie. "With you? Never! You're soiled! You're, you're …"

"Soiled?" said Gloria. "What in God's name—"

"I thought you were different. I told Farfel you were pure and chaste."

"Wait a minute," said Gloria. She crossed her legs. "You told Farfel? The dog?"

"Oh, this just keeps getting worse," I said.

"Quiet," hissed Cupcake. "I'm listening."

"Yeah," said Reggie. He steadied the gun, aiming at Gloria's pretty much naked bosom. "He's the only one I can really talk to."

"Reggie," said Gloria, in what she probably thought was a

soothing tone. "Farfel's a dog."

Here was the old prejudice rearing its head. I'm sure Gloria, behind closed doors or walking through the park, talked a regular blue streak with Cupcake, who—like any loyal dog—hung on her every word and offered up unquestioning, doe-eyed approval. But then, someone else admits to her that he converses with his dog—a dog, by the way, who offers the added benefit of talking back intelligently—and she goes all humaner-than-thou and pretends that she would never sink so low. For an intemperate moment, I was tempted to tell Reggie, "Go ahead. Squeeze the trigger."

"He's not a dog," said Reggie, tightening his grip and squeezing one eye shut. "He's my inspiration."

Sensing Reggie's earnestness, Gloria shifted on the sofa and uncrossed her legs. "Inspiration?"

"He helped me understand my mission."

"What mission?"

"To purge the world of sexual bestiality. To erase the fornicators. To hunt them down. To gut them like—"

Gloria stood, clutching her breasts. She had made the connection. She stared with fresh horror at Reggie.

"You? "Oh no!" she cried. "Oh my God, you're the one, aren't you? You're the—"

"Moses," said Reggie.

"Oh my God. You've been killing all those people!" Gloria went appropriately pale and seemed to sway. "Oh my God."

I caught Cupcake's eye. "You should do some barking now."

Cupcake cocked her head, normally a cute gesture, but in this case just irritating. "Barking? Why?"

"To distract Reggie. He's gonna kill her."

"Kill her? No."

"Yes!"

"No, this is just human foreplay, big boy. They do these sorts of things all the time. I've seen it on TV."

"C.C., for God's sake! This is *not* TV!"

DAVID BENJAMIN

Incited by Gloria's evident disapproval, Reggie launched one of his self-justifying Moses rants, twirling the gun barrel at Gloria. Barely able to stand, she had the frozen look of a doomed philosopher staring into Nietzsche's abyss.

Reggie blathered on about how he was always a gentleman who deserved the love of the women who turned away from him to throw themselves, like sex-crazed nymphos, at obnoxious drunken football players and horny Mexicans.

"Mexicans?" said Cupcake.

"He's not just a murderer," I said. "He's a bigot."

"You really know how to pick 'em, big boy."

I wasn't listening to Reggie, except to measure the depth and length of his harangue.

"As long as he's going on raving like this, he won't kill her," I said.

"Aw, he won't kill her anyway," said Cupcake. "This is just—"

"This, dammit, is not foreplay!" I snapped.

"There's the crime, you bitch," Reggie said. "The great crime of humanity in which you willingly partake every time to spread your legs. Yours is a crime that can never be forgotten, nor can any true gentleman forgive you. I always wanted to exact my revenge on humanity because all of you women turned away and forced me to live a life without love, with no one but this fucking dog to keep me company. But thanks to this dog, I found my way. His simple animal wisdom helped me to learn my purpose and realize my mission. Oh, no, it's not just revenge, not just the pleasure of ripping you open and denying you the filthy joys you lust after but deny from me. Beyond revenge, I will cleanse humanity of its whores and seductresses ..."

And so on. I could sense that Reggie was winding down. I had to make a decision. I faced a choice no supposedly simple animal should even consider. I had to decide whether, literally, I could go on being a dog.

Reggie, keening and gurgling in his throat in a way that chilled me to the tip of my tail, lunged back toward his "go bag" and pulled from it the huge razorback knife. He shoved the gun into his pants. He advanced on Gloria, literally baring his teeth, brandishing the knife. His sweat smelled like rancid vinegar. He was drooling like a junkyard Doberman.

"I gotta stop him," I said.

"You can't," whined Cupcake.

"I have to."

"If you do, you'll go to Hell."

This was too dumb to answer. Besides, my time was up. Gloria was rigid with fear. Reggie was carrying the knife low, as he always did, so he could enter her just below the navel and rip upward 'til her breastbone halted the blade. She would be, in a moment, pouring out onto the floor.

I leapt.

The knife was inches from her bare tummy when I clamped Reggie's wrist in my jaws and twisted as hard as I could.

"Ow. Jesus!"

Reggie dropped the knife. I let go. Reggie turned on me, clutching his wrist. I saw blood between his fingers.

"What the fuck is wrong with you?"

Gloria was still too scared to move. Reggie looked down and saw the knife. Reading his next move, I stood up on my hind legs and planted both front paws on Reggie's chest. He staggered back, landing on his backside halfway across the room.

Cupcake, reacting to the impact, crept backward, disappearing beneath the chair.

Reggie floundered on the floor. "Goddammit, Farfel!"

I turned toward Gloria and—trying to sound as much as possible like Lassie in mineshaft mode—barked. And barked again. And then, just for good measure, I said, in Dogspeak, "Lady, you gotta move. Hide! Call the cops. 9-1-1!"

Miraculously, she seemed to get my drift. After one

tentative step, she clenched her little fists on either side of her shoulders and spun away from Reggie.

Reggie was clambering to his feet, reaching to his belt, where he still had the gun.

Gloria fled to the bathroom, slamming the door. I heard the lock turn. I shook my head. A fat lot of good that lock would do against a 9mm semiautomatic. Reggie was erect, looking at the bathroom door. But he turned to glare at me, pointing the pistol in my direction.

"Boy, are you in trouble," whispered Cupcake from under the chair.

Afraid to further antagonize Reggie, I ignored this. So Cupcake added more: "I'm gonna make sure every other dog in Brooklyn knows what you did."

Now Reggie was talking to me. "Farf, how could ya?"

"Look, Reg," I began.

But he suddenly forgot me. Distracted by spotting the knife on the floor, he picked it up and tucked it carefully under his belt. Then, in a movement both swift and decisive, he turned toward the bathroom and fired through the door.

The gunshot was a thunderclap inside the little apartment.

Gloria screamed and began to sob. I looked around the room, hoping she had the wherewithal to take the phone and call 9-1-1 from the bathroom.

But there was her phone, lying on the coffee table in a little puddle of cabernet sauvignon. Great.

"Gonna bust the fuckin' door. Gonna gut her like a fuckin' ..."

Reggie crossed the room suddenly. He was aiming the 9mm at the doorknob. I no longer had even a split second to review my misgivings about the Code. It was too late to parse ethical abstractions. I was driven, unthinking, by the immediacy of protecting a life, whether human or dog, or any living creature (although, if Reggie had been drawing a bead on a cat, I might not have been quite so athletic). I bounded over the coffee table, sprang off the couch and landed on Reggie's shoulders, knocking him to the floor.

I landed hard myself, slipping on the hardwood as I tried to regain my feet. Reggie was upright before me. Not even looking my way, he reached the bathroom, stuck the gun barrel in the lock and blew it away. He leaned against the door. Gloria, shrieking in terror, pushed back with panicky, spontaneous strength. But Reggie continued wedging his way inside. As he did so, he pointed the gun at the door panel. Gloria was inches away.

"Sorry, Reg. But I gotta do this," I said, likely alienating myself forever from the brotherhood of domestic dogdom. I went for Reggie's gun hand again, closing my canines on his wrist and pulling backward. On the slippery floor, I made little progress. But the gun was pointed down now. I bit harder, desperate for Reggie to let go. He hung on, wincing and roaring with pain.

Holding his balance, he kicked upward at me, catching me square in the chest, lifting me and tearing his wrist free as I twisted in the air. I hit the floor on my side and lost all my breath. My head swam; my mouth writhed silently as my body struggled to remember how to breathe.

This was the moment Reggie chose to go completely rogue and shoot me. I felt the bullet in my shoulder. Searing heat followed a second later, along with a sudden, excruciating intake of air. For some reason, simultaneously, Cupcake decided to start barking—although maintaining safe refuge beneath her chair.

Cupcake's moment of empty bravado caused Reggie to turn away, probably saving my life. Apparently, Cupcake's yipping also stirred Gloria. She burst rashly from the bathroom, fleeing Reggie and, unfortunately, tripping over me. We both tumbled and sprawled in the same direction, causing Reggie to shoot wildly toward us. He missed Gloria with all five shots but managed to clip me one more time in the ear.

DAVID BENJAMIN

I know this sounds minor, but you simply cannot imagine how much a 9mm hole in the ear stings.

For a strange instant, none of us moved. Gloria lay on her back, half-in, half-out of the bathroom. Her pretty undies had been strained and twisted, but they were still hanging on. I was at Gloria's feet, bleeding onto her floor, wondering if I had long to live. Reggie stood a few feet away, between Gloria and the apartment's door. His gun arm hung limp.

"Farf," he said, noticing the blood. "You all right?"

"Hey," I replied, a little miffed, "you shot me, man."

"I did?"

"He did? Are you going to die?" This was Cupcake from under the chair. I paid her no mind.

"Aw, Jesus," said Reggie. "I didn't even think, man."

"This is obvious," I said. "Thinking hasn't been your strong suit tonight."

"I'm sorry, Farf."

With this, Reggie just dropped the gun.

Methodically, he reached to his belt, found the giant knife, wiped it once across his shirtsleeve and caught Gloria's eye.

He said, "Farf, I'll take care of you in a minute. You're gonna be fine. Just as soon as I finish with her."

He started toward Gloria. She realized what was happening and pedaled backward on her bottom, reaching for something to grab, to lift herself up.

"Oh, for Pete's sake," I muttered. Awkwardly, with my wounded shoulder burning, I fought the floor and made it to my feet, directly in Reggie's path.

"Hey, fuckhead, get outa my way!" he snarled. So much for feeling my pain.

"Don't, Reg," I said weakly.

"Got to," he said.

"No!" cried Gloria. She reached up, snagged a doorknob and pulled herself up. Finding herself wobbly on her one remaining high-heeled slipper, she kicked it off. Skirting past me, she headed toward the apartment door. Stretching out over me, Reggie swung the blade, raking its tip across Gloria's upper arm. She screamed.

Gloria was bleeding but not seriously cut. She could make it as far as the door, where she'd be trapped again. The door was secured by three locks—which are pretty much obligatory in Brooklyn. By the time she had turned the first lock, Reggie would be carving her into cutlets. I had to intervene again.

For a second, I considered just clamping onto his calf and trying to drag him down. But he was huge, and he had a knife that he wouldn't hesitate to use on me. My only serious hope, despite my damaged shoulder, was to jump up to his arm, bite down harder than I'd ever bitten a shankbone and hold on 'til Gloria could fumble her way out the door and hit the street in her underwear—which might earn the attention that we had not yet gotten from neighbors or police after several gunshots and enough banging around to bring down plaster dust.

New York, New York—it's a helluva town.

I can't describe the pain of extending myself across the room and leaping high enough in the air to close my jaws around Reggie's forearm. But the force of the impact, followed by both of us hitting the floor in a bony heap, rendered me senseless—blind, deaf, and incapable of smelling a thing—until I could feel Reggie struggling to free himself from my teeth.

I awoke just enough to tighten my grip, squeeze my eyes shut and endure as Reggie wrenched and squirmed to free himself, finally battering my head and wounded shoulder with his free fist. Each blow landed like the sharp end of a claw hammer.

I could finally hold on no longer. When I relented, Reggie bounded up, found his gun and ran into the hall, shooting several times. The shots echoed back from the stairwell.

I heard a voice speaking dog English.

"Hey, you were right, big boy. I think he was going to kill her."

The voice came from under the chair.

"Do you think it's safe? Can I come out now?"

I didn't answer. Instead, I asked Cupcake, "Where's Gloria? Did she get away?"

Before she could respond, Reggie was back in the room. "Shit," he said.

"Guess she got away," whispered Cupcake.

Reggie sat on the sofa, crestfallen and weary. There was blood on his arm where I had bitten him. He turned the 9mm's barrel toward his face and stared into the hole.

Cupcake, still under the chair, said, "You think he's going to shoot me?"

"One can only hope," I said.

"You know," said Cupcake, "I'm still going to tell on you."

Reggie was still staring down the gun barrel when I heard the first sirens. That's when I passed out.

30

"Now, as I walk in the street, I look at dogs with secret horror. Who knows what is hidden in their heads?"
—Mikhail Bulgakov, *Heart of a Dog*

I never thought Reggie would shoot himself. According to Cupcake, he surrendered without a struggle when the police arrived. I missed the moment because I was drifting in and out of consciousness. After nudging me awake, Cupcake told me that Reggie's exit was talkative—even after he was read his Miranda right to shut up and wait for a lawyer. He apparently spewed his tired rant about women being subhuman whores whose proper place was a concentration camp. He also mentioned his mother in less than complimentary terms.

"Crazier than a rabid polecat," said Cupcake. "But he was pretty entertaining. And he spoke more kindly about you than I would have."

I asked her what she meant by that.

"Well, he repeated all that weird stuff about you being his inspiration—he called you a guiding light and an idiot savant—for killing all those people," said Cupcake. "It's not often that you see a human sharing his glory with a dog."

"Glory?" I said.

"Sure," said Cupcake. "You hardly deserve it, but you're going to be famous."

"Famous?"

"Oh, come on, big boy. You rescued a damsel in distress and subdued the Brooklyn Ripper. The *Daily News*, the *Post*, even the *Times*—they're going to splash your whiskery black mug all over the front page. You're the biggest canine media star since Huckleberry Hound."

I lay my head back and closed my eyes. "I don't want to be famous," I said.

"You got no choice in the matter, Rinty."

"All I want," I said, "is first aid." I was still bleeding all over Gloria's floor as I sank slowly into a state of shock. I could hear Gloria in another room, talking to the police. Cupcake was lying beside me, not bothering to lick my wounds and looking like the pup who ate the cat who ate the canary.

• • •

As it turned out, none of my injuries were life-threatening. But Cupcake was right about my fifteen minutes of fame. Several animal-lover groups raised a small fortune to finance my convalescence at a luxury animal hospital on Fifth Avenue. The mayor came to see me (and get his photo taken). I got a lot of other celebrity visits, including a Kardashian who kept calling me "Falafel." But the best part was seeing Marilyn, my NYPD partner. She got all teary-eyed and gave me a huge hug. I was so happy to see her that I licked off all her makeup and ended up with an aluminum hydroxide aftertaste that lasted half a day. But it was worth it just to reunite with the human who truly made me into the dog I am.

On another visit, she brought along her new significant other. That's right! She'd finally gotten fed up and ditched her abusive husband. The new guy, tall with a mustache, named Mark, rubbed my chest in exactly the right spot and talked to me as though I were another person, not a brainless beast.

Marilyn, who had always confided in me as though I could understand (which I could), told me that Mark is also a K-9 cop from Nassau County. They'd met at a training seminar in Albany. I said a few words to Mark, hoping he might understand Dogspeak. But he just grinned at me ignorantly and ruffled my ears.

I doubt that I'll ever see Marilyn again. But, now that she's found a fellow dog-lover, I know I don't have to worry about her.

. . .

I'm living now with Luther.

Gloria volunteered to take me in after I was discharged from the hospital. She probably thought she owed it to me because I'd saved her from Reggie. I moved in, but the arrangement didn't last.

Gloria treated me well during the month or so I stayed with her. I've certainly never eaten better than I did at her place. But Cupcake drove me to the streets.

From the first day at Gloria's, the little bitch (excuse my French) was on my case, telling me that I was a traitor to all dogs. All quadrupeds. All mammals (except humans, who don't count)!

"But I saved your mistress," I argued. "From a murderer."

"That was my job," said Cupcake.

"You were hiding under a chair," I replied.

"Well, that was also my job," said Cupcake. "I'm no heroine."

"Wait," I said, trying to open Cupcake to the concept of logic. "Even though you profess absolute loyalty to Gloria, you were willing to let her die horribly without lifting a paw in her defense."

"Hey, big boy," said Cupcake. "Get real. Your crazy-ass master had a gun that was almost as big as me. Not to mention that enormous knife. And he was lookin' to kill anything that moved. He shot *you*. Remember?"

"Well, yes. He lost his head for a moment. But—"

"Besides," said Cupcake. "Where is it written that I should risk my adorable hide for any human, even the one who feeds me and bags my doody?"

"So," I said. "you're saying that you only have to be loyal to Gloria in comfortable circumstances?"

Cupcake nodded. "Look closely, big boy. I'm a poodle."

"So, it's perfectly okay for you to stick your tail between your legs and run when the chips are down? Because you're a poodle?"

"Because I'm a dog, you big dope. Survival is what dogs are all about. Living to fight another day is our forte."

"So, I should have run away, too?"

"Of course. That was your only moral option."

"Moral?"

"Yes, moral," said Cupcake. "It's in the Code."

"Cowardice was my only choice?"

"You got it, big boy. You knew your duty to dog and man alike. Look what happened. Against every standard of propriety, you inflicted grievous harm on your own master."

"Look, C.C., I risked my life for your mistress, saving her from rape and murder. But all you can see is that I violated the Code?"

Cupcake snorted. "Violated? Farfel, you broke the Code into a hundred pieces. You did so many things wrong you should be put down before you smell your next bowl of Beneful."

"For Pete's sake, C.C., I saved Gloria."

"No, no, no. You bit the hand that feeds you."

"I had to bite him. Reggie was crazy. Dangerous. Homicidal."

"Doesn't matter."

"He was murdering people."

"People, not dogs. Mere humans. And none of those people were your master. Reggie was your master."

"But," I said redundantly, "he was going to kill your mistress."

"That was none of your business."

"But if I hadn't stopped Reggie, Gloria would be dead. Dead!"

"Your point?"

"My point?"

"Yes, you keep harping on this whole issue of Reggie killing Gloria. So what if he did? What on earth does that have to do with you?"

I couldn't believe my ears. I tried a different approach. "Well, what about you, C.C.? I did you a favor. If Gloria were dead, you'd be homeless."

"Thanks, big boy. But even if that was true, it's still none of your business."

"But you're my friend," I said. I admit this was a slight exaggeration.

"Spare me. Friend?" said Cupcake. "You haven't humped me even once."

"Humping has nothing to do with friendship."

"Well, that's the dumbest thing I've ever heard," said Cupcake. "You've been talking to too many humans."

I tried to steer the conversation back to some measure of coherence, saying, "Look, C.C., whether we're friends or not, the fact is that, by saving Gloria, I saved you, too, from the pound. Maybe even from the needle."

Cupcake scoffed. "That's where you're wrong, big boy. Look at me. Look deep into my big, soulful eyes. I'm cuter than an apronful of baby chicks. Even if Animal Control picked me up and got me all the way to the pound, I'd be snatched up and living on Central Park West before you could say Rudd Weatherwax."

I lowered my ears and sighed. She was probably right about that. She was a born dowager magnet. She didn't really need Gloria. There was nothing I could do to change her mind about the Code, although, foolishly, I kept trying. We had the same circular quarrel a dozen times.

DAVID BENJAMIN

Life got steadily worse for me at Gloria's. Cupcake started to address me as "turncoat" and "traitor." When she found out that Hitler's dog was named Blondi, that became her name for me. If I didn't get to my food dish as soon as Gloria filled it, Cupcake would pee in it. She snarled and yapped jealously whenever Gloria even touched me. She developed a habit of nipping at the tender parts of my hindquarters while I was napping.

When I showed a fair tolerance for this treatment, she targeted my testicles. There are few worse sensations than waking from a sound sleep with a spiteful poodle gnawing your gonads.

Something had to give, and it had to be me. So, one day at Fort Greene Park, I pulled the slack-leash trick on Gloria, wrenched myself free and galloped over the hill. I didn't slow down 'til I was two blocks up Willoughby.

I knew where I was going. A fugitive dog, especially one as big and scary as a German shepherd, doesn't last long untethered on the streets of New York. I needed refuge, and I needed it fast. My devoutest hope was that the homeless guy who understood Dogspeak was still holed up behind the church.

When I reached the churchyard and squirmed through the fence, Luther was absent. But his flimsy shelter was intact, and it looked lived in. I crawled inside as far as I could, hiding from the inevitable Animal Control dragnet.

When Luther came "home" around dusk and found me there, he took my arrival in stride. He shared with me part of a stale meatball sandwich he had liberated from a dumpster behind a Subway in Flatbush. By and by, we struck up a conversation.

I learned that Luther had sublimated his aversion to the police long enough to report my information about Reggie to the desk sergeant at the 88th Precinct. He was careful not to mention that he'd gotten Reggie's name from a talking dog.

At first, Luther's tip led to no action at all. He was, after all, a drunken bum. But eventually, someone—I personally suspect Detective De Mars—connected the dots. Two dubious witnesses—a little kid who talks to dogs and a smartass doorway-dweller—had both fingered Reggie as the Ripper. This went beyond coincidence, and it prompted Driscoll and De Mars' second visit to Reggie's apartment.

If only the police had seen the light one day—or just an hour—sooner, Gloria would have been spared her near-death experience—and Cupcake might've left my nuts alone.

31

*"Outside of a dog, a book is man's best friend.
Inside of a dog, it's too dark to read."*
—Groucho Marx

For the last six months, Luther and I have shared a nice little room—a cot for Luther, a rug for me, a few appliances, even a secondhand TV—in the church basement. This came about after I talked Luther into voluntarily cleaning up around the churchyard, raking leaves, picking up litter, even helping me kill the occasional rat. (Did I mention? I hate rats.) The pastor didn't pay our efforts any attention at first. But then, one night, I sniffed out a couple of kids busting into the church, apparently looking for gold chalices, or sacramental wine, or just to empty the poor box. I used my police training and cornered them inside. My barking awoke Luther, who raised a fuss that woke up the pastor, Reverend Dave, who called the cops before the kids could get away.

The next day, Reverend Dave offered us shelter and an indoor toilet (and a little money from the Sunday collection). In return, Luther and I took on the jobs of watchman and janitor. Reverend Dave's only condition was that Luther had to stay more or less sober. I've been helping him with that.

Life with Luther isn't as affluent and cozy as it used to be with Reggie. But there's a lot less drama. Luther is a gentle master and—now that he's mostly off the muscatel—an erudite conversationalist. We walk to Fort Greene Park a couple of times a day, at hours when I know Cupcake won't be there. Thanks to Cupcake's loose lips, I get the occasional dirty look from other dogs. But current events appear to be rehabbing my reputation. Reggie's trial is all over the newspapers, and word has gotten out, even among dogs, about my small role in trying to save Gloria. It turns out that a lot of my fellow dogs aren't as stiff-necked as Cupcake about the letter and the spirit of the Code of the Dog.

I've seen Jesse once or twice in the park. The kid can still understand me, but I suspect it won't last. As Jesse gets older and starts suppressing his imagination, he'll probably forget our mutual language. He might even forget that we ever talked together.

I worry sometimes about Luther, too.

If he gets too sober and respectable, I wonder if he'll lose his ear for Dogspeak, and I'll be left with nothing but other animals to talk to. It's a funny thing about humans. They can be even more dangerous and brutal than Reggie—who, I hope is the worst human I'll ever meet. Humankind's passion for spilling one another's blood is inexplicable. They're warped by hatred, twisted by prejudice, filled with fear and driven by preposterous delusions. I know this is so. I've seen it, felt it, smelled it. I've suffered and witnessed the suffering of other dogs and too many innocent humans.

I'd change people's unfortunate tendencies if I could, but I know they can't understand what I'm saying—and, well would they listen anyway? I sometimes imagine that, if all of us dogs banded together, we could find a way to cleanse the planet of what Philip Roth called the human stain. Peace would prevail, and cruelty would be banished. God would be in his heaven, surrounded by billions of examples of his biggest mistake, and all would be right (at last) with the world.

But, after a moment of wishful thinking, I inevitably dismiss the notion of ganging up on people and wiping them out. Without human foibles rendering our existence a perpetual surprise, dogs would be stuck in an endless monotony of hunting, gathering, breeding and never quite figuring out how to turn pigs into bacon.

RELUCTANT ACKNOWLEDGMENT

Any masochist who has slogged through the online autobiography of spree killer Elliot Rodger, *My Twisted World*, might recognize remnants of Rodger's "philosophy" in the manifestos of Reggie Stockwell. Although I am a seasoned storyteller in touch with my dark side, I would have struggled to imagine as bleak and far-fetched an outlook on life and love as Reggie's. For that inspiration, I find myself perversely indebted to Elliot Rodger. He was a profoundly disturbed young man who—in vengeance against all the women who had rejected him in his brief twenty-two years of life—murdered six people and injured fourteen others in Isla Vista, California, on May 23, 2014, before killing himself. Were it not for Rodger's 137-page outpouring of self-pity, vindictiveness and sheer madness, I would have had far more difficulty conceiving a credible pathology for my story's antagonist.

ABOUT THE AUTHOR

David Benjamin is a lifelong storyteller, dating back to Mrs. Poss' second-grade class at St. Mary's School in Tomah, Wisconsin. His loosely told memoir, *The Life and Times of the Last Kid Picked*, was originally published by Random House and has been reprinted in a revised version by Last Kid Books. His Last Kid Books include a collection of his essays, *Almost Killed by a Train of Thought*, a collection of short stories and sketches, *The Melting Grandmother*, and fourteen novels: *Three's a Crowd, A Sunday Kind of Love, Summer of '68, Skulduggery in the Latin Quarter, Black Dragon, Jailbait, Bastard's Bluff, They Shot Kennedy, Fat Vinny's Forbidden Love, Woman Trouble, Witness to the Crucifixion, Choose Moose* and *Dead Shot*. As a journalist, Benjamin has edited newspapers, published and edited several magazines, and authored *SUMO: A Thinking Fan's Guide to Japan's National Sport*.

Since its launch in 2019, Benjamin's publishing imprint, Last Kid Books, has won thirty-two independent press awards. These include, for *They Shot Kennedy*, the Midwest Book Awards' 2021 grand prize for literary/historical/contemporary fiction, and a 2022 Silver Medal for Humor in the Independent Book Publishers Association's prestigious Benjamin Franklin Awards for *Fat Vinny's Forbidden Love*. His essays have appeared in, among other publications, the *Philadelphia Inquirer, San Francisco Chronicle, Los Angeles Times, Chicago Tribune*, the *Tokyo Shukan Bunshun* and *Wisconsin State Journal*.

Benjamin and his wife, Junko Yoshida, have been married for ages. They live sometimes in Madison, Wisconsin, and the rest of the time in Paris.